THE THINGS WE KEEP

the
things
we
keep

a novel

JULEE BALKO

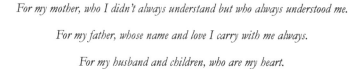

For my mother, who I didn't always understand but who always understood me.

For my father, whose name and love I carry with me always.

For my husband and children, who are my heart.

contents

prologue   i

chapter 1: beets   1

chapter 2: stone   21

chapter 3: clothes   51

chapter 4: dorothy   66

chapter 5: tom   76

chapter 6: cava   108

chapter 7: abigail   113

chapter 8: applesauce   143

chapter 9: horses   162

chapter 10: woodworking   175

chapter 11: maggie   182

chapter 12: sand   205

chapter 13: needles   229

chapter 14: robert   249

chapter 15: zygote   256

prologue

It was the smell of marigolds that brought Serena back to that day. The day Serena knew she could never make her mother happy. And then just like the memory comes, it leaves again. That's the thing with grief, it keeps you distant and then shockingly close all at the same time.

chapter 1: beets

Fifty-three cans of beets. Why these beets in particular enraged Serena wasn't totally clear. They were not her beets. They were her mother's. And her mother was dead. Serena had dealt with so much already, had taken care of so many things. And now, she, Serena, was going to take care of fifty-three cans of beets.

She pulled up to her father's house, noticing how it looked different. Even though the shrubs were still trimmed. The mulch still sloped where her father always ran it over with the car. The yellow flowers were still planted in a row. Yet to Serena, they all breathed a different air. A solemn air. The trees knew. She could see they bowed their branches ever so slightly to acknowledge the change. She nodded her head to them and took a deep breath before touching the handle on the door.

She glanced at her watch. She had an hour to get this done before she had to get to the lab. Her western blot would show if her last experiment worked, or failed, yet again.

"You here?" asked Serena as she walked into the house. Her parents' house. Barbara and Robert. Everyone always put Barbara's name first when they talked about her parents. Because her mother, Barbara, was such a force. Now it was just her father's name alone, just Robert, and it was also just Robert's house. Now it was all mentally renamed. The house greeted her with its strange smell of marinated roasts from years past.

"Hello? Dad?" She walked through the hallway and felt small.

The walls looked dingier than she remembered. A picture of her mom greeted her. Smiling from behind a sunflower and looking happier than Serena had ever remembered her.

"Up here," came a voice from her father's bedroom. She walked up the worn, carpeted stairs into her father's bedroom. He was folding socks. She had never seen her father fold socks in her thirty-six years of life until this day. She had never seen her father touch any laundry. Her mother took care of that.

"I'm here for the beets," she said with a smile.

As if it was something she was looking forward to doing. She didn't want the beets. She wanted to help her dad who was overcome with all the things her mother had left behind. He was lucky; he was left with material things. Serena was left with questions. She didn't have the "let's go shopping" type of relationship with her mother. She had space, hate, and uncertainty, and now a shit-ton of beets, which she planned on donating to a local food shelter rather than wasting them. Her mother loved beets. They were her favorite. She was also one of the most frugal people Serena had ever known. She could coupon-cut her way to free canned goods that began to stockpile because she couldn't say no to a good deal—even if it led to rows upon rows of cans that no one would ever eat.

"You sure you want them? I can just throw them away," replied Robert as he held up a sock to see whether it was navy or black.

"It's black," said Serena.

"Thanks. Hard for me to see that. The beets are in the basement. I was going to get them for you, but I lost track of time." His voice was stressed and high-pitched, as if failing to get the beets was a serious problem.

"Don't worry. I'll get them." Serena walked down the stairs and heard her father rush behind her.

"Let me get you some bags. I have lots of paper bags."

"Great. Thanks." And with more bags than necessary, she opened the door to the basement.

The click of the lock greeted her. She looked back. Her father had gone on to do some other chore. She walked down the steps slowly and deliberately. Her feet felt like they were wearing shoes too big for her—old-man shoes that were cumbersome, awkward, and heavy. The basement smelled of dust, wet wood, and old cement. Boxes half-closed revealed a graveyard of her mother's belongings. Sitting quietly. Whispering of being forgotten. Her father must have started cleaning out her mother's closet.

She gazed at her feet and walked slowly to the shelves. All that was left of her mother's once bountiful supply of canned goods were fifty-three cans of beets. Robert had emptied the shelves and relocated everything that was left to the kitchen. He picked through what he thought he would eat, claiming the green beans, corn, peas, the marinara sauce with the basil he liked, gravy, mustard, ketchup, boxed noodles, extra napkins, cream of mushroom soup, and those tiny pickles that the grandkids thought were fun to eat. What her father had kept was only a fraction of her mother's collection, which was impressive, considering all of the various sales, coupons, and deals she found at the store each week. Buying excess food to hoard downstairs was not her father's way though. He didn't even know what kind of sales the grocery store had each week. Knowing the sales, bulking up on canned foods—that was her mother's way.

And now that way was gone.

***

"What are those?" asked Serena, watching her mom chew a salad as if she were a cow. Lettuce and red beet juices dripping from her chin.

"Beets. You want to try one?" Barbara replied with a mouth full of food.

"No. They look gross."

"They're good. Grandma used to love them. Try one." Barbara handed her a fork with half of a beet that looked like a fat little burgundy moon. Serena took the tiniest bite she could. She wasn't grossed out by the beet. It was her mother who ruined her appetite. Serena was always aware of the slight dandruff on Barbara's shoulders, the smell of onions on her breath, the residue on her sleeve from a previous cold. Serena wondered how her father and sister didn't notice, or at least didn't seem to care.

Serena had never seen her mother shower. She knew she must. Somehow never seeing her do it always weighed heavily on Serena's mind though. Every morning her father came down, showered and ready for work. But Barbara did things on her own time and in her own way.

***

Serena packed all fifty-three cans of beets in the bags and brought them up in two trips. She whispered goodbye to her mother's clothes, closed the basement door, and walked outside.

"Bye," she shouted to her father as she finished packing the car.

Robert looked up from the paper. "See you later." His eyes looked puffier than usual, his face longer, his hair less neat around his ears.

Serena drove home fast and with the windows down to feel the cold of the late fall air. She took all four bags, overflowing with beets, to her front door. They were heavy and awkward, but she was determined to do it one trip. She set them down on the front porch and rubbed her back. She went inside and sat down against the stair banister. She stared at the white wall with dirty little hand marks and felt hot and sweaty with her coat on. Her husband, Tom, walked in.

"Seriously. Now you're a beet hoarder?"

"He was going to throw them away," said Serena, not looking at him, instead keeping her focus on a curly black scuff mark.

"And that would be bad, why?" asked Tom.

"Because I wasn't ready. And there are places that could use them."

"Sweetie, first the coats. Now beets? I know you're struggling. It's only been six months since she passed, and three months since—"

Serena interrupted him.

"Don't quantify. You quantify everything. Are numbers supposed to make me feel better? Bring me peace? I hate numbers."

"That's not what I meant." Tom walked into the kitchen and opened the fridge.

"Why are you here anyway? I thought you were staying at

Mike's."

It had been one week since Tom and Serena decided to take some space from each other. With her mom dead, Serena had so much more space. But now she wasn't sure what to do with it. She knew she should throw herself into her career as a molecular biologist. Looking for answers and the truth was what drove her. But now when she stared at the cancer cells, all she saw was her mom. And now the truth that Serena wanted to uncover most was why her mom seemed to hate her for most of her life.

"I came to check in on you. Make sure you didn't need anything. You need to go shopping. Unless you're planning on eating those beets for dinner. Want me to go get you something?"

"I hate beets," Serena said quietly to the wall. "And I don't need you to check in on me. You can't just waltz back in here whenever you feel like it."

"It wasn't my choice to leave. I thought we needed some space. Some time to think about things. We've been through a lot." Tom closed the fridge and looked at her. Her brown hair was pulled back in a ponytail, still wet from a late morning shower.

"What *we've* been through? Was Kara something *we've* been through? I think that was all you."

"We've talked about this. It wasn't what you think," Tom said.

"Oh, so we're done talking. Great. Great."

"I'm going." Tom walked to the door and headed to his old blue Honda Civic. Serena followed him outside and watched him from the front patio. She looked down at the bags of beets, bent down, and hurled one toward him. The can had a nice, graceful heft to it as it flew through the air, like a ballerina hippo. She missed by about five feet. Tom looked back and shook his head. Serena went inside and closed the door.

***

Serena and Tom met as undergrads at Boston University. Her major was science and he was on a path to finance; their common prerequisite of statistics found them sitting next to each other in a big hall of sloppily dressed lowerclassmen. Tom was cute, semi-tall with brown eyes that perfectly matched his brown hair. He wore button-downs and khakis in a way that seemed easy and approachable, without looking too frat-boy, because he hated frat boys.

Serena wasn't the type to notice guys in class. She paid attention to the teacher and little else; however, that morning she happened to stop by her favorite bagel shop to treat herself to a large coffee. It was that large coffee she accidentally spilled onto Tom's foot as she readjusted her notebook. Serena felt awful seeing his tan hiking shoes turn to dark brown and assured him she had just the stuff to clean them. Tom liked the no-nonsense way she talked and the way her eyes stole looks at him without being overly bashful. They walked back to her dorm room, and she got out her shoe cleaner.

"I can't believe you actually have shoe cleaner."

"Oh, I have everything." Serena opened up her closet to show Tom a variety of cleaning supplies with very specific uses. "I like purpose," she said and smiled as she casually put her hair up into a ponytail.

"Well, if my rug ever gets a stain on it, I know just who to call."

Their conversation was easy, like old friends. Before Tom left, they had talked about that awful lit professor nobody wanted, the nutritional wear of having cereal for dinner, which of the campus dorms were the worst, roommates, parents, missing their dogs—both having black Labradors to return to—aspirations of hiking the Alps, the lack of desire to take cruises or visit Cancun ever, the need for ethnic food and small art-house movies, the silliness of most freshmen, and finally, how they were going to meet up on Thursday to study together. After two months of being study mates, pizza mates, and workout mates, Tom finally asked Serena out on a real date. They were sitting in the dining hall talking about her roommate's new obsession with dating basketball players, when he asked,

"Hey, do you want to go to dinner on Friday?"

"Yeah, sure," Serena said without looking up.

"No, I mean like a real dinner. Like a date."

"Oh." Serena smiled and shook her head for a second like he had just mentioned a good idea for a game or asked her to pass the salt and pepper. "Yeah, sounds good. Where do you want to go?"

It was that casualness that Tom had first loved about Serena. She wasn't like other girls. She could always stay aloof. It wasn't until many years later that he'd see her walls come down with their daughter, Maggie. Then, he'd know that casualness toward him was something colder—detachment.

***

Serena made a mental list of everything that was around before or after her mother. The mulch. We put that down before she died. The bubbles. Barbara had bought those. This shirt. I bought that after. Maggie's doll? Was that before? No, her daughter's love of monkeys came after her mother had passed. And she went about her day not meaning to but keeping constant track of what and when objects came into her life. This ketchup. That coffee. This flower pot. That re-painted house down the street.

The thing that came after Barbara that bothered Serena most was her realization about how hard it was to raise a kid and how this impossible balance of parenting and marriage is what strained a marriage. Maggie and Barbara had overlapped. She had seen Maggie blow out her first candles. Saw her first steps. Heard her first words. It wasn't until after Barbara had died that everything fell apart. Serena understood more now. She thought about going to the cemetery to tell her mother. But the long, awkward road made her feel cold.

She wanted to tell her mom a lot of things. She wanted to tell her how she felt bad for her college years when Serena didn't have time for her. How when Maggie went through a short "daddy" phase, Serena's heart was crushed with the abandonment. Serena understood now how much love meant to a mother, and she felt awful she had withheld it so many times from Barbara. She wanted to tell her mother how she noticed all of the other grandmas in music class and wished she had taken her once. Even if Barbara would have called it a waste of money. Most of all, Serena wanted to tell her mother that if she could do it over again, she would try harder to understand Barbara's pain, the pain that kept her mother distant.

Serena tried her best to be a good mom. She was practical. Read all the books. Took Maggie to all the classes that make a toddler happy, bright, and overindulged. She sometimes got angrier than she should when Maggie wouldn't nap, or when Maggie was out of her control. Then there were the times Maggie would fall asleep in her arms, and Serena would put her nose close to her mouth and breathe in her sweet, stale-milk smell. Sometimes when Maggie laid on Serena's chest, Serena would close her eyes and imagined their hearts were connected. She could feel their blood pulse together as if they were one.

No one thought Serena was going to be a good mother. Barbara would often chide her about it once Serena had reached her thirties and had still not talked about kids. At the time, Serena could never tell if Barbara wanted to be a grandmother or not.

"It's not for everyone, Serena. And you are very focused on your job," Barbara would say. But after Maggie was born, she knew Barbara's true feelings. She couldn't mask her love for Maggie.

Motherhood did not fit easily into Serena's work life. She felt like she had to work doubly hard at being a mother and becoming a successful academic scientist. She had worked hard in grad school and during her postdoc and had recently published papers in the top journals in her field, *Cell* and *Science*. Long, intense hours meant progress. But now progress meant seeing less of her daughter. There was never enough time. It felt like an endless battle with no clear winner for her job or her family.

Serena pushed herself to understand all she could about

cancer. She had dedicated the last decade to knowing the details. Serena would spend hours looking in the microscope and watching how cells grew. She imagined them as slow, methodical dancers. It's true, she once called a western blot beautiful; every time crisp bands showed up on the film in the darkroom felt like a promise to her. Each band represented a microscopic protein present in cancer cells that might hold the key to understanding what goes wrong.

But that was before. And now here it was, her life's work, her mother dead, and so many unanswered questions. She felt betrayed by this. That the cancer that she devoted herself to, that she had thrived on learning about, had turned on her.

Cancer begins with a genetic mutation. A change in a cell that causes it to grow and multiply when it shouldn't. This is followed by more mutations, more changes, and then ultimately, when the cells grow out of control, a tumor. The endless change fascinated Serena. She could spend hours looking at the shape of the cells. She knew the inside of those cells held a secret. A secret that, if she could just figure it out, could help millions of people. Serena was driven to discover what caused breast cancer recurrence. Why did it go away and come back?

Fascinating is not how it looked in her mother though. Every day she went to see Barbara in the hospital, she looked as if she had aged another ten years. Her cheeks, which were already so sunken in, somehow managed to fall deeper within her face. Her skin let go. The bones in her wrists were noticeable. The cancer was winning. It won in her swollen legs. It won in Barbara's round belly that housed only painful fluid.

Serena would slide her hand in her mother's. Serena couldn't remember the last time she had reached out to Barbara's hand. Touching her mother, Serena could feel the gulf in their relationship. Years of life standing between them. She pulled her hand away, but kept it on the blanket nearby. Not quite ready to pull it all the way away.

"I'm sorry," Serena whispered. "I'm sorry."

Barbara groaned. Her now-sunken face turned away and gazed at the door.

"I know you want to let go. It's okay. You can. We'll understand."

Serena was surprised at many things during that final month of Barbara's life. How much she didn't know about her mother. How much she didn't truly understand about cancer. Mostly she was surprised that the woman she had spent most of her life being so frustrated with, so angry with, turned out to be someone she loved much more than she realized. A woman who had always managed to say the wrong things, cause a scene, and make life difficult, became heroic in Serena's eyes. Serena stared at her mother and said the words she had always wanted to hear.

"I'm so proud of you. You've fought so long."

Tears dropped on her mother's thin blanket.

***

"You're late," Barbara said as she sat, tapping her foot nervously as she did a Sudoku at the table. "Help me with my jacket. The zipper is broken. I need to step through it."

Serena helped her mom awkwardly step through the thick

black jacket. "Why don't you get the jacket fixed?"

"It's fine. Just help me." Barbara sounded angry. Or rather, normal. Her normal voice always had some anger in it.

The drive to the hospital was always quiet. Serena tried to think of things to tell her that would keep her mind off the chemo she was about to undergo. And Barbara was always agitated by how Serena would constantly talk about inane things.

"Maggie really likes to color now."

"You liked to color when you were little."

"I bought her some finger paints."

"You should buy some plastic mats to put on the floor, so she doesn't make a mess. I think your dad has a plastic tarp downstairs you can have."

"I think that's for leaves. Not sure I'd want that in the family room."

"Whatever. It's yours if you want it. Can you turn the heat up? I'm cold."

"Sure. Are you meeting with the doctor today or just getting chemo?"

"The doctor. Better not be that nurse practitioner. I want the real thing. I hate when they try to give me her."

"Some nurse practitioners are really good."

"I don't care. I want the doctor. I'm paying for a doctor. This is my life, Serena."

"I know, Mom. I know."

"Can we not talk for a bit? I don't want to talk."

"Okay."

The hospital always looked old-fashioned and dark, with its

tainted windows and people you couldn't see. Serena wondered who was in those rooms. How many were women, like her mom? Or kids, like Maggie?

"Why don't I let you out? And I'll park and meet you up there."

"Okay."

"I'll be up as soon as I park."

Barbara walked in without looking back, one arm sticking straight down, the other clutching her big purse. She walked swiftly and angrily, like she was in the army, the back of her black jacket dirty with fallen hair from months past.

There were never any open parking spots nearby, but Serena didn't mind the walk. If she waited long enough, she would miss the first awkward and intense minutes that Barbara had with the chemo nurse. Always slightly insulting the way she put the tube in her port. Always uncomfortable with the temperature in the room. Always needing a coffee made just the right way.

Serena had volunteered to take Barbara on Wednesdays. With their tense relationship, it helped Serena feel less guilty. It allowed her to point to a day and say, "See, I care. I take you to chemo on Wednesdays." Serena's sister Abigail helped out on all the other days, or so it felt like to Serena. Picking up groceries. Cleaning the kitchen. Making her soup. There was no way Serena could come close to Abigail's care.

As Serena found her way to the chemo floor, she thought about how if she had cancer, she'd do things differently. She'd embrace the world. Maybe take one last trip with her family. Maybe take everyone to Disney World. Barbara had been so angry lately.

She yelled at Serena when she didn't bring her medicine fast enough or rub her feet the right way. Barbara was even worse to Robert. She constantly nagged him and needed things, aging him with her demands. Serena opened the door and saw the nurse helping Barbara to the hospital bed.

"I'm scared," said Barbara in a whisper to the nurse.

"It's okay. I got you," said the tall nurse in pink scrubs as she gripped Barbara's thin arm.

Serena walked back out of the room before they saw her and felt tears well up in her eyes. She had never heard Barbara say those words. In fact, Barbara constantly told her the opposite. That she wasn't scared. That it didn't hurt that bad, even though Barbara popped Oxycontin like it was nothing and said she didn't understand why people thought that stuff was so great.

Serena stared at the hospital walls. The walls were not keeping her there. She wasn't a patient there. Serena didn't have cancer. She didn't know what it felt like to know her health limits. She dried her eyes and went back in. She sat down next to her mom and squeezed her mom's arm.

"Careful, Serena. That's the arm that hurts." Barbara's voice was jumpy and quick with fire.

"Sorry, Mom." Serena wanted to tell her mom so much at that moment. How much she loved her. How she was sorry she found her coat gross. How she wished she could scratch her back without looking away. She wanted to thank her for the time when Serena had been sick and Barbara had surprised her with homemade chicken soup. Serena had wanted the soup but was too afraid to ask for it because she knew it took all day to make and her mom was sick, too. It was times like those that Serena was so grateful for. When her mom was truly a good mom. Those times were few and far between. But instead of saying all that, Serena just sat there quietly, playing cards with Barbara to pass the two hours of chemo

.

***

Serena was not a great caregiver to her mother. There was just too much between them for compassion to come easily. It's true she sometimes had to hold her breath while helping her, because the mere smell of Barbara's skin would make her gag. Her skin probably didn't smell any better or worse than the average elderly patient, but because that skin was stained with a lifetime of rejection of Serena's touch, it held both pain and a musk to it. Serena's most troublesome nursing responsibilities were involved with the hair. When Barbara's hair began falling out, there was so much of it everywhere. It clung to Serena, even after she thought she had brushed it off completely, showing itself hours later while she made dinner, still stuck to her shirt.

"Mom, why don't we shave your head?" Serena pleaded after she moved Barbara's pillow and a clump of nighttime fall-outs stuck to it.

"It's fine. I want to keep what I have," replied Barbara matter-of-factly. As if the odds and ends of her gray-and-black hair were fashionable.

"It's falling out everywhere," Serena said with more force than normal. She was tired after being up all night with Maggie, and she was grossed out by the hair she couldn't get off her hands.

"It's not your hair to decide, Serena. If you're bothered by it, get the hell out of here," Barbara roared back with vengeance.

It was the typical full-throttle anger she was used to with her mom. Not the kind that came with cancer, but the kind of anger that had danced around all of Serena's relations with her mother. Conversations that had the quiet anticipation of fierceness were the ones that kept Serena on edge for most of her life. Like the person who was supposed to love you most was also the person who hated you most.

Serena fought the tears in her eyes. How she hated that her eyes gave her away. She was no longer a child and yet these stupid tears gave her mother's anger more power than it deserved. Serena left the room quietly and went downstairs. Her father was sitting at the table reading the newspaper. She heard the slow crinkle of the newspaper page and saw her dad's eyes peering at her.

"You need to do something about Mom's hair," she said quietly. The air between her and her father was much more forgiving.

"I've mentioned it. But it's her hair. She does what she wants with it."

"Maybe you could mention shaving it. I'll buy you a shaver. Or maybe she'd let Abigail do it?"

Her father didn't say anything. She heard the newspaper make a noise as he began reading the full page again.

Barbara always was more patient with Serena's sister, Abigail. But then again, Abigail was always more attentive to their mother. Always ready to help. Always showering Barbara with praise. Serena knew Barbara preferred Abigail over her. That was never a secret.

Serena was surprised the next morning when she came back

to their home to check in on the way to work and she heard laughter. The sound of her parents' laughter was so foreign to her that it made her heart race as she quietly walked through the house. She felt the same uneasiness she imagined people in a horror movie felt as they propelled their bodies forward to some unknown doom. What she found was entirely strange, if not one of the most beautiful moments she'd ever seen of her parents. She peeked around the corner and there was Barbara in a chair looking straight at the mirror. Behind her was Serena's father, wielding a clipper, moving slowly, carefully forward like he was mowing a small, precious lawn.

"It tickles," said Barbara playfully. And then, "Not too short!" Her mother's voice could oscillate from happy to angry so quickly that it always felt surprising to the listener—even if they had a lifetime of preparing for the quick switch.

"Shhh. I'm concentrating," Robert replied, unrattled by her tone or his task. "I think I'm doing good. I might be pretty good as this," he said as he methodically moved to the next patch of grass, or hair.

"Great. You can shave your next wife, too," Barbara retorted.

"Shush with that," Robert replied.

Serena watched as he put his hand on Barbara's shoulder and she held her hand on his and they just stared at each other in the mirror. And that mixed look of fear, love, and uncertainty was a look Serena knew she'd never forget and never fully understand. Serena watched her mom's hair fall to the ground and thought about how hair was nothing but the past. She shuffled her legs and both her parents twitched suddenly, noticing her presence. The moment broke as they let their daughter into their space.

"I bet you're happy," said Barbara with a snarl, wrapped in a little bit of insecurity.

"I think Dad's doing a great job and you'll be more comfortable. It's not about me being happy, Mom. It's about you," reminded Serena.

"This cancer of yours doesn't leave much room for happiness," said Barbara.

Serena hated how her mom had started calling it "this cancer of yours" as if because Serena researched it, she was somehow responsible for it invading her mother's body. She inhaled and could practically hear a therapist salivating at that comment and what it meant that her mom would choose those words. Oh, the field day a therapist would have with her after her mother died; so much to unpack, so much to let go, so much she probably would never share. Tom had been pushing this idea of therapy on her for a while. Serena wasn't sure she could ever open up.

Serena didn't have time for therapy anyway. She only had time for her mother and a bit of hope. A week before Barbara died, she looked better. Or rather, her sickness had become so normal to her family's eyes that they no longer saw it. Instead, they saw hope in the tiny morsels of food she was able to keep down. There was hope in her legs that looked a little less swollen. And hope that her pain seemed less. Abigail, Serena, and their father would take turns going to the hospital, sometimes even forgetting the pain that was around them. It wasn't often that Abigail and Serena would be together with Barbara at the hospital. It was easier to alternate who went; it reduced both childcare needs and the uncomfortable air that happened when the sisters were together with Barbara.

"How's Hannah-banana?" asked Serena.

"You know she hates when you call her that." Abigail rolled her eyes, never quite taking her sister's chiding to heart. "She's fine. She's at school. Doing well."

"Of course she's doing well. She's your daughter. She's brilliant," chimed in Barbara.

"I know. I don't know where she gets it from," said Serena.

"Stop, Serena. Girls, it's important you look out for each other when I'm gone," Barbara said, changing the mood in the room.

"Mom, stop," said Serena.

"Listen, to me. I'm sorry I did this to you. I wouldn't have done this—" but before Barbara could finish, she started coughing up blood. Serena ran to find a nurse.

Only my mother would think cancer was something she could control. Something she could have decided she wouldn't have done to us, Serena thought.

By the time she came back, her mother's blanket looked like a battlefield. And those were the last words she'd ever hear from her mother.

As her mother coughed up what seemed like gallons of blood, all Serena could think to do was kiss her mother's head and say, "I love you. I love you," over and over, as the nurse did her best to shove a tube down her throat to keep the blood at bay. It was only the second time in her whole life that Serena had kissed her mother's head.

chapter 2: stone

Nighttime is for wrestling thoughts. And Barbara always seemed to be at the center of those thoughts. There was the angry Barbara of Serena's childhood. There was the Barbara who showed during a year of opening up with Maggie. Then there was the Barbara who was dying. It was like Serena had three mothers and the picture didn't quite fit together. She'd stare at her ceiling, memories fighting, blurry, and yet pushing her mind to figure out what to think, confusing her heart with what to feel.

"Mamma. Mamma. Why are you sad?" Serena ran up to her mother who was sitting on her bed crying.

"I need to get away from here," Barbara said, staring ahead as Serena climbed next to her. Serena thought about wiping her mother's tears but didn't move.

"I need to get away from here. From all of you. I'm just so tired."

Serena sat next to her quietly. Her legs dangled above the floor and she folded her hands and looked down, trying to think of what she had done.

"Can I go with you, when you go?" Serena asked.

"No." Barbara stared ahead, and her cheeks turned hard. Serena waited for her to say more, but Barbara didn't speak.

Serena quietly left the room and went into her bedroom. She hid in her closet so no one would see her cry.

Serena woke up in a cold sweat and pushed the feeling

of insecurity from her childhood away. Her dreams were like a relentless friend, reminding her of how the past had hurt her. Not wanting her to open her heart to the possibility that someone could change, that her mother could be more than difficulty and hate. And just when she quieted her thoughts, a new one would pop in that showed love.

***

The hospital hallway. Her mind always took her back to the long hallway. Her mom's room was closed. A nurse ran up to Serena and said,

"You might want to wait a minute, sweetie. They're cleaning up in there."

"What happened?"

"Your mom pulled her tubes out last night. Made quite a mess. She kept saying she was doing you guys a favor."

Serena looked down at the floor.

"She's on a lot of pain medicine now. She hasn't said a word since last night when she was pulling those tubes out. Happens a lot. Patients are a little out of it and just rip them out. Looks worse than it is."

Serena understood why Barbara disliked nurses. They were chatty. They said too much without realizing this wasn't just another patient to Serena. This was her mother. Her mother ripping things out of her body. This was her mother's blood. Serena wished the nurse would go away.

When the nurses were done, Serena was surprised that her

mother looked even older. How could she change so much in a night? Serena spent so much time staring at journal pages describing what cancer does to mice. How mice get tumors. She realized she hadn't spent as much time seeing what it does to a human. She sat quietly by her mother. The room smelled of Clorox, dead skin, vomit, and blood. *This is why I need to work more*, thought Serena. She thought of the hours she had spent sequencing genes in recurrent tumors to look for new mutations that were not present in the primary breast cancer. It had been months of research. She vowed to remember this moment, why she was pushing herself so hard in her research. So that daughters everywhere didn't have to watch their mothers die.

Just last week she had come in to see her mother, who was barely able to move, taking tiny pieces of sausage off a disgustingly chubby slice of cafeteria pizza. Her mother had not eaten in days.

"What are you doing?" Serena asked as she watched her mother pick off the meat.

Barbara's dry, thin hands had globs of sauce sticking to them. Her bony fingers were shaking and after two misses, she grabbed a sausage ball and brought it to her mouth.

"Doctor said I needed more protein. My legs are atrophying. I figured sausage has protein, right?"

"Yeah. I can go and buy you protein drinks, too. There are some that aren't so gross. I had them when I was pregnant with Maggie."

"No strawberry though. Maybe chocolate."

"I'll go and get some tomorrow for you."

"Serena, help me." Barbara took a plastic cup and was filling it with the little sausage balls. "It's for later. I can save it for later. I can't eat anymore."

"I'll do it, Mom. It's okay." Barbara's red sauce–stained hand fell back against the white cotton blanket.

"Serena, hand me the plastic bowl."

Barbara grabbed it and threw up.

"Clean it out for me. Just put it next to the bed here so I can grab it. I need to rest. I'm tired. Turn off the phone."

Serena closed her eyes and took the bowl into the bathroom. She turned on the water and dumped it down the sink without looking. She pressed the soap container five times and scrubbed her hands viciously. In the corner of the bathroom sat an unused commode with metal handles. The shower had a plastic seat. A long, black hair on the wall was blowing from the fan.

Serena came out of the bathroom and said,

"Okay, Mom. Sleep. I'll probably leave soon to go check on Maggie. But I'll come back."

But Barbara was already asleep. Serena touched the top of her hand with her fingers, careful not to get dirty. As she left the sterile hallway, she saw the doctor.

"Serena."

"Yes, hi. Have you seen my mom?"

"Yes, I saw her earlier. Serena, she's not doing well."

"Yes, she told me about the protein." Serena looked down at her feet and concentrated on the dirty part of her shoe. Her mind flooded with research papers that detailed how cancer causes the body to waste away.

"Serena, your mom hasn't kept food down in weeks. We have

her on an IV. Her bloodwork came back, and her liver enzymes are elevated. We're trying to combat the fluid, but . . ."

"I know. I know how it ends. Have you talked to my dad?"

"No, I was looking for him."

"He should be here any minute. There. There he is."

Serena's father walked through the hallway as if he was going for an enjoyable trip. He had magazines, soda, snacks, and some playing cards.

"Hi, Serena. Is your mother up?" Robert asked.

"She just fell asleep," Serena said.

"Hello, Dr. Orenstein," said Robert.

"Hi, Robert. I was just talking to Serena about... Actually, let's step away and go into this room."

Serena, her father, and the doctor went into an office. There were brochures and someone's lunch sitting on the desk. The office was small, and the orange-and-brown chair looked like it was thirty years old. The wrinkles of the chair's fabric had been sat on over and over, while the doctor shuffled ever so lightly, year after year of giving out bad news to a family. The chair, too, became sunken by the weight of every sob.

"Barbara isn't doing well. Her body is shutting down." The doctor stared down at the desk. Serena stared at a coffee mug sitting on the doctor's desk. The rings of the spilled coffee radiated outward onto a piece of paper. Cancer is a lot like a seeping spill. The drip that had started in her mother's breast had spread to her liver and now was leaking into her whole body. Serena had studied recurrence so much, and here it was, in front of her, in an experiment she couldn't control.

"How long does she have?" Serena's voice asked the question her father couldn't.

"My guess would be within the month. Barbara's strong-willed—she's a fighter—maybe longer."

"Thank you, Doctor."

"I'm sorry."

The doctor shook Robert's hand and gave a gentle wave in Serena's direction. Serena walked up and hugged her father. They both cried, and Serena's father said,

"These are tears of love. They're just tears of love." He wiped away the tears, straightened up and said, "I should call your sister and tell her this."

Everyone was always worried about Abigail. Her presence was always in the room even when she surprisingly wasn't. Serena wasn't sure if it was fear or sadness that kept her away. Abigail would say it was babysitter issues, but Serena knew it was more. She had expected Abigail to be by their mom's side. She had expected Robert to be by Barbara's side. In her mind, and at least in movies, a husband didn't leave his wife's side. But if care was calculated in bedside minutes, it was Serena who cared the most for her mother in those final days.

Serena had never understood her parents' marriage. They seemed to have more things out of common than in. Her dad loved sports, new movies, good food, traveling, books, museums, friends, and antique shows. Her mom loved old movies, solitaire, diner food, and Abigail. They had an old-fashioned marriage that meant Barbara cleaned, cooked, and washed while Robert worked, came home, and complained about the way Barbara cleaned, cooked, and washed. He wasn't wrong. Barbara cared more about playing cards than cleaning house. Once in a while, Serena heard them giggling together and it gave her faith that maybe she didn't understand them.

***

Serena was not there when her mother died. She was with Maggie. No one was with Barbara. The daily therapy dog, Bailey, was making his rounds, wagging his big black tail, when one of the volunteers, Sheila, came into the room with him. She brought Bailey up to Barbara and the dog sat down and nuzzled his head into her arm, and her arm fell down hard. Cold. Machines began to beep. Sheila ran with the dog to the nurses' station to tell them something was wrong.

Serena was washing dishes when Abigail called.

"Hello?"

There was no voice on the other end of the phone. Only sobbing. Such strong, forceful sobbing that Serena didn't even realize it was crying. She thought it was an odd background noise, like construction equipment on a busy highway. She started to hang up the phone when she lost her breath. Somehow her heart had figured it out first.

"Is it Mom? Is it Mom?" her voice came out high, totally out of her control.

She waited for the answer from whoever it was on the other end of the phone. A shuffle. A pause. A switch of whoever was holding the phone and then Serena heard a quiet breath that she realized was her father's voice.

"I'm sorry, Serena. Abigail couldn't." He paused.

"She's dead. She's dead." Again, Serena's voice left her and became something more like the squeak of her daughter's.

"Yes. The nurse said it was peaceful. Abigail and I were on our way. Abigail had to stop and let Hannah—"

"Abigail is always having to stop and go somewhere. I should have been there. Someone should have been there." Serena was holding her phone tightly, trying to keep her chest from tightening with every word her father said.

"We did our best. We were here a lot. You were here. We did our best."

"She died alone. She hated being alone." Serena grabbed a towel and dried a mug over and over.

"Do you want to come here?"

"Yes. Let me call the neighbors or Tom and see if someone can watch Maggie."

She hung up the phone and walked into the family room where Maggie was playing with her toys.

"Maggie, want to watch TV?"

Maggie's eyes shined bright. "Yeah!"

Serena grabbed the remote clumsily and quickly found the first cartoon she could find.

"Mommy will be right back, okay? Sit and watch."

Serena ran to the bathroom and looked in the mirror. She closed her eyes. Her heart beat fast, as if a lifetime of emotion was pumping it. Slowly, tears began to slide out her eyes. Her chest heaved in and out. Everything she had bottled up came pouring out. She put her hand to her mouth to quiet her sobs. After a few moments, she gripped onto the sink and steadied her shaking.

"Alone," she whimpered to the mirror as if her reflection would understand. "She died alone."

"Mamma? Mamma?" A little knock on the door.

"It's okay. Mommy is almost done. Just one second."

Serena wiped her tears and opened the door, forcing a smile to the brown eager eyes of Maggie. She bent down and hugged her little frame. "I love you."

"Mamma come sit?" Maggie's tender voice found its way into Serena's chest and echoed there. Her tiny, soft hand led Serena's to the TV. Maggie pointed to the ground next to her. "Mamma?"

"Sure, baby. Mamma sit."

Serena gazed at the TV. Trying not to cry. *Is this what motherhood is?* she wondered. *Is it all an act? Is it all a bold lie? Trying to smile when you have tears? Trying to show happiness when you are too exhausted to repeat the ABCs one more time?* Her eyes glazed over as she tried to remember what it felt like to watch cartoons and get lost in them. To be lost in anything and not be so aware. The phone rang.

"Serena?"

"Tom? I—" She couldn't say it.

"Your dad called to see how you were."

"I'm sorry. I should have called. I just—"

"It's okay. I'm on my way home. I'm coming home to you now."

"Okay."

***

As Serena sat waiting for Tom, she couldn't help but think through how her mother's illness had progressed. The cancer had started in her breast, and there were some cancer cells in her lymph nodes. But it was not an advanced tumor. Serena knew cancer. Her mother was doing fine.

The tumor was small, her surgery had gone well, and she was responding well to treatment. It was Stage III. Staging was developed to help doctors know which treatment to follow. It just referred to what organ the cancer started in, the size of the original tumor, and if it had spread to the surrounding lymph nodes, or if it had spread to more distant areas of the body. *It's just a number*, she thought. A number she had seen millions of times. It didn't have to mean the end. It didn't have to be a big deal. Serena never thought anything was a big deal. Her mother thought everything was a big deal. Maybe that was why they never got along.

Serena wondered how Abigail was doing with it all. Serena and Abigail were only a few years apart in age. But it was more like an endless abyss because of the tragedy that had happened between their births. Serena always thought the death of their other sister, Dorothy, must have changed their mother. How does one get over the loss of a child except by losing yourself? It wasn't until Maggie that Serena would truly, deeply understand this. But as a child, Serena accepted that the warmth Abigail knew and grew up with in her early years was just not there for her. Serena would watch out of the corner of her eye as Abigail lavished their mom with hugs and kisses. Serena didn't hug and didn't kiss. Serena stayed away, quietly playing. This strange dichotomy of motherly love didn't make the sisters' relationship colder; if anything, it made them more attached. Serena always looked out for Abigail, knowing she was precious to their mother. Abigail loved Serena, often making up for the lack of motherly kisses with sisterly ones instead. And the death of their sister that no one dared talk about bonded them together like glue.

As Maggie concentrated on *Elmo's World*, Serena got up and went to the kitchen. Instinctively, she started making dinner. Grabbing vegetables. Chopping. Cutting with such focus her back teeth hurt from gritting them.

***

"Serena?" She could hear her mother's voice yelling from the kitchen. Angry.

"Coming, Mom." The stress of dinner and a clock.

"Here, you wash and cut these." Her mom handed her green peppers.

They cooked silently.

Her mother had a determined anger toward whatever meal they were preparing. Slaughtering tomatoes. Banging pots. Pressing the life out of meat with a spatula. Serena always cooked beside her quietly. Her mother never asked Abigail to help. And it used to bother Serena that she always had to be the one to help. Then she realized that it was because she was a good cook, a better cook, a faster slicer. This realization made Serena happy. The angry dinner preparation was something the two of them shared, silently. It was something that Serena was better at than Abigail.

***

Serena became so absorbed by the rhythmic cutting of vegetables that she didn't even hear Tom come in.

"Honey? You okay?"

She turned, looked at him, and let the tears fall down her cheeks. Without a word, she turned back to her vegetables and kept cutting. Tom came behind her and hugged her. She stopped and said,

"I'm just getting dinner ready, and then I'm going. It's almost done."

"You don't need to make dinner. You should go. Serena, I'm so sorry. I'm so sorry. I don't know what to say. I love you."

"I love you. Just take care of Maggie. I don't want her to see me sad. She won't understand."

"It's okay. She'll be fine. We'll be fine. Go be with your family."

"Okay. Okay. I'm going."

***

There are some drives that take longer than they should. Drives where the sky seems grayer. The clouds seem to whisper. Every car seems to glide as if on ice. Serena felt her hands on the wheel but felt nothing else. She drove past the familiar grocery store, that old stone house on the corner, around the back of the woods. She thought about taking the back roads, but she was afraid she would forget how to get to the hospital, even though she had been there hundreds of times. The pace of the highway felt uncomfortable. So many cars with places to go. So many people who don't notice that one person's life has just ended. Grief is like that. It's a lonely road forward, where the world seems to be moving at a different speed.

***

Just a few weeks ago, her mother was alive. Just a few weeks ago, it was her mother's birthday. Serena had frantically chased the happy birthday balloon that escaped her car through the parking lot.

"Don't do this to me," she screamed at the balloon. As if losing the balloon meant losing hope for her mother.

It finally wrapped itself on a car rearview mirror, bobbing happily in the wind, taunting her. What do you get for someone's birthday when you know they aren't going to live? Clothes? Serena's mom now lived in a world of hospital gowns. Jewelry? She would only be buried in it. Abigail, like every year, had bought her mom pajamas. Her mother loved pajamas. It was her and Abigail's thing—a PJ party Serena was not included in. Serena decided on a balloon to cheer up the room and some flowers. And a picture of Maggie. Her mom did not want Maggie to visit.

"Maggie is like sunshine. The happiest baby I've ever seen. I don't want to see that go out when she sees me like this," Barbara said.

"She's asking for you. Maybe just for a second, she can come by and say hi."

"You mean goodbye."

"Stop, Mom. Don't talk like that."

"Serena. I want you to have this ring. Grandma's ring." Serena was touched, but her heart stung because she knew her mother had already given her favorite ring to Abigail. She tried to let go of the feeling of jealousy, as she thought that any gift of her mother's was something to cherish.

"Mom."

"This is important, Serena. Save it for Maggie. She may want it one day."

Serena's eyes teared with a mixture of disappointment and appreciation. Of course, the ring was not for her, but for her daughter. At least Barbara loved Maggie. They had that joy to share between them.

"Okay, Mom. I will." She slid the ring on her finger and made a fist.

***

Serena looked down at her fingers as she walked through the cold parking lot. She would wear the ring until Maggie was old enough. Suddenly, she was glad to know that a piece of her mother and grandmother would be hers. Even though her relationship with her mother was complex, there was something about family lineage that felt beautiful to Serena. The passage of generations was now so apparent as she thought about Barbara, herself, and her own daughter, Maggie. Women representing life's continuous movement of time. Serena passed two elderly people sitting in wheelchairs waiting to be picked up. She saw the familiar sign on the elevator reminding you to wash your hands. She pressed the number three button without thinking. She had walked this path many times. It wasn't until she heard the ding of the elevator that she was reminded that this was not the same path. She was not walking to see her mother. She was walking to see her mother's body.

The hospital door was closed. It looked heavy. Serena paused and saw one of the nurses glance up at her. She looked away quickly, bowing her head and turning the knob. Her mother's body, rigid with her mouth opened to one side, greeted her. She walked straight into Abigail's arms and cried. The two sisters kept each other from falling to the ground by hugging each other tightly. A nurse came and closed the door respectfully, to keep other patients from hearing their cries. Robert shifted his weight and finally came up and put his arms around his daughters.

"I'm sorry," he said.

Serena caught her breath, blew her nose in her sleeve, and went over to her mother. She went near her mother and put her hand on her heart; it was hard like a stone.

"I love you, Mom," was all she was able to get out before she moved away from the hardness that was no longer her mother.

Abigail, Serena, and her father all sat in chairs near her mother without talking, each one taking turns from time to time to go over and sit next to her.

"We should call some people," Serena said, breaking the silence. "Aunt Patty. Uncle Tom. Janice."

"We will," Abigail said.

Serena was surprised Abigail wasn't crying more. Abigail was always crying over something. And yet, here in front of her mother's body, she seemed oddly calm.

Some time passed before her father got up and put his hands on Serena's and Abigail's. He looked like he was going to say something but didn't. He removed his hands and started walking to the door.

"I'm going to go talk to the nurses about what's next," he said quietly.

***

"Let's go for a walk."

The way Robert said those words to Serena wasn't demanding but more of a subtle offer of help. Barbara was in one of her moods and Serena's teenage attitude wasn't helping.

Robert and Serena walked down to the woods behind their house, carrying the weight of the day's fight with them. Neither of them talked as they made their way slowly down the familiar paths of leaves and dirt. The trees swayed in the wind. Serena looked up at their gentle movement, listening closely for the secrets in their branches. *Maybe that's how my father survives with my mom*, Serena thought. *He bends to her, lets her storms pass through.*

Serena passed an old white oak and put her hand on the thickness of the bark. Robert came next to her.

"Tough exterior," he said. Serena nodded. A tear slipped out as she noticed the grooves within the bark's protection.

"Sorry," she said. "She makes me frustrated. And then I just make her mad."

Robert put his hand on hers, and if hands could talk, Serena thought his were telling her, "It'll be okay." But instead, he said, "Come on, let's walk back."

***

Feeling sorry changes as you get older. The guilt you carry as a child gets more complicated with every wrinkle as you age. It would be months after Barbara died before Serena would feel sorry for things. Sorry for the times she treated her mom poorly when she was alive. Like the night of the high school dance when she didn't want her mom to come take pictures. Or when she was embarrassed by the food on her face at her wedding. Serena was also sorry for treating her mom poorly when she was sick. Like when she was short with her mom because she was self-conscious when her mom was unruly with nurses. Serena was sorry for never getting the recipe for her mom's chicken soup. She was sorry for never truly appreciating how nice it was to have someone smile at Maggie with love. The list of things she was sorry for went on and on. Mainly, she was sorry she didn't have the perspective she had now that her mom was dead when her mom was alive.

As Serena stared at her mother's body, she didn't feel sorry and she didn't feel sad. She almost felt exhilarated. Like her mother's body or soul was swirling about her and filling her up. She wanted to ask Abigail if she felt the same thing, but she kept quiet. She didn't want to know. Serena wanted it to be her thing, something that her mother was making only her feel.

The next few days went by like some odd dream. Things were slow, like thick pecan pie filling. They did the things they were supposed to do. Call family and friends. Talk to funeral homes. Decide on a time and a date for the funeral. Pick out a casket. Serena found she was not good at calling people. She couldn't get her tone right. She felt she never took value in the words she was saying.

"Hello, Janice?"

"Yes, hello?" Serena wondered what Janice was doing. How she had interrupted her day.

"This is Serena. Barbara's daughter."

"Yes. How is she?"

"Well. My mom passed away yesterday."

Silence. There was always silence. Maybe because of tears, maybe because there is no response that seems right. No words that seem to have enough weight.

Janice was crying. "I loved your mom. She was a dear friend."

"I know. She loved you, too. You were so good to her."

"She wouldn't let me visit."

"I know. You know my mom. She was private. She didn't want people to see her sick."

"I can't believe she's gone." More crying.

"I'm sorry." Serena sat holding the phone. Why did Serena always apologize? She said "I'm sorry" too much, and every time those words escaped her mouth, she vowed to herself she wouldn't let them slip out again so easily. Yet here she was, listening to another one of her mother's friends cry and feeling like the most awful person on the earth. She should have let her dad call everyone. He was better at this. He wouldn't say much. But he could turn simple words into meaningful statements. He would leave people remembering Barbara and feeling happy they were a part of her life.

Serena wondered if Abigail was just crying through her calls. She put a line through Janice's name and looked at the list. Only four more people to call.

She decided to call Natalie next. If there was anyone who would make Serena feel better, it was her friend. Natalie knew how to talk and fill the empty spaces. Conversations with her always flowed; they were never work.

"Serena, I'm so sorry. What can I do? Let me take care of dinner Saturday. I'll drop off Sages, I know you love that place. Does 5:30 work?"

Serena agreed because Natalie made it easy to accept help. She had a specific idea of how she would help instead of a general "What can I do?"

"Also, if you need me to watch Mags, I can."

"Thanks, Natalie. I'll let you know. I appreciate you being there for me."

"Of course, you're stuck with me girl, always."

Natalie's casual breeziness felt like a welcome exhale to all of Serena's other conversations. Serena's whole posture relaxed and she was ready to take on the rest of her calls. Good friends are powerful like that. They can share their strength with you without you even knowing it.

***

One time, Serena's cell phone showed the caller's name as *MOM*. Serena dropped to her knees like someone had punched her in the gut. It was her dad; they had shared a phone. In that brief moment, she had forgotten. It felt so familiar. Her phone ringing with her mom's voice. Grief can do that to you. Turn the familiar into the enemy. Bring you to your knees when warm memories suddenly sharpened into daggers.

There were times Serena found herself looking around the kitchen, feeling like she forgot something. She'd check the stove to make sure it was turned off. She'd look in the fridge to make sure they had milk. She'd check the washer to make sure she hadn't left it full of wet clothes. And then it would hit her, that feeling she felt, the feeling like something was wrong—it was there because her mother was dead.

***

The day of any funeral is an odd day. There are friends and family dressed up. So many people you are happy to see. Yet it isn't a wedding, or a bar mitzvah, or some other pleasant occasion. You are all there because one of you isn't.

Serena didn't have anything to wear to the funeral. She had an old black skirt that was faded to gray. The thought of buying a dress or new clothes for such a day seemed awful. She would never want to wear them again. They would always be the clothes she wore on that terrible day. But she had to, so she drove to the mall the afternoon before the funeral and tried on clothes. Everywhere she looked, she saw mothers with their daughters. She grabbed three black dresses and ran into the dressing room. She put her hands to her eyes and wept as quietly as she could. The third dress was expensive, but it fit. She bought it without ever looking at the salesperson.

As she put on that dress the morning of the funeral, the fabric felt different. Not elegant. Not pretty. Just black fabric that hung on her like sadness. She blow-dried her hair, but she didn't worry if it was just right. She put on lipstick, though it felt strange to be putting on make-up for such an occasion. She wiped it off and found some Chapstick to put on instead. She didn't look in the mirror. She came down the stairs and saw Tom looking handsome in his suit. Maggie was in the flowered dress Barbara had bought her just a few months before.

Serena pulled Tom aside and said, "I don't want Maggie to see me upset. You'll make sure your sister Alice takes her away when we get started?"

"Yes, don't worry."

"Do you think it's bad that I want her to go?"

"No. It's okay. I understand you wanting her there."

"My dad should be here any minute. I'll meet you at the cemetery."

"Okay, sweetie. I love you." He squeezed her hand and gave her a hug like someone who's relieved it's not their mother who is dead.

There is nothing friendly about gravestones. They are hard and cold, standing in rows upon rows of grass that seem sad to be there. Serena kept track of the names as she walked past them. Beckett. Silverstein. Simons. Purple flowers. Little garden gnomes. An American flag. An old baseball. Little trinkets of remembrance trying to make the graves seem less cold, less hard, less final.

Serena looked down at the grass and thought how it probably

wished to be on a hill somewhere or in a park, anywhere but stuck between dead people. Barbara's grave was like an open mouth of dirt waiting to swallow. The casket looked wooden and hard. The heel of Serena's shoe kept getting stuck in the dirt below her. Her legs felt uncomfortable and tired. There was a row of metal folding chairs meant for her elderly family members. Serena looked at them, thinking this would all be easier sitting. Tom found his way through the small crowd and took her hand. Serena saw Maggie playing in the distance. She smiled and waved. Playing hopscotch and unaware of her surroundings. The grass seemed to smile where Maggie was, happy to feel joy upon it.

Next to where they stood sat the small gravestone with Serena and Abigail's sister Dorothy's name on it. It read: *Dorothy Solomon. Our sweet angel.* There was no date on it. Serena's aunt had told her once that her mom couldn't bear to see the same year begin and end on the tombstone, so they left it off. Serena looked at her baby sister's grave and felt a chill. She saw the little rocks on top of the tombstone—stones of remembrance and respect for the dead. Would Serena ever know the truth of what happened now that her mother was dead? They never talked much about her dead sister.

Barbara had wanted a small graveside service. She did not want an open casket. Before the ceremony, Serena went to the funeral home to make sure everything was in order. She had brought the clothes her father had given her in a brown grocery bag the day before.

"You forgot shoes," she told him.

"She doesn't need shoes, Serena. Besides, I couldn't pick."

Serena had wanted to go upstairs and get some, but Robert seemed angry. Serena stopped and bought shoes on the way to the funeral home. She couldn't think of her mother shoeless in the dirt. She knew Barbara would be mad that she spent money on such a stupid thing. She tried to find a pair in the clearance section, but none looked right. Her mother loved a good clearance deal. Thirty-nine dollars later she had shoes that no one would ever see. Serena also brought a picture of her mother. Even though no one was going to see Barbara, Serena wanted the embalmers to know what she looked like. She didn't want her to be in the ground forever looking like someone she wasn't.

At the funeral home, Serena saw Cindy, the lady who was in charge of running the facility. The two women shook hands. Cindy wore a cheap blue blazer suit, and Serena could see her stomach rolls over her pantyhose. Cindy was overly solemn. Too solemn to be real. Serena felt a little freaked out as she thought about how this lady lived here all the time with dead people in her basement. The house had a lot of pictures of wooden rocking horses. Serena wondered if that was supposed to remind mourners of childhood or a happier time.

"Your mother is ready. Do you want me to close the casket or do you want to see her? She's in there." Cindy pointed casually to a room.

Serena stopped for a moment. She desperately wanted to see her mother again, to touch her. Everyone had agreed it was not what Barbara had wanted. Serena knew Abigail would be upset if she got to see her and she didn't. Serena nodded; no words came out and she walked into the small, dark room. Her mother, or the hardened, strange shell of a body that looked vaguely like her mother, lay in the room. What was left of her hair looked over-sculpted. Her lips looked swollen. Serena thought to herself, *She looks like a dead body*, and then shook her head at what an obviously stupid thought that was. She put her hand above her mother's heart and let it levitate there. She wanted to touch her but was afraid. She was glad to be alone with her. The round buttons on her blue blouse were buttoned to the top. Instinctively Serena unbuttoned the top two, just how Barbara would have worn it. She kept her hand on the second button, touching her mother slightly over her heart.

Serena knew a lot about the embalming process. She had seen her first dead body when she was twelve years old. Her grandfather's funeral. He looked handsome and quiet. Not at all like how her mother looked now, her suffering apparent through her swollen face. Her grandfather had a heart attack—quick and done. After the funeral, Serena's curious scientific nature made her look up the embalming process, and the facts now ran through her brain as if she'd be quizzed on it.

Arterial embalming—injecting embalming chemicals into the blood vessels, usually via the right common carotid artery. Drainage. Cavity embalming—replacing the internal fluids inside body cavities with formaldehyde by using an aspirator. Hypodermic embalming—injecting embalming chemicals into tissue with a hypodermic needle and syringe, to treat areas where arterial fluid was not distributed during the main arterial injection. Surface embalming—using chemicals to preserve and restore areas directly on the skin. Serena looked at her mother's poor swollen body and wondered who spent the time doing this to her mother, as if she were just another body. Someone spent hours with her mother's body, touching her elbows, her knees, her skin as if she was nothing more than today's work.

"It's time." Cindy's voice broke her from her moment.

"Thank you. She's all set," said Serena, and she left for the cemetery.

***

Serena stared at the casket now and thought about her secret last moment with her mother. Her ears heard the words of the service, but they felt tiny, like fuzzy newspaper print. She looked around at all the faces. She knew her mom would be pissed that cousin Alex came; she never liked him. Barbara always said, "I never understand why people who don't want to be part of your life want to come to your death."

She was right, Serena thought as she looked around at the many people who hadn't taken the time to even call Barbara when she was sick. Yet they were all standing here looking sad. Serena counted her breaths to keep her mind from listening to the service and getting sad. She heard Maggie's name and looked up, as if suddenly the world had regained its color.

Her aunt was talking, "Barbara had always wanted to see her daughters have children of their own. When Serena did, Barbara said, 'It's okay, whatever happens to me will be okay. I've seen both my girls have girls. There's nothing a mother could want more.'"

Barbara had never told Serena that she had wanted her to have a child. That would have been too easy, too warm. Instead, she spent more time questioning all the years Serena waited to get pregnant. Serena found Tom's shoulder and hid her heart from the small crowd and cried for how much Maggie meant to her, and to her mother. She thought about taking longer solace in his suit and never looking up again until the service was over. Robert started to say a few words and stopped. Serena and Abigail went over to him and put their arms around him. Their neighbor sang a song, and it was done.

Serena looked up and desperately wanted to find Maggie. "Where is she?" she asked Tom. "I don't see her."

"I'm sure she's fine."

"Can you find her? I need her. I just think, maybe my mom—I don't know. Maybe I was wrong. Maybe Maggie should say goodbye. I don't know if she'll get it. But my mom loved her. Maybe she needs this memory? Maybe I do. I don't know if any of this makes sense."

"It's okay. I don't think anything needs to make sense. But if it feels right, it feels right. I'm fine with whatever you want to do. I'll go get her and be right back."

Serena watched a small spider make its way across her mother's coffin. She wondered if it would survive being lowered down with the dirt. A life being lowered down with death just didn't seem right. She crouched down and let the spider crawl onto her finger and then she released it onto the grass. She felt Maggie's little arms hug her back from behind.

"Hey Mags. I know you probably don't understand this. But I want you to know Grandma, who came by and fed you cereal, she's not going to be able to do that anymore. But the thing you need to know is she loved you so much." Serena didn't know if the words she was saying were important for her to hear or if she just wanted to know that Barbara had heard them. She also didn't know if she believed Barbara could hear them, but she stuffed that thought back inside her head to make this moment what she thought it should be. Funerals were not a day for rational thought. Funerals were not a day when anything made sense.

Maggie's eyes got big like she did when her mom read her a good book.

"And I just wanted you to have a chance to say goodbye to Grandma, Maggie. Because she loved you."

Maggie waved to no one, not really sure where Grandma was, but happy to oblige her mother's waving wishes.

When Serena finally said her last goodbye to her aunts, uncles, and parents' friends, she made her way home. Tom and Maggie were sitting on the couch snuggling.

"Mamma!" Maggie jumped off of the couch and ran to Serena and put her arms around her neck and patted her back. The magic of Maggie's touch, a tiny body of exquisite squish, all elbows and knees, was just what Serena needed. Like an octopus releasing its tentacles, Maggie pushed off and ran into the other room and came back with a fistful of flowers that drooped over. Maggie encouraged each flower to stand back straight, but they were worn out from a day without water and the not-so-gentle grip of her fingers. She held out the bouquet, a gift of love and gratitude for the unspeakable everything between them.

Serena took the dandelions and smelled them. "My favorite," she said.

Maggie's face beamed.

"Thank you so much. This was just what Mommy needed. But it's a little late for you to be up, isn't it?"

"I figured you wanted to see her. I gave her a bath already." Tom looked tired as he turned off *Elmo*.

"Yeah, thanks. Come on, Munchkin, Mamma go read you stories and put you to bed."

Maggie's fingers found her way into Serena's hand and they made their way up the stairs—Maggie's short, thin legs trying to take the steps two at a time like a fearless mountain climber and Serena's hand holding her tight to keep her from falling back as she made her ascent.

Maggie found her little monkey doll and sat in a chair and pointed next to it, "Mamma?"

"Mamma's coming. Let me get a good book to read."

Serena's mind wandered as she read the words to *Amelia Bedelia* as she had many nights before. She thought about how her mother had read her that same book and how much her mom seemed to laugh at it. The little chicken dressed up. The towels all cut. She was struck how, in that moment, she was remembering only good things about her mother. Maggie's body curled into her, and she squeezed her warmth tight. Serena felt grounded in the corner of Maggie's little pink room. She imagined she was tucked in one of the angles she used to study in geometry. And the whole world was in front of her like some vast obtuse opening into space. Maggie arched her little head and looked past Serena's shoulder and smiled. Serena imagined her mother's spirit playing peek-a-boo with Maggie from behind the chair. Serena nuzzled her nose into Maggie's soft cheek. She adored Maggie's cheeks; she could have touched them all night, with their warmth and fuzz like a Labrador puppy.

As she laid Maggie down in her bed, shadows from the window danced across her sheet. Serena knew it was just the leaves from the tree blowing. It looked like a hand waving hello. Her lungs went cold. She looked out the window and whispered, "I miss you."

In her head, she chastised herself for missing her mother. This person who Serena had spent years thinking her life would be better without. This infuriating woman who had made her life stressed and miserable and then decided to show love in their last year together. It wasn't fair. Serena's heart ached with confusion about the new person she saw when Barbara was with Maggie. It ached with the thought that maybe if they had more time, Serena could have mended the past. Or at least understood more about the Barbara who had raised Serena and how their relationship had grown so out of control—like ivy on a tree, that clutched and wound until it wasn't obvious if the tree was dying from the ivy's grasp.

Serena kissed Maggie's forehead and watched her squeeze her monkey tight. Serena scratched Maggie's back lightly and watched her body relax. Normally, she would kiss her goodnight and leave, but Serena stayed, quietly stroking Maggie's back softly with her fingers. Maggie's eyelids grew heavier and heavier, trying so desperately to resist the sleep that was coming. Serena watched them bob open and closed like two tiny ships on the ocean. Finally, her eyelids gave in and they closed tightly. Serena thought about how her mother's eyelids did the opposite today. Her mother's eyelids gave in and hid, leaving her eyes open forever. Serena closed the door quietly, walked down the stairs, and found Tom on the couch and snuggled into him and wept. He petted her hair and said, "I'm sorry. I'm so sorry." Serena tried to remember what her mother's eyes looked like at the hospital, but couldn't.

The next day Serena got her first batch of "I'm thinking of you" cards. Friends. Family. Distant acquaintances. She was amazed at how many people felt compelled to write her yet not actually write her. "Thinking of you." "My thoughts are with you." The statements people wrote didn't mean anything. *Really*, she thought. *Could nobody think of something personal to write?* Many of these people knew her mother well, yet they showed no emotion, no feeling. No anecdotal story to make Serena smile and remember the good times. Serena's favorite was "Things will get easier." When she read that, she knew it was from someone who had never lost someone close to them.

How will it get easier? she wondered. *My mother is dead forever. I'll never understand her. Her death will not change. Maggie will not have a grandmother forever. That is not easier. That is the same.* She hated the cards' muted colors. The sad gray flowers. The seagulls over dreary oceans with gray stones. The overly scripty writing. It was as if all the greeting cards had agreed on the same dull color palette that exuded both mournfulness and quietness. One by one, she threw them in the trash.

chapter 3: clothes

Going through someone's closet is like going through a photo album. Old shirts that remind you of a specific day. A good lunch. A trip to Tennessee. Serena looked around her mother's closet and could practically see her standing there. She couldn't understand why her father wanted to get rid of her clothes so quickly. She would have kept them hanging there for the rest of her life. Just so she could walk in from time to time and still see her mother. But maybe her father didn't want the reminder. Maybe it hurt too much for him.

Serena knew this task wasn't going to be easy for her. It wasn't just the memories. It was having to touch her mother's things. The mess of it all made her insides feel on edge. But closure is never tidy. She saw her mother in the white shirt with the ketchup stains from one too many hotdogs. She saw her in that old black sweater that was ratty from wearing it too much. One dark gray shirt still had a clearance tag on it with the original price crossed off and then the sale price crossed off and then a clearance sticker marked $7.99. She could hear Barbara's voice, "A true find in the racks. What a deal." Shoeboxes of never-to-be-worn shoes gathered layers of dust that made Serena uneasy. Smells of musk, old sneakers, and stale perfume on silk blouses filled Serena's nose as she gently touched a sleeve of a cream-colored cotton sweater.

Abigail went right to work, methodically going through old purses and taking out old tissues, cough drops, and sugar packets.

"You're being really thorough." Serena handed her a garbage bag.

"Mom always hid money. I figured we could give it to Dad—it just seems silly to throw it away. Mom would have wanted me to look." Serena noticed the wetness growing in Abigail's eyes and wondered if Abigail still felt the pull of Barbara even from the grave, and the need to honor her wishes.

"Oh. I didn't know that. About the money." Serena looked down and tried to go through a purse, but the dirtiness inside made her feel sick. She wondered what else she didn't know about her mom that Abigail knew.

Serena looked down and saw a familiar jewelry box. "Remember this? It used to be Grandma's. I used to play with it when I was little."

"Take it."

Serena put the box in a bag along with some other random things. Perfume, which she never even liked to wear but for some reason felt bad throwing out. An old hot water bottle she had bought for her mother that was in the shape of a dog. A little girl's shirt that might have been hers when she was little. A birthday card that her mother had written a recipe on. A picture that Serena had made with a note on the back that said, "Happy Mother's Day. I'll try to be a better daughter."

"How's it going, girls?" Robert peeked in the closet and handed them more bags.

"Good. We've gone through this side."

"Great. Great progress," he said with genuine enthusiasm as he left the room.

"Don't you think it's weird he isn't helping?" asked Serena.

"He's been weird since Mom died. Not helping doesn't surprise me," replied Abigail.

"I just don't see what his rush is. And if he is in such a rush to get rid of her things, why doesn't he help, too?" Serena wanted nothing more than to be able to go home and stop touching the dusty boxes and old clothes, but she didn't want to leave Abigail alone. Every time Abigail called her these days, she was crying. Yet, here in the closet, her eyes were dry.

"Grieving is odd. It's all part of the process, isn't it? Getting rid of the past." Abigail threw a cleaned-out purse into the heap of searched-through accessories.

"What's that pile over there?" Serena asked.

"Consignment stuff. I figured some of this stuff is too nice to donate. We can take any money and put it toward the grandkids."

"Good idea," Serena said as she looked at the pile of formal clothes that were huddled up as if they just finished a football play. "She wore that to my wedding. The gray dress." The dress's shimmering fabric twisted and turned within the pile.

"You want it?" said Abigail.

"No." Serena went back to work and pushed anything too dusty near Abigail to look through.

"Hey, look," Abigail said, gesturing toward the bathroom.

"What?" Serena asked.

"The toilet seat is up. Mom would have killed him." The girls laughed, but Serena's eyes stayed looking at the seat. Somehow the big round O of the seat seemed to sum up everything that had changed—there was zero left of her mother.

"Have you noticed he doesn't say her name? It's been two weeks and we don't say her name," Abigail said without looking up as she shoved her hand into a purse that had been used so many times the leather was soft like linen.

"Yeah. He hasn't mentioned Mom to me at all."

"We never talk. He never calls me. I waited a week, and then I finally called him and all he talked about was having us come over to clean out the closet. He didn't even ask about Hannah."

"Who knows what he's going through? Maybe this is how he deals. Remember after Grandpa died, he never really talked about him. Think about how hard it is for us. It must be even harder for Dad. I mean, they were married for so long." Serena could see that Abigail's face stiffened.

"You always did stick up for him."

"I'm not sticking up for him. It sucks. All of this sucks. It sucks way worse than I ever could have imagined."

"At least you were there for her when she was in the hospital last week. I feel like Hannah got sick, the babysitter canceled— so much time was taken away from me." Abigail looked away and controlled her tears.

"You were there for her when she was alive. That's when she needed you. You were there when she needed support. We couldn't all be there 24/7. You were there a lot. All you missed that last day was—"

Serena closed her eyes as she thought of all the blood and said, "You wouldn't have wanted to see what I saw, Abigail. And besides, she never would have left if you were there."

The girls got quiet and breathed in the dust flakes of their mother that were circulating in the air around them. Serena looked at Abigail and tried to find some common ground in her eyes. Her hazel eyes were cold. Her dark brown hair was disheveled and up. And she wore a black T-shirt that was misshapen from too much wear and wash. Yet, even so, Serena thought Abigail was the prettier of the two sisters, and she was sure everyone else thought that too. It didn't matter that Serena ran twelve miles every week and Abigail had never exercised in her life.

Abigail had started every type of sport when she was young: soccer, softball, basketball, volleyball, tennis, even fencing and badminton. Although she never finished up the season, Barbara always stuck up for her. "If she doesn't like it, she doesn't like it." Yet every year, Abigail would come with some sort of form for some sport she just *knew* she was going to love. But when Serena got really good at softball and made the traveling team, Barbara decided that all the games were "taking up too much family time," and so she encouraged Serena to quit. For Serena, that meant staying up in her bedroom and reading in her closet so Barbara wouldn't come and nag her to clean. Abigail never had to clean. Although, being the good daughter that she was, she was always offering to help Barbara with laundry and making beds. Serena hated making beds. She saw no point in doing something that was just going to be undone in the same day. Whenever Barbara called from her bedroom, Serena would climb under her bed and hide.

Barbara's bed was made now and looming behind the two sisters and their clothing piles. Serena would steal glances at the green, flowered bedspread. Sometimes she would look back and squint her eyes and she could almost see her mother lying there. She couldn't imagine how her father lay in that bed every night.

"I was thinking we should do something every month in honor of Mom. Something fun. Something that reminds us of her," said Abigail as she put a navy sweater in the giveaway bag.

"Sure," said Serena, looking at her sister and trying to hide her bewilderment. Abigail never wanted to do anything with her lately. She always had things to do with Hannah. And even when Serena tried to get Hannah and Maggie together, Abigail would always say the girls had too many years between them to have anything in common.

***

The first sister date commemorating their mom was to the Blue City Diner, a silvery old diner with big uncomfortable booths finished in bright red plastic fabric and orange-and-brown tables. In the middle of the other dining room, which had tables and no booths, sat a big salad bar where Barbara used to fill her plate with chopped liver, cottage cheese, and beets, and rave about the half-stale raisin bread like it was gourmet brioche. Barbara never liked to sit in that room. "We'll wait for a booth," was always her reply when they offered it up.

"Doesn't this feel weird?" asked Serena. "I keep expecting to see her."

"It feels okay. It's good to be near places that she was near," said Abigail.

Serena took a good look at Abigail, who seemed remarkably calm for someone who usually perfected the stereotypical stressed-out-single-mom look.

"Is that Mom's coat?"

Abigail shrugged and touched the black peacoat softly and said, "It seemed like a waste to give it away."

"I thought you were going to take it to the consignment shop."

"Oh, yeah. Well, whatever. I liked it, so I kept it. You kept clothes."

"I know. I just don't think I could wear them."

"Can you get us a table? I have to go to the bathroom."

"Sure."

Serena watched Abigail walk through the restaurant in her mother's black coat and thought her shoulders looked small and sunken, like the coat was swallowing her. The old hostess, Betty, came to the podium, and Serena thought she was going to remember her. She was hoping Betty remembered her. Her heart raced in anticipation. She wanted so much for her to ask about her mother so she could tell her she was dead and have someone react. Serena had stopped sharing her pain with anyone; she had bottled it up so tight that she thought if the hostess just mentioned her mother, it would rip her chest open with a stab. Even though Serena didn't talk about it, she missed people reacting to it. She missed the release of emotion. Now it was just an accepted fact that she had no mother. No one cried, no one said sorry. No one even acknowledged it. The world just went on and accepted she was motherless.

"Want a table or a booth?" The same scratchy-voiced woman with platinum old-lady curls didn't even look up at her.

"A booth," Serena said quietly and followed her to the table.

"Dining alone?" the waitress asked, with a rehearsed, false tone.

"No, my sister just went to the bathroom."

"I'll bring back some waters for you two then." She returned shortly with two small glasses and Serena started to sip on hers while she waited for Abigail.

She stared at the old couple in the booth next to her and thought about how her dad no longer had someone to share a booth with. She felt like she should try to remember that when she didn't understand why he was acting so strange. The old lady got up and went to the bathroom and was back before Abigail. Serena wondered if she should go check on her. *She's probably calling to check up on Hannah*, she thought. The old lady sat down and touched her partner's hand.

"There's a young girl crying in the bathroom."

"Is she okay?" he asked in a grandfatherly way.

"Shh. Shh. Here she comes."

Serena watched as Abigail and the old woman shared solemn nods. Abigail sat down at the booth and said with a smile, "What do you think? Order the salad bar?"

The two girls walked around the salad bar multiple times but put nothing on their plates. It was like neither one could make the first move. That somehow putting food on their plate signified their mother was not there. She was not over their shoulder saying, "Ooh, put a few pieces of cantaloupe on there for me." Or "This noodle salad looks great." Or "Don't forget to get some raisin bread; it's delicious here. I wonder if they make it. I should ask." Instead, there was silence and empty white oval plates. Serena stared at the container of beets. They looked like huge platelet's swimming in a pool of blood. *Mom had too many platelets*, Serena couldn't stop her brain from thinking, *and she got that bad leg clot. That was the beginning of the end.* She stirred the beets, trying to break them up as if she could stop her mother's thrombosis.

"I thought you hated beets," said Abigail.

"I do," said Serena as she silently piled lettuce, garbanzo beans, and cheese on her plate. She wasn't even that hungry. She didn't even really like salad.

The girls said little through the lunch. They did talk about their daughters, mainly about Hannah—the one subject Serena knew would make Abigail happy. They did not go up for seconds. Neither sister touched the raisin bread, even though they had both gotten extra pieces. They hugged and departed, both sisters saying how they should do it again. Both sisters feeling utterly sad and isolated from the world and each other.

Serena decided to stop at the grocery store on the way home and was surprised to see Abigail's car go past. She didn't live that way. *She's going to see Mom*, she thought to herself. The community graveyard was down the road. As Serena shopped for pasta, cereal, milk, kale, and the remainder of her grocery list, she couldn't help but feel guilty that she had not visited her mother. She wanted to laugh at herself, that she could still feel the guilt that Abigail was the better daughter because she was taking the time to visit her mother. As if her mother's dead body was keeping a tally of who came and when. Serena drove by the cemetery on the way home and stopped across the street. She could not go in. Abigail's car was still there. She could see Abigail sitting next to her mother's grave—a rectangle of soft dirt amid gravestones. Her knees to her chest like a little girl. Their mother's black coat was around the gravestone next to her gravesite as if Abigail put it around its shoulders so it would not get cold. Serena started her car quickly so Abigail wouldn't notice her.

When Serena got home, the house was quiet. She saw the light blinking on the answering machine and pressed it.

"Hi, honey. It's me. Maggie is having fun at the playground, so we're going to stay a bit longer. Hope you had fun with your sister. I'll call you on the way home." Tom's voice sounded relaxed. It had been a while since she had heard that happy tone in his voice. Lately, it seemed like all she heard was stress and work and frustration at her.

"Three old messages. Playback?" the robotic-sounding answering machine inquired.

Serena pressed play. "Hi, Serena. It's Abigail . . ." Delete.

"Hello. We have been trying to reach you to . . ." Delete.

"Hi, Serena. It's Mom. Give me a call when you get a chance." Serena stared at the answering machine, her hand shaking as she pressed it again. "Hi, Serena. It's Mom. Give me a call when you get a chance." *How long has this been on here?* she wondered. She pressed play again: "Hi, Serena. It's Mom. Give me a call when you get a chance." She closed her eyes and in that moment her mother seemed real. She could imagine Barbara on the other end of the phone, calling her from the couch. If she closed her eyes tight enough, Barbara felt alive. "Hi, Serena. It's Mom. Give me a call when you get a chance." This time Serena noticed her mom sounded out of breath. "Hi, Serena. It's Mom. Give me a call when you get a chance." Her voice sounded like she was forcing herself to sound happier than she was. "Hi, Serena. It's Mom. Give me a call when you get a chance." *How couldn't I have noticed that?* thought Serena. She's trying so hard to sound happy; she's stuck on a couch, for God's sake. Serena pressed it one more time and closed her eyes. This time she just listened to the voice and thought nothing. She walked over to the desk and wrote a note, "Do not erase message," and taped it to the machine. It made sense to hear her mother's voice. Not hearing it anymore made no sense, to her head or to her heart. She had to save it for the times when she would be alone and needed to hear her mother's voice. Even though when she listened to Barbara's voice, Serena felt an indescribable, shaky combination of ache, love, and uncertainty.

Serena had stopped talking to Tom about her mother. She didn't want to share her grief with him. She wanted to hold her grief close to her, because the pain of it at least felt like love. But it showed up in places where she did not want it to. Like when she was in the lab, running a western blot, and used the wrong buffer on her gel. Instead of neat little black bands that could prove her scientific quest, it showed a smear of black that revealed only what her current emotions felt like inside.

How stupid, Serena thought to herself.

Mostly it crept up on her when she was driving somewhere. When she had just dropped Maggie off at daycare, her car filled with quietness and loneliness, and she cried. She did not expect to miss her mother as much as she did. Serena tried to plan for Maggie's second birthday, but her heart wasn't in it. She didn't feel like making invitations. She didn't have the energy to make the pony cake that Maggie wanted. She didn't feel like smiling with the other moms. Serena realized so much of what drove her to be a good mother was to impress her mother. And with Barbara gone, Serena just didn't care to try.

***

Barbara was a real pill at Maggie's first birthday party. She wasn't feeling well, and she never did have much of a stomach for socializing. Serena knew Barbara would hate all her polished mommy friends with their organic food, nursing shawls, and two-hundred-dollar diaper bags. Serena pushed herself to be the alpha mom. She made the monkey invitations from scratch and even cut out banana-shaped labels for the envelopes. She took two days off of work to make an organic and healthy monkey cake. She even made mini monkey cupcakes for the kids. She made all the healthy wraps and salads from scratch. And she had presented all the food as if, on that day, it was about her mothering and not about Maggie turning a year old.

Barbara came in and fingered a sandwich and asked, "What is this? Spinach?"

"Yes. And there's tomato and plain wraps, too."

"You didn't put much meat in there." Barbara popped a piece of cheese into her mouth and sat on the couch. "Make me coffee," she said.

"Already made it. Give me a sec, okay, Mom. I got to get a few things ready."

The party progressed as Serena knew it would. Serena watched as Barbara talked with her friends and controlled the conversation like a hungry raptor.

"And what is your daughter's name?

"Aurora."

"What?" Barbara's voice heightened loudly to show her disdain.

"Aurora."

"You don't hear that very often," Barbara said to Robert and laughed a short, insulting chuckle. "Kids these days, feel like they have to name their children something to stand out. Whatever happened to nice normal names like Sara and Rachel? Now those are the abnormal names."

Aurora's mom smiled nicely, with her short, perfectly coifed hair, and offered her pink-cheeked child another organic kale puff.

She remembered feeling jealous when Aurora's mom brought out a fancy sippy cup with a straw. Maggie couldn't drink through a straw yet. And yet there was Aurora drinking through the straw while her mom looked on like she was a prize-winning pony. It's amazing how much the small things got in the way of motherhood. How many times had Serena thought about the "straw" milestone? As if any forty-year-old person grows up and can't drink through a straw. And yet Serena would practice with Maggie. She'd buy milkshakes and try to share to encourage her.

"Come on, Mags, you got to sip like a big girl to get the chocolate milkshake."

Always in a rush to move Maggie along to the next bigger stage—as if straw-drinking was like a game of soccer where she could keep working on her skills and improve. Maggie refused. She put the straw in her mouth and would just smile. She laughed now and thought how different life would be if someone could just tell all the moms in the world that it was all going to be okay. All the stress, all the small worries, it'll all end up being small.

And wasn't that what Barbara had told her that day: "Don't worry about straws, Serena." For a moment, on the couch, their relationship felt almost normal. A mother reassuring a daughter. That was the magic of Maggie. A bridge of joy that let Barbara and Serena talk in ways they hadn't talked. Serena's guard came down. And Barbara's time was almost up. While Serena worried out loud about milestones, Barbara worried inside if Maggie would even remember her.

***

As Serena drove to the store to pick up food for the party, she couldn't stop thinking back about Barbara. Things weren't fun when she was around, and they didn't seem as important when she was gone. Of course, at the time of Maggie's first party, Serena felt like she couldn't breathe. Just waiting for Barbara to attack another friend. Maybe that is why Serena missed her so much. Barbara was so much of a presence that the air seemed to not know what to do without her.

When Serena got home, she went to Maggie's baby book and searched for a picture. She found the one she was looking for after page after page of smiling, tiny Maggie pictures. Maggie's first Thanksgiving. Barbara was wearing her wig and actually let Serena take a picture of her.

"You're not in Maggie's book yet, Mom. I want a picture of

you with her," Serena said without looking up at Barbara for fear that Barbara knew what she wasn't saying. Who knew how long Barbara had left? Who knew how many picture opportunities she had left?

Barbara held Maggie tight and said, "Take a picture."

Serena loved that picture. A true smile from her mother. She looked at the picture now and it grounded her. She did exist. *My mother did exist*, she thought to herself. How could this person feel so far away, like such a faint memory that maybe never was? Serena went to her closet and took out the maroon sweater she had kept from the pile of her mother's clothes they were going to give away. She had slid it into her bag, not wanting Abigail to notice her being sentimental. She was unsure of putting it on. She hadn't washed it. It was like a symbol of their changing relationship. In that picture, in that moment, Maggie linked them together. A mended arc in a lifetime of broken coldness. If only they had more time to fix it. If only Serena could understand why her mother had always been so hard. Serena touched the sweater again, then hung it up in the very back of her closet.

chapter 4: dorothy

When Serena was young, she would think about things as "before Dorothy" or "after Dorothy" when it came to their mother. Serena was the sister who came "after Dorothy." She was careful not to use those words in front of their mother, only with Abigail. The one time Barbara overheard her, Serena found herself met with a broomstick to the butt and locked in her room for an hour. Dorothy was alive for only twelve days. But that was enough time to change everything, especially their mother.

"Before Dorothy, would Mom have gotten mad like this?" Questions like that were what Serena would pester Abigail with. As if Abigail's short time of a happy childhood with no death revealed a mother that only she knew. But really what Serena wanted to say was, "If Dorothy had never been born, do you think Mom would have gotten mad like this?" But those words seemed too harsh.

Abigail would answer with hyperbole that only a child could conjure. "Before Dorothy, Mom would make milkshakes," Abigail said. "She made vanilla milkshakes with chocolate syrup. We'd have milkshake parties. I swear I remember milkshake parties." Serena had never seen her mother make a milkshake, nor did she think her mother would give a young child ice cream. In fact, she thought her mother hated ice cream. She felt like Abigail made a lot of stuff up. Abigail always seemed to have blurry remembrances of happiness and food. But how could Abigail really remember anything before

Dorothy when she was so young? Serena wondered if Abigail painted this happy picture for herself and if she truly believed it.

Serena wasn't sure when she first learned about Dorothy, but she remembered looking at a picture of a baby swaddled in a hospital bed whom she assumed was herself. "I was a cute baby, Mom, wasn't I?"

"Where'd you get that?" Barbara snatched the picture out of Serena's hand.

"It was in the drawer. Next to the others," said Serena, but her mother had already left the room. Her father looked up and said, "The picture was of your sister. She passed away when she was a baby." Serena wanted to ask him so many questions but the sadness on his face kept her quiet. He walked over to her and put his hand on her shoulder and kissed the top of her head. "Some things are too tough to talk about. She was loved, like you."

Serena was left with only the faint picture in her head that she and her sister had looked very much alike. That was the thing with Dorothy—Barbara never talked about her. Robert never talked about her. And yet her presence was always there. A big black box that her parents walked around in every room of their home and in all aspects of their lives. Only when Serena would push Abigail would the sisters talk about Dorothy, Serena always wanting answers to questions. Abigail not actually having answers. Childhood memories are slippery, like fish. And death was not a memory that Abigail's young synapses had held on to or wanted to discuss.

Over the years, Serena pestered Abigail more and more to ask their mom about it. Aware that Abigail's relationship with her mother was different—they shared more, talked more.

"Why do you care so much about it?" Abigail asked.

"I don't know. Don't you want to understand?" Serena answered.

"Unlike you, I'm fine with not knowing every answer."

Serena looked at her sister and started crying. It surprised Abigail to see her sister sad.

"It means that much to you?"

Serena nodded her head. "Maybe it would help me understand?" Serena got quiet but Abigail knew what Serena meant. Serena and her mother had been fighting more and more lately.

"When the time is right, I'll ask, okay?" Abigail gave her sister a side hug.

Abigail was always able to ride her mother's moods like a surfer, knowing just when to jump off and when to stand up. But even so, on the day Abigail finally brought up Dorothy, she was shocked when Barbara answered her. They were on the couch; Abigail had made Barbara tea and they were watching a soap opera with a sad storyline. Abigail asked, "Is that what Dorothy died of?"

The words were out in front of her, and she could see them in the air between them. But instead of the "I don't want to talk about it," Barbara said, "No. She had Edwards syndrome," and said nothing more. They watched the rest of the show in silence. Abigail repeated the name of the disease in her head so she wouldn't forget when she told Serena. Together, they went to the library. Together, they looked it up. With shaky hands, Serena opened the book and searched the glossary for Edwards syndrome, trisomy 18. She flipped to the page and they read the passage with their heads as close as possible. A genetic disorder where a person has a third copy of genetic material from chromosome 18, instead of two copies. It's more common in girls and causes severe heart and kidney problems.

When Serena had Maggie, she truly understood why Dorothy's death affected Barbara as much as it did. Maggie made Serena almost forgive her mother for the distance that was between them for all of her childhood. How hard it must have been to hold a child whose life would end any day. How hope must have made her heart want to believe that there was a chance. Abigail had been through that painful experience with Barbara. It made sense to Serena how Abigail's relationship with Barbara was different, or at least she had accepted it long ago. Abigail was born before heartache; she was imprinted on her mom with happier times. Serena was only after—after her mom had been broken. That brought up the other hard question Serena often thought but didn't dare speak out loud: would Barbara have been happier if Serena hadn't been born, too?

Comfort finds its way in families like water through a tea bag, seeping where it's needed. And for Serena, that comfort flowed from Abigail, and from Barbara's sister, Eileen. Eileen loved both girls dearly. She was one of the few people who could put Barbara in her place. Barbara would serve it right back. One day after Barbara's funeral, Serena went for coffee with her aunt Eileen. Unlike Barbara, who had few but harsh words, Eileen had an excess of pleasant words.

"How are you doing, really?" Eileen put her hand on Serena's hand.

"Honestly?"

"Honestly."

"Confused. Mad. Sad. All of it. I feel like if I had an easier relationship with my mom, this wouldn't feel so complicated."

Eileen nodded her head, looking for the right words when there weren't any to soothe the situation.

"Your mother was complicated," her aunt said, and then added, "She changed a lot after Dorothy."

Serena looked up from her vanilla tea and scanned the coffee house of adolescent kids with expensive clothes and big purses. Boys being silly and showing off. Girls gossiping and trying to act aloof in front of the boys.

"I know. I mean, everyone tells me she changed. I never knew her any other way," Serena replied. She watched some kid try to take a straw out of his drink using only his teeth.

"Your mother was a strong woman. Can you imagine giving birth to Maggie and just days later having her gone? This child whom you carried for nine months, you finally get to hold in your arms, with their whole future in front of you, and suddenly nothing."

Serena looked down. Just the thought of it made her stomach sick.

"Your mom loved Dorothy, and I think she buried a piece of herself when she buried that child. Never was the same."

Serena always felt guilty when she heard about Dorothy. Like somehow it was her fault she came along next and wasn't enough to erase the pain for Barbara. That if she had just been better, if she had been more like Abigail, maybe she would have been able to get Barbara to change back to her former self. But Serena did try as a child, in her own way.

***

"Mamma, I made this for you." Serena had a fist full of marigolds.

"Serena, your dad planted those and now you ruined them. They'll die. Why would you do that?" Barbara shouted.

"I just wanted…" Serena grew quiet looking at the orange-and-yellow blooms. They looked like happiness to her. They smelled of dirt and summer play. In her head, she thought of how she'd hand them to her mom, and she'd smile and put them in a vase.

Barbara stood up and went inside.

Serena put the little bouquet next to her on the grass and sat beside it like it was her friend keeping her company. She felt the warmth of the sun and the coldness of her mother. She picked up one of the flowers and fingered the petals in her hand until all that was left was a green stem with nothing. The smell of marigold hung on her fingers as one by one she crushed their petals. One beautiful flower remained. Serena picked it up and smelled it. *This one is for me*, she thought.

***

"She loved you, Serena, she did. More than you'll probably ever know," Eileen said, and Serena looked down at her white cup, not wanting her aunt to see that just the thought of that made her sad. "I mean, she always had this connection with Abigail. It's like they were kindred spirits. I'm worried about her. About Abigail."

Her aunt looked around at the kids being loud.

"Everyone is always worried about Abigail." Serena rolled her eyes. She loved her sister, but she got tired of everyone worrying about her. Serena was always seen as the tougher of the two sisters. If one was crying, it was Abigail. And even as they got older, Serena barreled ahead at the world, taking on college and her career. Abigail was always tentative, switching colleges, switching careers, never knowing her next step.

Serena finished up coffee with her aunt and drove home thinking about all the different women in her family—Eileen, Abigail, Barbara. No one was simple.

Dorothy had changed Abigail, too. Or at least the aftermath of her did. It brought Abigail and Barbara together, but it also brought a strange quietness that settled over Abigail. A quietness she never grew out of. As if she were always waiting around for loss. As she grew up, Abigail was scared of death like most people were scared of spiders. As a child, she constantly worried that she was going to die. Every time Barbara sneezed, Abigail would run to her and pat her back to make sure she was all right. As an adult, the fear persisted as an obsession. Abigail listened to the news intently and counted the daily number of victims she heard during each telecast—because of gunshots, or a fire, or a deadly car crash. Feeling the weight and sadness of every death until she had to turn the news off just to repeat the same news ritual the next day. Maybe that was why Abigail was so tender with Serena because she felt the possibility of her slipping away and dying, too.

Abigail did not have an easy role in the family. She seemed to be the only one who could love Barbara the way she needed. And her big heart also wanted to take care of Serena. When Serena was young, she would crawl into bed with Abigail when she got scared at night. Abigail would never tell her to go. She would just make room for her. Serena would stay there, lying straight, and sleep there until morning. The girls never talked about the many nights Serena crawled into bed. Serena clung to Abigail's warmth. And Abigail clung to Serena.

Years later when Serena was in college, she learned about Harlow's experiment with baby rhesus monkeys, and she realized why she needed Abigail so much. One group of monkeys had a terrycloth monkey, and another group had a wire monkey. Serena went home and read over and over about the monkeys. How the little monkeys held on to the cloth monkey whether it had food or not. How the monkeys from the other group were scared and did not go to the wire monkey. *I have a wire-monkey mother*, she thought.

But it was not fair to diminish Robert's role. Though his voice was meek, his love was steady. Both girls had a fine relationship with Robert. He listened to their stories. He hugged them when they scratched their knees or needed reassurance. He tried to ignore Barbara's obvious preference for Abigail. He made up for it by taking Serena on small errands and trying to show her the value of small things. The peace of going to the bank and balancing your checkbook. The joy of a warm pretzel and soda. The smell of fresh mulch. He tried to encourage her curiosity and look for museum exhibits that she'd be interested in. Robert was a man of few spoken words. But he cut out articles about nature or the way stuff worked and would leave them on Serena's bed. They never talked much about the articles. Serena would smile when she saw the tall, skinny newsprint on her pillow—a quiet sign that someone cared.

But grief has a way of changing all relationships and all families. Robert had not called Serena much since Barbara had died. Serena had called him a few times. She was met with only awkward silence and lame discussions about the cold weather making the grass turn an early brown. Sometimes Serena would look through the newspaper and cut out articles she thought her dad would like. She put them in a pile and she'd use them as an excuse to go over to her father's house and be near him.

"Here is that restaurant we talked about. They had a write-up on it."

"Oh yeah?" Robert was downstairs making an omelet for lunch. Serena wondered how often he ate eggs for lunch. She wasn't sure what her dad knew how to cook. He had tried once to make French fries when they were kids. They turned out to be more like burnt potato sticks.

Serena sat at the table and looked out the window, trying to think of something else to talk about. Robert didn't add much to the conversation. He sat there slowly scraping the eggs off the small skillet so they wouldn't stick. The two sat in silence with only the small scratching sounds of the spatula between them.

"Well, I have to run and pick up Maggie. Why don't you come over for dinner on Sunday?"

"I'm supposed to meet Steve for dinner. It's wing night at Foster's Inn."

"Some other time then. Let me know what works for you."

Serena closed the door and got in her car and felt sad. She looked in the mirror and tried to quiet the insecurities of her youth.

She tried to see the person she was right now, an adult, not a child who needed love. Not the child who came after Dorothy who was never enough.

chapter 5: tom

Tom didn't know when he last felt connected to his wife. They were in the thick of marriage now. The time when lace panties turned to period-stained Hanes. Bras weren't bought from Victoria's Secret but grabbed from the endcap of Target as they rushed through the store. When late-night cuddles turned into gropes of hopeful sexual desperation that were turned down in favor of sleep. It felt like Serena always chose sleep over Tom. Or Serena always chose Maggie over Tom. When was the last time Serena chose Tom? He couldn't remember. He tried to remember the last time they even paid full attention to each other. Not half-listening while checking emails on their phone. Not wiping the counter while feigning interest in a work story. Not a quick peck on the cheek. Their relationship felt beaten down by every, "Did you pay the water bill?" or "Where's the plunger for the toilet?" or "Did Maggie poop today?" exchange. He could feel their marriage thinning like his hairline.

It wasn't always like this. It was different before Maggie was born, and when he was deeply lost in thought he could feel his memory reaching for what he and Serena used to have a long time ago. He could remember a night out at the Oak Tavern, a cozy restaurant down the street that served microbrews and free-range food. The place was crowded and dark and Serena's leg was pressed into him at the bar, and she had more than her normal one drink. She was bashful yet alluring, tucking her hair behind her ear as she laughed at his analysis of everyone else in the restaurant.

"That girl over there. I bet she's a first-year resident. Young, with an ego. Thinking she's going to save the world, one hemp shoe at a time. And that guy, he couldn't care less. He's not even listening to her. He's probably some marketing guy who sells shit he doesn't even understand. And he's probably sleeping with his secretary."

"Nice, Tom." Serena laughed a real laugh, taking a chip and putting it in her mouth. They could talk about anything—a movie, a book, the news. Conversation always flowed easily. Tom was always attracted to Serena. Her athletic frame, her sensuous full lips, and the way she moved as if she didn't care if anyone was watching. That night she had a bit too much to drink and was more aggressive and assertive in bed. Tom thought back on that night often. It was not at all like the times when they were trying to conceive. Serena always had a schedule and a plan. Too goal-oriented to "waste time" as she put it. Tom feeling like nothing but a sperm provider. Maybe that was when things changed. When Serena saw Tom more as a means to an end rather than as her long-time friend, let alone her husband.

Right now, their relationship felt like the neighborhood pool in the middle of a cold winter. A big gaping hole where so much happiness, splashing, and joy should be. Tom knew Serena's grief was pulling her away from him. But he didn't know what to do. Marriage was hard. Every day you had to work at it. He knew it took just one hand, one small gesture, to begin filling up the pool again. Some days he tried, but some days he didn't. And now here they were.

There had been plenty of warm days. Beautiful days spent

under Serena's favorite willow tree where the two of them would hide from the world and talk. Talking is what they did best. Underneath the cover of leaves, they would confess their love and their past.

"I used to hide in this willow tree when I was little," Serena shared. "Away from my mom when she was mad." Serena reached up and gently stroked the long willow branch. "I always trusted these limbs to protect me." Slowly, she would feel the tree bark with her finger, scribbling what looked like letters. Tom loved to watch her write on trees. She would do it without thinking. Her fingers tracing invisible letter after letter. "I'd send secret messages to the trees this way," Serena confessed. Tom never asked what her messages said. She never offered to share. One day when he was lying next to her, he felt her fingers on his back and he could feel her drawing letters onto his skin—I, then L-O-V-E and Y-O-U. It was after this secret silent confession that Tom knew he wanted to wrap Serena in his love forever.

And now, he couldn't remember the last time he touched her without wondering if she wanted him to. She never leaned into a hug anymore. She was a hard shell, and he was most definitely on the outside. When he had first met her, he had loved her fierce independence. She needed nobody, was never irked by friends; she lived in her own world and her world was always moving forward with conviction and passion. Now that same independence made him feel less needed and less like a man. And the more he thought about it, the more he could pin every insecurity on her security. What did she need him for? She never called on him for any projects around the house, or to hold her tenderly, or anything in between. His insecurity began to kick and scream, reading into even the smallest gestures of her taking out the trash or falling asleep on the couch as soon as Maggie was down for the night. Tom wished he felt more secure. But all his thoughts splintered him like a stick that had been gnawed on by a rabbit until it disintegrated. He felt like a failure. A failure in love. A failure as a father. A basic failure in his career—where was it going these days anyway? Even his clothes hung on him like he was a failure. His slightly shrunk, green sweater with a few wrinkles clung to his body in an odd, uncomfortable way.

He remembered when he used to care about clothes. When he used to be on a quest to be unique, to stand out more than the average. When his purpose was to rage against conformity. Now he succumbed to the string of cars on the highway. He was one of the lemmings in lines that seemed to suck out the soul of his life— the grocery store, the gas station, the restaurant. Now the constant waiting drowned him slowly. Every long line, every long business meeting quieted his desire to be someone. The constant drudge of life was smoothing away his edges until all that was left was sameness. He felt it in his khakis. In his blue button-down shirt. In his typical brown shoes bought from the typical mall store. Who he was, or wanted to be, was lost.

Then his relationship with Kara started. It started slowly, but there was no denying the instant connection. Tom had never thought of himself as one of those men. The kind who cheated or had an emotional affair with a woman. He valued family. When he was young, he dreamed about owning a black lab and a shore house in North Carolina where he would spend the summer with his kids and wife and grill burgers and shish kebabs. They would play with the kids down the street and enjoy the sand at their feet and the purity of youth and ice cream.

Kara was out of college and studied accounting. She was smart and friendly, without being overly friendly in a flirty kind of way. Tom felt bad for her because most of the people in the office were men or older judgmental women who didn't want to befriend her. She sat alone at lunch, reading. One day when there were no other seats at his usual table, he sat down near her and asked,

"Do you mind?"

She put her book down and said, "'It's all yours."

They didn't talk much that day. He learned mainly how she missed her family who lived out west and that this was her first job. She told him about the challenges of finding an apartment that was affordable and not in the basement. They had very little in common. She had nice long, dark, shiny hair and that was all he thought about her that day.

***

At home, Serena found herself staring at Maggie's dead goldfish, Sally. Sally was only one month old. A whim buy when Maggie was having a hard day. But Maggie lost interest in her little fish after a week, and Serena had been taking care of it instead. Its little orange body was frozen stiff in the water, slowly drifting nowhere.

All dead things look alike, thought Serena, seeing its puckered mouth open to one side, breathing nothing.

Serena brought the bowl to the toilet and flushed the

hardened orange body down the toilet. She quickly took the bowl to the sink, washed it out, and put it away before Maggie might notice. Maggie hadn't asked about the fish all week anyway; maybe in her little mind it was already gone. Maggie seemed to either attach or not attach to an object. A random blue spoon could suddenly be the most important object in the world to her. Days later, the spoon was replaced with something else. Serena hid the fish food in the medicine cabinet. All evidence of Sally was gone. Disappeared from the world, just like her mother. Serena felt silly as her eyes welled with tears. She tried to call Tom on his phone. He didn't pick up. She texted his phone, Sally died. I feel awful. Tom did not text back.

As Serena got Maggie ready for a nap, she was happy that Maggie seemed to want to snuggle with her. She ran her finger through Maggie's little curls and watched her eyelids settle down into a relaxed half-opened stare. *What a little wonder*, she thought. Her hair so soft and perfect; it brought back memories of a boy she lived next to when she was in high school. Curly, sandy hair and a smile that was always big and filled with sincerity and slight foolishness. Serena always had a crush on him and was always filled with feelings of inadequacy and excitement when they would spend afternoons together. She always thought she could have married him. Serena wondered if everyone had a fork in the road in their head and heart—where life could have been completely different. But she would never choose any road that didn't bring her here, to Maggie. As she combed Maggie's hair with her fingers, she thought, *Maggie, don't have regrets. I hope you do everything you want and don't look back wondering about anything.* She gave her a kiss and put her in bed. Her little mouth opened slightly to breathe in her sleep.

When Tom came home that night, they were both in a mood. Tom complained that the tomato sauce was sour; Serena took it as an insult and didn't think he had a right to say anything since he never cooked. Serena cleaned up and took her frustration out on the pot.

Tom, trying to make up, came behind her and put his arms around her. "'What's wrong?"

"You'll think it's stupid. I don't want to talk about it," Serena answered, adding more soap to the sponge.

"What? Tell me," Tom said as he watched Maggie play her little guitar in the other room.

"I texted you about it. You didn't respond."

"Oh my gosh, Sally. I'm so sorry. I got stuck in this meeting and then . . . ugh. Serena, I can't believe I didn't text you back. I'm a jerk." He put his arm around her, trying to comfort her. "Are you okay?"

"It just upset me more than I thought it would."

"I totally understand." Tom gently patted her hair the same way Serena did to Maggie.

"Seeing her like that. And I felt like it was my fault. I mean, maybe I didn't feed her the right way."

"Wait? What?" asked Tom.

"Sally."

"Your friend, Sally?"

"No, our fish. Maggie's goldfish."

Tom started laughing, which made Serena start laughing. She hit him with the dish towel and teased, "Don't make me laugh when I don't want to laugh." It felt so good for Tom to hear Serena laugh.

And just like that their relationship went from winter pool to hot tub for him.

"I'm sorry the fish made you sad. I'm glad it's not your friend who died. No offense to the fish."

"I just don't want to see something dead again. It's hard to explain. I know it's a fish. It got to me. I hate that things get to me."

"Why don't you take a minute. I'll go take Maggie and play outside to give you room to breathe." Tom went out of the kitchen. "Come on, Maggie, let's go play outside." Maggie was in no mood to be told what to do.

"No, Daddy."

"Yes," said Tom, more sternly than he meant.

Maggie ran from him. "Noooooooooooo."

Tom scooped her up and tickled her as he brought her outside; her wriggling body pushing against his dissolved into laughter.

Serena smiled and took a deep breath.

***

Maggie was not making it easy for him to put her flailing body into her swing. She was more centipede than two-year-old girl—with all her legs and arms moving wildly about.

"Maggie, I'll give you a big underdog push."

Something in Maggie softened and her legs relaxed into a wet noodle. "Daddy. Big!"

And even though Tom was already exhausted, he gave her underdog after underdog, daringly running under her swing as he pushed her up just to be rewarded with an "Again! Again!" Until one time he didn't do it high enough, and she started crying and wanted to come in.

It was so much easier when she was a baby. You have to be nice to babies. Their smiling innocence. The made-up dialogue where you can affirm your parenting prowess. "What a good daddy," he'd make her say as he jiggled the baby in his arms. How easy she'd laugh at tummy kisses. Now, there were endless *No*s. Now just the task of putting Maggie's shoes on could end in a tantrum. And it was wearing Tom down. Some days the struggle of her felt like a mountain of parenting failure he carried with him all day.

That night, Tom put his arm around Serena in a hopeful way that she might want to talk or kiss. Serena stayed curled in a ball and pretended she was asleep. She wasn't mad; she just wanted to be alone with her grief like a turtle inside her blanket. She was surprised at how much she was struggling with her mother's death. It seemed so stupid. After all, Serena knew better than anyone how her mom was going to die, how long it would take, how it would progress. Yet, she lay there still thinking it couldn't be true. She still couldn't believe her mom was dead. She thought there was a difference between knowing it and believing it. She knew her mother was going to die, but even those last few days, she realized she never believed it. Tom turned the other way and fell asleep.

***

On Saturday, Tom and Serena took Maggie to the park. Tom was always good-spirited and went down the slides to Maggie's delight. Serena always liked the quiet time to sit on a bench and stare out at the people, the road, the sky. Today she watched one woman who was pushing forty years old but wore the clothes of a twelve-year-old—holding desperately on to a youth that her body no longer believed in. But then Serena instantly felt too judgmental and pushed her mind to be kinder—whatever makes her happy. Serena watched the road as a car drove past with two grim kids in the back, teenagers annoyed and uninterested in wherever their parents were dragging them to.

***

"Ugh. Why do we have to go?" whined Serena.

"Because I said so," replied Barbara. "Just be quiet back there and enjoy the trip."

They had seventeen hours in a car together just to go to a wedding of some cousin they had never even heard of. Abigail fell asleep quickly and sprawled out all over the back seat, digging her hard sneakers into Serena's side. Serena kept pushing them away. Abigail's feet would just spread out more into her lap.

Serena read most of the drive. Slept for some. Complained about having to go to the bathroom most of the time. They stopped at a cheap motel that seemed to be the place deer hunters stopped during the season. Serena was starving. Abigail was tired and wanted to go right to the room.

"Mom, I don't feel good. Come with me," Abigail pleaded.

"I need to eat. I won't be able to fall asleep this hungry," Serena whined.

Barbara marched into the restaurant and found the hostess.

"Can my daughter sit at a table, and I'll join her in just a minute?" The hostess led Serena to a table as Barbara said, "Go sit down and I'll be back as soon as I help dad bring in this luggage."

Serena sat down and felt small, in a room full of gruff-looking men. The waitress came and gave her a menu. Serena was twelve. Old enough to be left alone but also young enough to search the kids' menu for her favorite food and order from it. It was in the corner of the sticky, plastic menu, next to a freaky-looking clown. She ordered chicken tenders and chocolate milk and waited for her mom. A man across the room kept looking at her and made her nervous. He was tan and skinny, and his teeth weren't quite right. One was a bit crooked, and it threw his whole mouth off when he smiled. Serena kept her eyes glued to the table and picked at where a hole had been made by a burning cigarette. Every so often she looked up at the door to search for her mother to come in. Her heartbeat quickened and she looked at her tiny pink-and-orange fairy watch. The waitress brought her food, but Serena couldn't eat. She felt scared and wanted to leave. She was worried the waitress would yell at her for not paying for the food. The man across the room smiled at her again and licked his lips. Serena looked around the room for the waitress, or for an adult who could help her.

Suddenly, Barbara appeared and sat down.

"Abigail threw up. Why aren't you eating?"

"I'm not hungry anymore."

"You're probably getting sick, too. Let's find the waitress. We can box it up and bring it to the room. Your dad might eat it later."

Serena was quiet for the rest of the trip. Barbara nagged at her to be social and spent most of the wedding saying, "This one here has decided to be mute this whole trip."

***

On the way home from the park, Serena pointed out every animal she could find for Maggie. "Look, a dog." Serena put on her happiest, most excited voice. Funny, how she could fake excitement and happiness for Maggie.

"I just saw a cow. Way up there! Did you see it, Mags?"

Serena could make the world suddenly magical, just for her daughter. Every farm or drive home, an adventure to see. Serena wished the world always felt the way it felt when she dictated it for Maggie. Usually, it felt cold, drab, and less colorful.

Tom decided to stop at the expensive town bike shop. The type of place that sold high-end bikes to people who had never ridden once.

"Why are we in here?" asked Serena.

"I don't know. I just thought it would be fun. You know, to have a hobby."

"I have a hobby," said Serena. "It's called taking care of Maggie."

"Funny." He bumped her hip with his and got her to smile. "You know, it'd probably good for you to have a hobby, besides Mags."

"Oh, I do. It's called science," Serena snarked back.

"Besides Maggie and science," Tom quipped. "Wow, this one is cool." He slid his hand down a thick, black bike that had big tough-looking wheels and a bigger price tag to match.

"That one's amazing, isn't it?" A salesman, who must have smelled Tom's enthusiasm, approached.

"Yeah. It's nice."

"You a rider?" the salesman asked casually. He was a young guy, well-built, and probably had been riding bikes and running and doing whatever else it takes to get a toned body like that all his life. His brown, shaggy hair fell down over his forehead in just the right way that made him look authentically hip.

"No," said Tom. "Thinking about getting into it."

Meanwhile, Serena put Maggie on a bike and tried to make motorcycle noises to keep her interested in the shop. She shot Tom a look like, "hurry the hell up and let's get home," so Tom thanked the salesman and they left. Later in the day, while Maggie was napping, Tom said, "I think I'm going to get that bike."

"You should," said Serena. Even though she didn't think he should. They had plenty of bills to pay off and plenty of other things they needed to do with their money. They still hadn't taken care of that leaning tree in the backyard, and every time there was a storm and Maggie was out in the yard, Serena worried it would fall on her.

"You sure?" Tom said, with giddy excitement like he was an eight-year-old boy who had just been told he could get a video game.

"Yeah. Do what you want," said Serena as she folded the clothes in the laundry.

Tom stiffened. Whenever he heard the words "do what you want," he knew they meant the opposite. Tom could never do what he wanted. Serena always had an opinion or a plan for what they should do. Even if she never said the words out loud, she would subtly hint at it. For instance, when Tom tried to think of what to eat for dinner, Serena would answer with, "Oh, tacos, that's a good idea." Even though it was clear that tacos were not what she was thinking.

That Monday during lunch with Kara, he mentioned the bike. This time Tom was glad that Kara was sitting with the chubby guy with one lazy eye from legal. It made the lunch feel way less intimate. Kara's reaction was more enthusiastic.

"I love to bike," said Kara. "I just bought a new bike, a Trek—"

She rattled off the model number of her bike, but Tom wasn't listening. Had Kara mentioned she biked earlier? Is that what made him want a bike? "Yeah, I figured it'd be good exercise. Stress relieving."

"Oh, it is. I was thinking of bringing my bike and doing it during our lunch break. Maybe we can ride together. I mean, if you want."

"Yeah. Yeah, that would be great," Tom said as he finished the tuna sandwich that Serena had made for him with too much mustard and not enough relish.

After work, Tom came home with the bike.

Serena said two words: "Nice bike." Tom knew she wasn't happy.

Maggie was more excited. "Bike for me!" she squealed as she pushed it over and got scared.

Serena heard it topple and came running out and scooped Maggie up. "You okay, sweetie?"

"Bike go boom," said Maggie, her eyes wide with excitement and fear.

"It happens," said Serena. "Want to go color with Mamma?" Serena took Maggie's hand and left Tom outside with his super black, super cool, super overpriced new toy.

Serena hadn't been talking much lately. She sat quietly and so Tom didn't talk either. He tried to interest himself in the latest political blog or go mow the lawn, but it bothered him. The way she sat there comfortably in her quiet, like she would be fine never talking again. When Maggie was awake, Serena was like a different person: lively, chatty, and happy with energy to color, blow bubbles, play ball outside. It's like she saved all her energy for Maggie and didn't want to use any of it on Tom. Tom was trying to be patient. He knew things were hard for her, losing her mother. He didn't know what to do or how to fix it, so instead he did nothing. He gave her space because he felt so uncomfortable trying to fit in her quiet space. There was no room in there for him.

"I'm going for a bike ride. Is that okay? Maggie's napping anyway?" Tom said.

"Of course," said Serena. "I'm tired. I'm probably going to lie down." But inside she thought, *Please, don't go.*

"I'll be back in an hour—before she wakes up."

"Doesn't matter," said Serena. But in her heart, it did matter, but she didn't want to tell him that.

She watched Tom leave, and her stomach tightened because she knew he'd pull the door too hard and make a loud noise that could wake up Maggie. She checked the monitor; Maggie flipped over and remained asleep.

Serena did not move. She stared straight ahead. She was feeling empty. Maggie drew a cute picture that morning, and instinctively, Serena said, "We can bring it to Grandma." But Maggie no longer had a grandma. It bothered Serena that she still wanted that relationship for Maggie, even though it would never happen. That she could still hear the phone and think it was her mom calling to check in. It made her feel like her mind was cruel. Trying to hurt her.

She felt herself digging into the past, trying to understand, trying to go back and figure out why their relationship was not as good as it could have been. She cursed herself for the last two years, not because they had been bad, but because they had been so good. She had gotten along well with her mother. They had bonded through Maggie, and now that made her miss her mother like she never thought she would. Seeing all the places that her mother could fit so nicely in her life. No longer as a nag, but as someone to go to the playground with. Someone to sit on the couch and talk to as Serena played Legos with Maggie. She stared ahead and remembered again the hardness of her mother's body. That last hug. One of Maggie's toys, a little yellow smiling vacuum, stared back at her.

How can I feel so sad when I am surrounded by such cute things? she thought. Serena got up and turned the vacuum around so she did not have its little yellow face smiling at her. The vacuum came alive with the ABC song, and she heard Maggie stir. *Dammit. That's just my luck.* Serena checked the video monitor and, sure enough, Maggie was standing.

Tom came back from his ride sweaty and feeling good, like he had accomplished something on this lazy Sunday. He tried to quietly open the squeaky front door. He heard Maggie upstairs playing horse. *Uh-oh*, he thought. *I'm in trouble.* He knew that whatever had woken Maggie up, even if it had nothing to do with him, would be his fault somehow. He knew it from the time he took his first pedal that Serena had not wanted him to go on a bike ride. She wanted him to stay. Why? It's not like they would talk. He probably should have stayed and helped do something around the house. He left anyway. He left and did not want to think about her or her somberness. He only thought about the trees that passed him. The lawns he passed, and whether they had a lawn service to make them so green and weed-free. The fact that he was getting gray hair. The way Kara looked at him when he talked. The way Serena never looked at him anymore. And before he knew it, an hour had gone by and he was back home to meet his wife's anger and his daughter's joy.

"She woke up like five minutes after you left," Serena said without looking up.

"Sorry. That sucks."

"Sucks more for her 'cause she's tired and cranky, which is great because I'm supposed to meet my sister and Hannah today."

"So, cancel."

"I'm not going to cancel. We've planned to take them to Pizza Play for a month. I wouldn't do that."

"Well, what do you want me to say?" asked Tom, bending down to stroke his tired calf muscle.

"Say it sucks. Say she's going to be cranky. Say it's ruined."

"She'll be fine. She'll be tired, but she'll be fine. She loves that place. Why don't you call your sister and move it earlier if you're worried?"

"Hannah has ballet first. We can't move it. Whatever, you're not going. It's not like you'll have to deal with her meltdown."

"I don't like fighting in front of her," Tom whispered.

"We're not fighting. We're discussing," said Serena. Serena gave him a big smile but even she didn't buy it.

Meanwhile, Maggie was taking her little horse and galloping around the room. "Giddy-up, giddy-up, giddy-up, up, up," she squealed with delight.

"Hey, Maggie. Want to go get some ice cream?" Tom asked.

Maggie smiled and raised her horse in the air and screamed, "Ice cream! Yayyy!"

Serena shot Tom a look and said under her breath, "Why would you say that? She's already going to the pizza place tonight and eating crap."

"I figured I could take her, and you could spend some time alone. I was trying to be nice. You can come with if you want."

"No. I should stay here and get stuff done. Ice cream is fine. We just think so differently," Serena said.

Maggie ran to Tom, who picked her up, and she happily waved goodbye to her mom. "Chocolate," Maggie sang.

Serena gave her a kiss on the cheek. As they left, Serena went and grabbed the bleach and took out her frustration with life on the bathtub, but each scrub frustrated her more. The dirt from Tom's feet, the fact that no one else cleaned the bathtub or worried about it, the fact that she was so tired—it all just left her bitter. Cleaning the bathroom always made her feel like she had a layer of dirt on her. Tom always laughed at how she showered right after she cleaned. As if she wanted to be the first to enjoy it before it got dirty again. But that's not why she did it. The dirt that she felt on her sat on her skin like a new layer, and she could think of nothing else but removing it. She scrubbed as hard as she could, and it brought her peace, a release of all that was wrong. Only after hot water, soap, and a washcloth that was rough and angry would she feel relaxed and like she had let go of all the dirt she had seen. Maybe it was her knowledge of mold and mildew that made it so much more disturbing. Or maybe it was because her mother was never that into cleaning and so Serena was always left noticing the dirt, the grime, the stains on the toilet that other kids didn't have. She'd secretly clean things before a friend was coming over. And she kept a roll of paper towels and Lysol hidden under her bed.

Serena was actually looking forward to pizza night with her sister and Hannah. Not just because she wanted to get away from Tom and his restlessness, but because she wanted to be around someone who was feeling the hurt of her mother's passing like she was. And she knew that however hard it was for her, it was five million times harder for Abigail. After all, Barbara had been Abigail's real spouse all these years. Helping to raise Hannah. Always making her dinner or picking her up more underwear or socks, or whatever else she needed. Sometimes it would upset Serena how close those two were.

She decided to take advantage of her time alone and use a gift certificate to a hair salon that Abigail had given her. Serena absolutely hated getting her hair cut. She didn't mind the actual cutting, but she hated the fake conversations. She never felt less like a woman than when she was in a salon. She didn't wear makeup. She didn't enjoy being fussed over. She hated answering banal questions knowing the person didn't care. And she was pretty sure even if she spent two hours doing her hair, it would still look the same—dull and lifeless. Sometimes Serena felt like doing her hair was some big, failed experiment that someone else was monitoring. As if they were taking scientific notes: we gave her tools today, but no change in the quality of her hair styling. If Serena could sum up her beauty skills, they would all be listed in the failed experiment category. But nonetheless she picked up the phone and called. They had an appointment open, so she decided to seize the moment and cut her too-long locks.

The hair salon had big white walls with artistic drawings, trying to be cool for the younger generation, but artsy for the older clients. They offered cucumber-and-lemon water or a cappuccino while you waited. Serena wanted none of it. She already felt awkward in the sleek, modern leather waiting chair. The woman across from her had beautiful, shiny blonde hair. It already looked amazing and yet she was here to get it cut again? Serena wondered what she did for a living. There was a whole female world that Serena did not understand. She felt like a species of bird that accidentally got placed in the wrong nest and just looked around, trying to grasp why she was so different. Finally, her name was called.

She sat down and hoped her lack of eye contact would signal she didn't want to do the usual meet-and-greet. But the blonde hairdresser was chewing gum and not paying attention. Her shirt was black, tight, and hung off her shoulder just the right amount. Serena could never wear that shirt without it looking like a costume. But on the hairdresser, it looked flattering and appropriate.

"Hi there, sweetie, what would you like done?"

"Just a trim," Serena said and put her hand beneath her shoulders to indicate where she wanted it.

"Any layers?"

"Nope. Keep it simple. I don't tend to do much with my hair."

"Gotcha," the hairdresser said. But her overdone blonde hair with perfectly coifed bangs made Serena feel like her lack of hair attempts meant she was less of a woman. Or at least not the type of women who were portrayed in magazines.

Not many scientists on the front page of Glamour, Serena thought to herself. But her silence was interrupted by the typical questions: "What do you do for a living? Do you have kids? Going on any vacations soon?"

With every response, Serena's answers got shorter and shorter until finally there was just uncomfortable silence between them, and the haircut was done.

She got into her car and looked in the mirror, expecting to see some more beautiful version of herself. But there she was, still Serena, but with slightly nicer hair—all set for the sister dinner.

***

Serena heard Hannah before she saw Abigail in the booth. Maggie squealed with delight,

"Hannah-banana!"

Hannah scampered out of the booth and ran toward Maggie, who was half her size. Hannah was all limbs and elbows. She made

Bambi's first steps look graceful. She had happy brown freckles on both cheeks and sweet, curly pigtails. Abigail looked tired—swollen, puffy eyes hanging on a face that was pale with either sickness or sleeplessness.

"You doing okay?"

"Yeah. I'm hanging in there," Abigail said as she quietly scolded Hannah to sit down. "You got your hair cut?"

"Yep. Finally used that gift certificate you gave me."

"Looks good," Abigail said quietly.

Maggie was standing up in the booth trying to bang the salt and pepper shakers together.

"You talk to Dad lately?" Abigail asked.

"Nope. He never calls and I'm tired of always calling him," Serena said. She knew she sounded like a bratty child, but her father's snubbing hurt. She thought he'd rely on her during this. She thought she could be there for him. They could talk, reminisce. She never imagined he'd want to be left alone.

"I stopped by the other day and you know what he was doing?"

"Do I want to know?" Serena grimaced.

"No, nothing gross. He was drawing."

"Drawing?"

"Mom's gravestone. What it should look like. He had, like, fifteen sketches."

"That's weird."

"You know Dad. Everything needs to be perfect. He kept asking me questions, but honestly, I don't care. Whatever he wants. Do you want to know the worst part?" Abigail looked over at the girls to make sure they were playing nicely and not paying attention to them.

"He's putting his name on it."

"Already?"

"Yeah, he felt like it looked odd without it, and it's cheaper or something. It creeps me out. It just looks like a born date and then a huge dash with nothing after it. Like it's just sitting there waiting. Waiting for when—" Abigail was interrupted by the waitress.

"One large cheese pizza," she answered. Serena nodded. They always got the same thing. Neither of their daughters was very adventurous, and they got tired of trying to put on green peppers or some vegetable just to watch the two girls pick them off.

"Wow. I can't believe he's putting his name on it. What if . . . ?" Serena looked down and took out some crayons and paper and gave it to Hannah who, like a nice older cousin, helped Maggie color.

"What if what?" Abigail said as she twiddled her straw paper between her long, bony fingers. Serena noticed her nails and cuticles were chewed off.

"What if he meets someone else? Gets married. What if he decides to get buried next to the new person? Does he just leave his name there, waiting? Mom would be pissed."

"I love that you have Mom getting mad. Do you think he'll get married?" asked Abigail. Her eyes looked teary.

"I don't know. I don't know anything about him anymore. He doesn't talk to me."

"He doesn't talk to anyone. He's just being . . ." Abigail searched for a word.

"A stupid man."

"That's what Mom would have said."

"I know. It's funny; Mom always told me how he behaved unemotionally like a stupid man. And I just thought she was being dramatic. That he needed to be that way so all her rants and raves wouldn't affect him. But now, I see how it could have hurt her. His detachment hurts."

Serena was interrupted by Maggie serenading her with her cheese pizza song as the waitress put the pizza on the table: "Cheese pizza. Mmmmm. Cheese pizza. Yum. Yum. In my tum. Tum."

The four girls all ate their pizza—Maggie with it cut up in many tiny bites, Hannah with her slice cut in half, Serena crust-first to get it over with, and Abigail with a fork and knife. Barbara had always folded the pizza and eaten quickly, creating an oil-and-tomato-sauce waterfall down the back and usually onto her hands and knuckles. Their mom never cared about appearances, only food.

On the way home, Serena decided to give her dad a chance and call him. The phone rang and went to voicemail. The message was changed. It no longer said, "You have reached Barbara and Robert Solomon." Now it just had her dad's voice sounding overly serious when he said his name coldly, "Robert Solomon," and the computerized voice of the answering machine said, "Is not available."

I'll say, Serena thought to herself.

***

Tom never knew what to do when Serena was out of the

house. She always told him what to do. If not directly, there was always some indirect instruction of sorts.

"What do you need to get done while Maggie naps?" she'd ask. Tom didn't know that he needed to get anything done. But then he'd guess at what Serena may have noticed.

"Grass needs cutting, I guess," he'd respond. But with Maggie and Serena gone for pizza, Tom was happily sitting eating tortilla chips and watching basketball. When Serena got home, Tom heard the door slam and felt his shoulders tense. He knew he was in trouble. The kitchen was a mess. The bag of chips lay open like a big-mouthed bass. Some random crumbs were spread across the counter. A knife with peanut butter dripping off it lay half on a plate. The soda was out, and its cap sat next to it. Serena glanced in and rolled her eyes.

"What?" Tom said from the couch.

"Nothing. I'm going to give Maggie a bath," Serena said.

"I want to help. I missed her." He gave Maggie a little squeeze and ruffed up her curls.

"Okay." Serena marched up the stairs and started the bath, loudly throwing in Maggie's toys.

"Oh no. What did I do?" Tom said as he followed behind Serena.

"It's what you didn't do. You couldn't have done anything while I was gone? You couldn't have at least cleaned up your mess in the kitchen?"

"I'm going to clean it up." Tom sulked and looked down at his feet.

"I'm just tired. I'm so fucking tired. I wake up tired. I go to sleep tired. And I don't have the energy to do all of this. You. Maggie. Work. You just have no idea."

"Let me help you. Instead of trying to do everything. Just go downstairs. I'll give Maggie a bath."

"What, so I can go clean up your mess in the kitchen?"

"No. It's a chip bag and soda; it'll take two seconds. I meant go sit."

"You just don't get it."

"I'm trying, Serena. But you're right, I don't get it. Look, I've never lost a parent. And I know your relationship with your mom was complicated. But stop taking it out on me." As soon as those words slipped out of Tom's mouth, he knew he had gone one step too far.

Serena simply looked up and said, "I would like to give Maggie a bath. Alone."

Tom turned around to leave the bathroom and knocked over Maggie, who was running into the bathroom carrying her towel and washcloth. Maggie put on a huge frown, and her face turned red.

Serena quickly hugged Maggie to calm any tears and said quietly, "Just go."

Through the splashing of Maggie's tub play, Serena heard Tom slam the front door.

"Maggie, time to wash your hair."

"No!" Maggie tilted her head away in defiance.

"Yes. Your hair is like crazy snakes. We need to make it smooth," Serena said, trying to mask her frustration. Her back hurt as she tried to get the cup of water over Maggie's little head without gravity turning it into a waterfall over her eyes.

"No hair. No hair." Maggie's little chubby body squirmed and wiggled. Serena grabbed Maggie's wet arm hard and pulled it closer to her. Her little body capsized into the water.

"Owwww," she whined.

"Sorry, Mags. I need you to come closer to me. Now please stay still so we can finish and get you to bed. Mommy's tired." Roughly, Serena finished the bath and pulled Maggie's little wet body out and circled it with a towel, the weight of her body pulling hard at Serena's back muscles. She found pajamas quickly and put them on fast before Maggie could argue they weren't the ones she wanted.

"Daddy. Want Daddy!" Serena pushed Maggie's body into bed.

"No. Daddy isn't here." Serena gritted her teeth. "Let's read this book. The bear one."

"No, roo-roo."

"What?" Serena didn't understand what Maggie was saying. She just wanted to go to bed. She just wanted to pull up the covers and hide under them. But Maggie was being a roadblock at every move.

"I don't know what roo-roo is. This book?"

"No, ROO-ROO."

"This one?"

"NO!" Maggie started to pout.

Serena couldn't take it anymore. She was done for the day. "That's it. No book tonight then."

Maggie started to cry louder, but her eyes lit up as Tom walked in the door. "Daddy!"

"I'll put her to bed," Tom said, his shoulders puffed out as if he were a superhero saving the day.

Serena went to the bathroom and washed her face, hard. Water splashed. She scrubbed her cheeks with her nails, letting the dead skin of the day go under them. She rubbed her face dry with her blue towel and stared at herself for a moment in the mirror just to see the day's wear on her. She put on her pajamas—the ones she had bought herself. She climbed under the covers and turned on the monitor. She heard Maggie laughing as Tom was pretending to make one of her purple stuffed monkeys climb all over the bed. *It's time for bed, not play*, Serena thought to herself. Serena was bundled under the soft flowery cover with her hate and anger. Serena knew she took out her frustration with Tom on Maggie. She'd been a shitty mom tonight, she thought.

Tomorrow I'll do better. I'll try harder tomorrow, she promised herself. How could she let her frustration get at her when all she could see was Maggie's happy eyes on the monitor? She hated it when she failed Maggie as a mom. But she hated hearing Tom's winning, goofy voice more.

***

Tom went downstairs and cleaned up. He saw one of Maggie's old applesauce pouches and thought about the day, and without thinking, his stressed hand squeezed it. Applesauce flew everywhere—on him, the cabinets, the floor. He grabbed a paper towel and cleaned it up, defeated by all the places it splattered. On his hands and knees, in the kitchen of his own home, Tom felt like his life and relationship with his wife were slowly getting messier and messier, too.

The next day at work, Tom wore his favorite blue shirt. It became his favorite blue shirt because he wore it once and Kara commented that it made him look "J. Crewish." Tom had forgotten what it felt like to receive compliments. And Kara's blushing as she said it made him feel like he was a young college guy again. He met Kara for lunch and sat down, feeling secure in his blue button-down. This time Kara didn't greet him with a compliment.

"You look tired," she said.

At that moment, Tom realized he was tired. He had been so tired from dealing with all of Serena's emotions. Tired from running around with Maggie and never having a moment to himself. Work was his most restful escape.

"Yeah. Things are still just rough lately."

"Oh yeah? Is everything all right?" Kara put her hand out instinctively to touch his but stopped and pulled it away slowly. They sat awkwardly looking at each other among the din of the crowded lunchroom.

"Did I tell you Serena's mom died?"

"No. Oh my gosh, I'm so sorry. I didn't know. That's awful." Kara looked stressed by the news, and suddenly Tom felt guilty that he wasn't more supportive of Serena. This was a big deal. Losing your mother is a big change.

"Serena's just been, well, not herself and it's just been hard. I can't do anything right."

"She's probably just really hurting. I'm sure I'd be devastated. I talk to my mom every day."

"The thing is, Serena didn't even have a good relationship with her mom. I don't get why it's so hard for her." Tom felt guilty for what he just said, but he couldn't stop himself. He was angry at her. "I swear she complained all the time when her mom was sick. And before she was sick, Serena has endless stories about how her mom was nuts. I mean, in college, her mom never even visited her. Not once. She was mad because Serena chose such a faraway school, and she didn't support her decision since she had also gotten into the state school close to home. Oh, and when she was little, her mom used to not bathe her or keep her clean. Her mom just had her sister do it, but one day her dad saw her sister spraying her with the hose outside and realized what was going on."

Tom wasn't sure why he was telling Kara any of this. Tom never understood Serena's relationship with her mother, and it made him sad for Serena. Made him want to love her more. And he saw how it made Serena try even harder as a mother.

He also saw that over the last year, Serena was more and more dedicated to being Barbara's nurse, always going over there to do small things. Once Barbara called while Tom and Serena were having sex, because she couldn't open a can of soup.

"I'll be right over," Serena said, getting dressed and leaving Tom under the covers. "You just don't understand," she'd say. "I need to do everything I can now to make things right."

"But you weren't the one who made things wrong," Tom pleaded with her and grabbed her arm to pull her back into bed.

"No. Tom. I need to go."

Tom focused back on Kara. Her adoring smile. Her sweet eyes with just a little bit of brown eyeliner and a hint of mascara. Serena never wore makeup. "Why can't women just accept themselves?" Serena had said to him many times. "I don't look any prettier with paint on my face. I'm fine looking just like me." But Tom thought it looked good on Kara. Maybe the gloss on her lips was a bit shinier than it needed to be, but her eyes looked accented.

"You know last week we got in a fight over a tea bag," Tom said, shaking his head and eating half of his turkey sandwich that Serena had made for him the night before.

"A tea bag? Did you finish her tea?" Kara guessed.

"No. I was driving Maggie somewhere in Serena's car 'cause mine was in the shop. I was probably dropping Maggie off at daycare or something. It was cold, so I brought a mug of tea. But the tea was getting too strong, so I took the tea bag out and put it on her car seat. They're black leather and they're always covered with all of Maggie's raisins and milk. I mean the car is filthy; it's like ten years old. Anyway, I forgot the tea bag."

"And Serena got mad?" Kara asked.

Tom knew he was complaining too much. He knew he shouldn't be telling Kara any of this. But he went on anyway, "Well, you see, Serena doesn't get mad. Not directly. She said nothing. But then yesterday, when I forgot to put away the soda, she just puts it away and says, 'I'm not surprised.' Which annoyed me."

"Yeah, that is kind of annoying to be branded like that," Kara said with approving eyes that communicated she would take his side of the matter no matter what.

"She goes on to say, 'There are two types of people. One who would leave a tea bag in a car and one who wouldn't.' You would have thought I killed someone with that stupid tea bag."

"Sorry. It sucks fighting. Hey, I have an idea. This lunchroom has been depressing me. It's supposed to be nice tomorrow. Do you want to go for a bike ride tomorrow during lunch? It might do you some good. Work off some stress."

"Yeah, sure. I'll bring my bike in."

And that's how it started—their daily bike trips together. Sometimes they'd go during lunch, sometimes they wouldn't have time, so they'd go after work. The bike trips together were exactly what he needed to feel alive again.

chapter 6: cava

There are friends who you need to tell when something is wrong. And then there are friends who just know when it's time to show up with dinner and wine. Serena's friend Natalie was the second type of friend. Serena got two texts, one right after the other. The first was from Tom, saying he would be working late that night. The next was from Natalie: dinner + drinks. Don't say no. Serena was tired of being in a funk and she thought a night with Natalie could be just what she needed, so she sent a text back: yes.

When the doorbell rang, Serena was doing laundry as Maggie played with some magnetic tiles on the ground. Serena could feel her friend's smile even before she opened the door.

"Hello, look what I have," Natalie beamed, holding up a bag of food and a bottle of Cava—a Spanish sparkling wine the girls had grown to love when they traveled to Spain together in college. Serena couldn't help but smile at the bottle and the memories it evoked. That warm night on the beach in San Sebastián where they rolled up their pants and skipped through the water. The walks through Park Güell—enjoying Gaudi's whimsy. Serena never felt more alive than on that trip. She was 3,972 miles away from her mother and could be anything she wanted. The girls would eat Padrón peppers and pluck off the tops like daisies as they talked about their lives and who they wanted to be.

"Come in, come in." Serena gave Natalie a big hug. She took the food and put it on the counter while grabbing two wine glasses.

"That's my girl." Natalie smirked. "Wine first. Talk second."

"Ha. I just figured we could go chill for a little and catch up."

The two friends sat on the couch. With Maggie absorbed in her play, Serena quickly put the folded laundry into the basket.

"Hold on there." Natalie stopped and pointed to a neat stack of all nude-colored underwear. "Seriously? That's the most boring underwear I've ever seen. No polka dots? No pink?"

"Do I seem like someone that would have fun underwear? Do you not remember me in college?"

"No. That's true. But pleeeasse tell me there's at least one lacy one hiding somewhere. For Tom's sake. Or for yours. Your body rocks, even after having a baby. You should love it, or at least not bore it with plain underwear." Natalie laughed. Serena did, too, but just a little, because the thought of Tom and all that their relationship wasn't stung a bit too much.

"Did you really come all this way to talk about my underwear?" Serena joked.

"No, of course not. I came to see how you were." Natalie put her glass down and put her hand lightly on her friend. "How are you? Really? Do you want to talk, not talk? I'll do anything. I just know when I lost my Paps, it was hard. And, well, I can't imagine losing a parent. I mean, I loved my grandfather but..." Natalie quieted down to let the rest of the words be said silently.

"Honestly. I'm grouchy. Sometimes I'm pissed off. Some days I'm fine. Some days I think if I have to look at cancer cells at work one more time I'm going to scream. But then there's Mags. That helps. You can't totally lose it if you're a mom." Serena laughed as if to lighten that statement.

***

"Where is Mom?" Serena asked. Abigail had gotten together a bunch of crackers and cheese and dumped them on the table.

"I don't know. She left this morning."

The girls ate the food quietly, not sure what to do next. Four hours later, they repeated the crackers and cheese for lunch. Every so often keeping an eye on the door. At last around 4:30 that afternoon their mom came through the door. She saw the girls and said, "Keep playing. I need to lie down."

When their dad came home for dinner that night and found Barbara in bed, they could hear his worried voice. They didn't tell him they had been home all day alone. But he made them all grilled cheese sandwiches and let them have cookies after dinner. Then he taught them how to call their aunt on the telephone in case it ever happened again.

***

Natalie instinctively got up and started taking out the food she brought, getting out plates and opening each drawer to find where the utensils were.

"You don't have to do that. I can help," said Serena, getting up.

"Yes. You're very capable. Let me dote on you. It's what friends do." Serena sat at the counter, always amazed at how her friend could make her feel relaxed. "So. You'll never guess who I saw last week? Twigs!"

"No way!" Serena started laughing at how much they hated Twigs in college. Her real name was Jessica; the name Twigs came from her extra-long arms, which were always extended because she knew the answer to every tough question.

"Twigs was damn smart," Serena admitted. "How is she doing now?"

"No idea. I literally saw her coming and hid in the freezer aisle. Like, pulled the door open and pretended freezer waffles were so interesting until she passed."

"You should have talked to her!"

"No. Just so I could tell her that I hate my job, and she was right, math was not my strong suit? No way. Plus, I was wearing crap clothes and hadn't done my hair." Serena grabbed her phone and searched up Jessica Hoffman. And there she was, smiling on Facebook with her two sons in matching argyle sweaters. "Excuse me while I vomit," Natalie said but pulled the phone closer to inspect the picture. "She's a fucking surgeon."

"Shhh. Maggie can hear you." Serena checked, but Maggie was playing with her toy, oblivious to them or their language. "Yeah, I kinda knew that."

"What? How could you not warn me that she was lurking in our hood?"

"She does a lot of breast reconstruction surgery for women who have had cancer."

"Fuck. And she's honorable." Natalie hid her head in her arm in defeat and mouthed, "Sorry about the fuck."

The Cava and easy conversation had gotten to Serena and she

just couldn't stop giggling.

Natalie laughed too. "Cheers to Twigs."

"To Twigs," said Serena and she smiled in a way she hadn't in quite a while.

chapter 7: abigail

Abigail had started seeing Andy again. She hadn't told Serena because she knew what Serena would say. Or rather, she knew the look Serena would give her, and she didn't want to see it. She was sad, and Andy made her feel better. Abigail knew it was going to end the same way it always ended—he would never commit to dating just her, and he'd say something stupid, and she'd wonder why she was with him. They had met online. And it was that simple and it was that hard. Andy and Abigail didn't have a lot of history. There were no romantic dinners with candles. No trips to the beach with friends. They did have the casualness of calling each other up and going for a movie and, well, after-movie activities that went on for most of the night. Right now, all that Abigail cared about was that there was someone out there who she could call when she needed to. Someone who would sit on the other end of the table and pretend she existed.

There were many things Abigail wasn't telling Serena lately. She didn't tell her how much time she was spending at the cemetery. How one night while Hannah was at a sleepover, Abigail decided to go to the cemetery. She needed to see their mother. She lay down on the soft earth and hugged it and fell asleep stroking the soil beneath her. The birds had woken Abigail up, and she rushed home. Abigail caught sight of herself in the downstairs mirror and saw that her cheek was browned with dirt. She took a warm shower and erased the night's trespassing.

Abigail did not tell Serena about the guilt that was wearing a hole in her stomach because she was not with her mother when she died. She did not tell her that she went to the doctor to get medication for her depression. Abigail did not tell Serena about the nightmares she was having of her mother screaming at her. Last night she dreamed they were at the grocery store and Abigail was moving slowly. She saw her mother at the end of the aisle, but she just couldn't get there any faster. Her cart had an odd wheel that squeaked and made the cart move in a funny zigzag. No matter how hard she pushed, the cart wouldn't go forward. Abigail could hear her mother screaming angrily at her,

"Abigail. Move. Move. Move. I need you." And then Barbara's face turned to tears in her dream as she sobbed, "I needed you. I needed you."

Abigail woke up in a cold sweat. She found the pajamas she had bought her mother for her birthday, the soft white-and-blue ones that Barbara had worn so many times that the elbows were worn through, and snuggled them and cried herself back to sleep.

Abigail certainly did not tell Serena about her daily breast exams that seemed to take up more and more of her mornings. Obsessively, she'd check for lumps, then recheck. Serena would just talk to her like a scientist, with data, numbers, and survival rate percentages that were supposed to make Abigail feel better but didn't.

Abigail would stare at her breasts in the mirror. They were not big—certainly not the kind that came with free drinks from admirers from a bar. They were not small—not the kind that could swing freely without a bra. They were average. The kind that filled a sweater in an unassuming way. The kind that meant she didn't need to hide cleavage in a V-neck shirt or worry about overexposure in a bathing suit. Abigail mentioned nothing of her visit with her gynecologist. The one where she discussed having a double mastectomy because all she wanted was for her breasts to be gone, for the chance of breast cancer to be lower, even though the doctor said the kind her mother had was not genetic. She didn't tell Serena how her breasts no longer felt part of her body but rather like grenades that could detonate a deathly cancer blow at any moment. She read through the pamphlet the doctor gave her. She visited sites online where women discussed what it felt like to have no more breasts. She looked at their scars and viewed them as badges of strength—their ability to cut themselves free from their womanhood. She became increasingly agitated at how society seemed to adore breasts more than any other part of a woman. And when Abigail wasn't thinking about breasts, or lack thereof, she was thinking about how to protect Hannah from breast cancer. And always in the background were thoughts of her mom, always her mom.

Abigail couldn't go anywhere anymore without seeing things that reminded her of Barbara. She'd put on the radio and there'd be a song that they used to sing. She'd turn on the TV and her mom's favorite soap opera would be playing. Sometimes when she was trying to fall asleep at night, she'd put one of her mom's old black-and-white movies on her computer and keep it playing all night. *The King and I. The Student Prince. The Little Princess.* All the classic old movies that her mom would watch over and over were like voices of friends to her now. Abigail would stare at the movies and become lost in them until a part where the movie was dark and she'd suddenly see herself reflected in the computer screen. Her hair not as sleek as she remembered. Her face older than she expected. Her overall beauty not at all the woman she thought she'd be. The movies both comforted her and shamed her.

Suddenly, Abigail's belongings seemed meaningless. That red chair she had saved up to buy. Her pale-yellow dishes with an antique finish. Everything she carefully picked out to define who she was or who she wanted to be seemed to just sit and mean nothing. There was no one to look at the chair and compliment it anymore. Nobody but she and Hannah ate on the dishes. Hannah's father never had and never would eat on the dishes. Hannah's father didn't even know that Hannah existed. There was Andy, who once in a while did come around, but he never noticed those things— he just ate her food. Her job as a project manager seemed vague and unimportant. The world felt rainy and cold, even when the sun shined clearly. One day after dropping Hannah off at ballet, Abigail stopped by her dad's house. The door was open but no one was home. She went to the kitchen and saw a note on the table:

Pick up Bounce, glass cleaner, yogurt.

And then at the bottom, it was signed Robert. On the counter was another note:

Blue shirts on sale at Kohl's on Tuesday. Buy two, get one free.

At the bottom in the right-hand corner was his name, Robert, signed again. Abigail made her way through the dining room and noticed a few more signed notes detailing events in the community.

Park concert 8:00 on Wednesday, Robert.

Movie with Paul on Friday, Robert.

Looking at Robert's signature made Abigail frown. He used to leave Barbara notes and sign them. Abigail wondered if it was out of habit that he did it, or out of comfort. Maybe he didn't even realize he was signing a note to himself. She went upstairs to her mom's closet and closed the door. She breathed in deep and tried to smell her. The darkness of the closet, the quietness of the house, all made her feel like her mother did exist. She was here. Abigail could almost feel her.

When Abigail and Serena were little, they'd have secret tea parties in their mother's closet. They'd find the box of jewelry that was their grandmother's. Serena would always be quick to get the fuzzy white clip-on earrings. Abigail always went right for the fake diamond bird ring. Adorned with bracelets of all sizes, shimmering brooches and necklaces made of beads and glass, the girls would quietly drink their pretend tea. Both girls knew they'd get in trouble for playing with the jewelry, but the coziness of their mother's closet made them feel safe.

Abigail hugged her knees to her chest and tried to regain that safe feeling. She looked down at her watch: six o'clock. Still a half-hour until Hannah would be done with ballet. She opened the closet and noticed some papers sticking out of her mother's side dresser. She grabbed the end of one paper and nudged it out. It was a birth certificate. Dorothy's. She hugged it to her chest, thinking about how the paper had lived longer than her sister.

She looked at the paper tenderly. But her eyes stopped at the birthdate. It was wrong. It was two years later than it should have been. *That's weird*, Abigail thought. *They must have made a mistake.* She folded the paper up and stuck it in her pocket to show Serena later. Somehow it felt like a secret just waiting in her jean pocket. Abigail started to poke through the other files that were in the drawer—lots of papers, some old school report cards, health records—when she heard her dad's voice.

"You up there?"

"Yeah, coming. Was just looking for something." Abigail tried to close the drawer quietly, but it wouldn't budge. She smashed the folder down with her hand and pushed it down as hard as she could. She caught her finger and instinctively said, "Damn." She walked down the steps, nursing her finger, and saw her father. He looked normal, wearing his favorite blue pants and striped shirt.

There were no formalities between them. No "hello" or "how are you?" Robert just started talking about a movie he saw. "Saw a movie at the local theater. Some artsy French movie. Had a good mystery to it. Your mom would have figured it out right away. Not bad. A little slow though."

"Oh, yeah. Who'd you go with?"

"A friend." Robert started making piles of old magazines. "You want any of these?"

"Nah. I'm fine. Thanks."

"Where's Hannah?"

"At ballet, remember? Tuesday night? I've invited you to go watch her, like, a million times."

"Oh, yeah. Still have to get there. Maybe next week. Oh, wait, no I have plans with the guys to try some new Italian place. Supposed to have amazing pizza. Thin crust, interesting toppings or something. I don't know. Hank was all excited by it."

"Well, maybe some other time."

"Yeah," Robert said without much conviction.

"Well, I guess I should be going." Abigail moved toward her dad for a hug, but he just stood there looking around the house for things to move from one place to another.

It's like he's forgotten how to be a father, Abigail thought to herself.

On the way to pick up Hannah, Abigail called Andy. She was pretty sure he had, like, three other girlfriends. And that he even lived with one of them. His voice was quiet on the phone when he picked up.

"Hey, what's up?"

"Nothing. Just wanted to call and say hi and see if you wanted to get together." Abigail imagined he was in some corner of his apartment having this secret phone call while his girlfriend lay naked, waiting in the bedroom.

"Uh, maybe. Just now is not a good time to talk. I'll call you sometime this week."

"Sounds good." But Andy had already hung up the phone. *Stupid*, Abigail thought to herself. *Stupid, stupid girl. Why do you call him?* But she knew why she called him. Because he was cute. Because on her best days when she did her makeup just right and her hair looked shiny, she felt pretty enough to be with him. And she liked how he looked at her.

Abigail had never had good luck with men. She dated a lot in high school and always had a steady boyfriend to go to school dances with. She always had valentines on Valentine's Day. She never had to worry about asking people to parties because they always asked her. College followed the same pattern. Fraternity brothers adored her long, curly locks and slim figure. She was quiet enough that she seemed alluring, and it always took a few months before the boys would decide that there just wasn't much more to her and the excitement would fade. She was never overly sexual but was good at doing what she did. None of the boys were brilliant or marriage-worthy, though none of the boys were thinking about marriage either. Most had neat hair, semi-ironed khakis, and expensive shoes. It wasn't until her first job at UrbanAid that she met Ben.

***

Ben was older, rougher, and wore faded T-shirts, not at all Abigail's usual type. He ate things like sandwiches with bean sprouts and read political magazines. The bottoms of his jeans were ripped in a way that made them look fashionable. His dark brown hair always fell into his eyes when he was concentrating on something important. He cared deeply about delivering education to underprivileged urban areas. When he spoke about kids, his voice had a way of convicting anger and passion.

"Did you know children of poor families are six times more likely to drop out than wealthier kids? I mean, these kids just don't have a chance. That's why we need to work harder on development programs that keep these kids' attention. We need to give them a safe haven where they want to come to learn and escape the realities of their lives."

Abigail would nod her head in agreement, but she was happy to go back to her apartment and sit on her nice couch and forget all about the world where things weren't as pretty. She had taken the job at UrbanAid because they had come to her school recruiting, and they were looking for an account coordinator. She had no idea what that really meant, but she was organized and had gotten a marketing degree, which the position had said was a plus. And it was the only job offer she received. Although she didn't send out many résumés. She figured she'd work there a few months and look for better jobs that paid more, but then on the first day, she met Ben. When he shook her hand to greet her, it was firm and manly. She could feel herself blush deep inside. She spent her first three paychecks on new clothes that she could wear that would convey to Ben how interesting she was. Skirts with patterns that she thought he would like. Expensive shirts that were intended to look inexpensive and earthy. She started their first direct mail outreach program. She led their most successful email campaign targeted to past rich donors who felt guilty in their big, glorious houses and therefore generously opened up their wallets, thanks to her pictures of sad kids and startling statistics. Abigail would then go home to her prettily painted green-and-beige apartment and eat fine treats she'd picked up from the bakery or specialty chocolates she had seen in the city that cost fifty dollars for a box of ten hand-crafted truffles.

It wasn't until they decided to organize a ten-day-long road trip that she made any progress with Ben. They were going to go to different cities to try to raise awareness and funding for their organization. They targeted different festivals where they could get a booth cheap. Abigail was hard at work developing the booth graphics and giveaways. She couldn't believe she'd get to spend ten days with Ben. Sure, there'd be other staff, but still, chances were, they'd have to spend a lot of time near each other. She already had figured out the perfect outfits that she was going to wear to show off her ability to be travel-ready and efficiently prim. Skirts that didn't wrinkle. Dresses that could be worn inside out. She had opened a credit card at the nearby mountain climbing store to outfit her trip.

The first day of the trip was long. They had rented a school bus to take all of the staff going on the trip. She didn't get to sit near Ben, so he couldn't even notice the book she was reading that showed off her love of literature and her interest in both short stories and environmental issues. She had picked it especially because she thought it would impress Ben. She sat instead next to red-haired Susan, who was super annoying and super self-assured for someone who was so red and pudgy that she looked like a combination of Shirley Temple and Strawberry Shortcake but smelled like earthy mushrooms. Abigail was pretty sure Susan hated her. They argued over everything. Susan was in charge of their graphics department, or rather, she was their only graphic designer, and so she felt that she was in charge. She was always giving Abigail some lame, artistic reason why she wouldn't change a brochure or signage. "I just really feel the blue helps balance out the structure of the piece." Or, "I feel like this design helps lead the eye to our message." Susan was always leading the eye to someplace that Abigail just couldn't see. Their conversations tended to end the same way. Abigail would give up and say, "You're the expert—just get it done," and walk away in a huff that showed off her leadership and her skirt's flowy-ness.

That night, the team rallied in the conference room, but one by one members peeled off to go to bed. Abigail pushed forward, opening up boxes of rubber bracelets that showcased their web address, organizing pamphlets to hand out and T-shirts to sell. Ben was in the corner working on his computer when finally, the last team member left the two of them alone.

"Dammit," Ben said as he hit his computer.

"You okay?" Abigail asked as she tried to pretend that she was doing something important by re-straightening the brochures for the seventh time.

"My Excel spreadsheet keeps crashing. We're supposed to keep track of all this inventory, and it keeps wiping clean. I should just go to bed. You should go to bed, too."

Abigail smiled, trying to pretend that the thought of him worrying about her sleep habits didn't make her insides shake with excitement.

"I know. I just want everything to be perfect for tomorrow," she managed to say without a hint of trembling.

"You're really dedicated. We need more people like you."

Abigail blushed at the compliment. "Thanks," was all she could muster as she came behind Ben to look over his computer. She put her hand on his shoulder in the most casual way possible, which was anything but casual, and pointed to a cell in the document. "You just need to expand it here. You're collapsing the cells. The data is there."

"I'm an idiot."

"Nah, it happened to me before. That's how I knew it." Abigail's face felt warm to be so close to Ben. She breathed in the smell of shampoo from his hair. And looked at the soft hair on the back of his neck. Ben moved back, and the sudden straightening of his shoulders reminded Abigail that it was time to move her hand.

"Well, I think I am going to go to bed," she said.

"Yeah, I know I'm the one who brought up sleep, but I'm thinking about having a beer and decompressing for a bit first. You in?"

"Yeah, sure." Abigail pretended as if this offer didn't make her heart beat five million times faster than it should. She smiled to herself. *The outfits worked. I knew he'd notice me*, she thought. As they walked to his hotel room, Abigail tried to think of things to say, but she was tired and was trying hard to fight any showing of her true fatigue. When they got to his room, Abigail sat awkwardly at the end of a stiff chair, trying desperately to look relaxed. He handed her a dark, short-bottled beer, and Abigail did her best to look at home with it. She was normally more of a mojito, cosmo, or whatever-drink-was-pretty-sweet-and-popular-at-the-moment kind of girl.

"You know, I don't get you," Ben said.

Abigail frowned.

"No, sorry, that came out wrong. Not in a bad way. You're just different than the other girls that work here."

"Because I shower?" Abigail said and crinkled her brow.

Ben laughed. His lips curled into a smile, and Abigail felt good.

"Well, yes. You do tend to smell better than most of the girls that work here."

He notices how I smell, Abigail thought and put another check on her mental Ben-wants-me list.

"So, how am I different?" Gaining confidence, Abigail leaned over to get closer to him.

"I don't know. You just are." Ben laughed short and rubbed his eyes. "I don't know. I'm too tired to describe it."

"Different bad?" Abigail inquired, making her eyes look big and hurtful.

"No. Different good, I think."

He smiled, and she moved over closer to him.

"I really do appreciate how hard you work," he said as his hand fell near her knee. He looked up, realizing he had touched her.

She put her hand on his and said, "I'm glad you notice me." If Abigail's eyes were sticky notes, they would have said: "MAKE A MOVE" in big black Sharpie ink.

He kissed her. His lips were soft and full. He kissed softer than Abigail would have expected. His lips reminded her of the bottom of warm, chocolate chip muffins. The kissing grew more intense before either of them could deny what was happening next. She only had time to notice his nice shoulders and to enjoy kissing his neck, and before she knew it, they were done and on opposite sides of the bed staring at the ceiling. There was no more talk about what was different or special about Abigail. There was no more talk at all. They fell asleep. Abigail woke up early and left before he woke up to avoid any awkwardness or view of her not showered.

Once she had gotten ready for the day, she went down to the booth at the Manayunk art festival, and the crowds were already swarming the streets. Little tent upon little tent of brightly colored jewelry, paintings, lawn art, photography, and more sat quietly waiting for acknowledgment. Amid them was UrbanAid's tent trying to stop people from shopping for overpriced artisanal crafts and take notice of the schools in the area that were losing students to drugs, violence, and poverty. Ben was nowhere in sight. Abigail felt relieved by this. She didn't even care that Susan was there already and being critical of how everything turned out.

"The brochures should have been printed on better stock. This doesn't do the artwork justice."

"We're a nonprofit, Susan; we can't be spending money on high-quality paper."

"I didn't say high-quality. I just said quality." Susan walked away in a huff. "I'm going to get coffee. You want some?"

"Yeah, sure. Thanks. One sugar, no cream." But Susan had already walked away.

It wasn't until two hours into the festival that Ben showed up. Abigail was glad she had a crowd of three elderly people who seemed interested in the cause and possible donations. They had gotten a fair amount of random bills and change in their donation box. She was going through the program with the three older people when she saw Ben. She straightened up her shoulders and tried to increase her enthusiasm and earnestness.

"For just fifty dollars, you can ensure a youth in poverty has access to an after-school program. This will help keep him out of the streets, away from drugs. For a hundred dollars, you can sponsor a whole summer of camp where someone can learn, do art like this"—she gestured to the booths around her—"and be inspired to break out of the world they live in."

She caught Ben's eye and smiled without trying to seem overly excited to see him. He nodded and grabbed a bunch of pamphlets. Her elderly posse had left, putting brochures in their oversized purses.

"How's it going? Looks like a great crowd. I can't believe how many people there are. The streets are packed," Ben said with a cool casualness that only he could pull off.

"Yeah. It was a good choice on this one. I think it's a really receptive crowd. We've had a lot of interest. And already some camp donors." Abigail frowned internally at her overenthusiasm. It was so obvious she was trying too hard. She tried to stare ahead and make her heart go cold.

"That's great. Hey, Abigail." Ben's voice dropped.

Ugh, Abigail thought. *I know that tone of voice. He's going to let me down.*

"Don't, Ben. You don't need to say anything." Abigail suddenly felt sick to her stomach and tired. She had never been so happy to see Susan walk up with coffee. The hustle and bustle of the crowd and endless change of workers kept Abigail and Ben from being alone for the rest of the day.

***

That night they were all supposed to meet up at a small café to celebrate the day's work and the number of sponsors they had achieved. Abigail was busy getting ready in her room when she heard a knock at the door. She stood quietly, breathing fast, and didn't move. The knock came again. She was sure it was Ben, and she didn't want to talk. She knew he was going to say it was a mistake, and she didn't want it to be a mistake. She wanted to keep it feeling like love just a little bit longer. After one more light knock, she tiptoed to the door and looked out the peephole. He had left.

The café was painted a deep orange. There were candles and warm burgundy accents that made it feel like they were in some ancestral cave. When Abigail walked in late, she was happy to see ten of the staff members were already sitting, and the only chairs left were on the opposite end from Ben. There were hummus platters and warm bread with olive oil brimming with fresh herbs and red pepper waiting on the table. Abigail sat down and grabbed a square nub of bread and picked at it nervously. She smiled and nodded and pretended to listen to the conversations around her. She was glad that Ben was sitting on the same side as her so that they didn't even have to look at each other. Just then the door to the restaurant jingled and a tall, beautiful, African American woman came walking in. Her dress was a black-and-white pattern that was busy but artistic. Her neck was adorned with a big, turquoise piece of jewelry that accented the dress in a way Abigail thought looked artistic and cool.

"It's Ruby," said Sam, who was sitting next to her.

"Who's Ruby?" asked Abigail. But the answer was clear. Ruby walked right up to Ben, who was already standing, and she kissed him on his cheek. He pulled a chair from the table next to them, and she sat right down next to him. The rest of the meal was an awful blur. Abigail managed to order a falafel dish and eat half of it. As soon as the first person got up to leave, she excused herself, explaining she was tired from working the table and "Too much heat." She smiled and kept her eyes down so as not to see the attractiveness of Ruby or the look of Ben's eyes. By the time Abigail made it back to the hotel, she was tired. She fell asleep on the bed and didn't even take off her clothes.

Abigail woke up feeling sick the next morning. She wasn't sure if it was the falafel or Ruby. Either way, she closed her eyes when her alarm clock went off and fell back asleep for two more hours. She took her time when she woke up, showered, grabbed breakfast at a coffee shop, and made her way to the booth as if ten o'clock was the time she was scheduled to arrive.

"Thanks for coming in today," Susan said.

"I had some things I had to get done this morning. I had a call with an administrator who wants to open up an after-school program," Abigail retorted, even though it was clearly a lie.

"Ben was looking for you," Susan said with attitude.

Serves him right, Abigail thought to herself. Just then, she saw the flash of height and gorgeousness walking toward the booth with Ben.

"Hi guys," Ben stammered. "Glad you made it, Abigail. I was worried."

"Sorry, I should have told you that I had a call this morning. Came up yesterday," Abigail said without looking up. She busied herself with folding T-shirts for sale.

"Ruby offered to help out, too. She knows the program well. And we're down a person 'cause Roger got sick." Ben glanced at Abigail to see how she would take the news.

"That's great. Thanks, Ruby. Let me know if you have any questions." Abigail put on her biggest fake smile.

As Ruby went to the front of the booth, Abigail muttered under her breath to Ben, "You're an asshole."

Susan opened her eyes wide and pretended not to hear. Ben

grabbed her elbow and brought her to the back of the tent.

"Just getting more brochures!" he exclaimed too loudly. Then, quietly to Abigail, "I was going to tell you. I came to the room the next day to tell you. But you weren't there. I don't know what I was thinking. I made a mistake, okay? Look, Ruby is my fiancée."

"Fiancée!" Abigail exclaimed and then quieted down. "How could you do that to me? And what about her? Honestly, I don't know what to say. I'm just . . ." Abigail was too upset to talk. Even though she had many words in her head that she wanted to say—yes, a whole list of words like "prick" or "cheater"—that she wanted to scream at him.

"Look, I'm sorry, okay? Don't let this ruin everything you're doing for UrbanAid. I like you. I do. I was just tired and confused. And I've been apart from Ruby for the last few months. I slipped up."

"Leave me alone," Abigail mustered and walked to the front of the tent to pretend she gave a damn about UrbanAid. Somehow Abigail made it through the rest of the trip. By the end, she had her hair in a ponytail and thought about returning some of the clothes since she hadn't taken the tags off. When she got back from the trip, she immediately sent out résumés, and her experience at UrbanAid at least got her an offer to be a project manager for a small marketing firm. She took the job and gave her notice to UrbanAid.

"I hope this isn't 'cause of me," said Ben.

"No. It was a better offer. More money. I wanted to move on from nonprofit anyway," Abigail said as if she had actually thought about her career goals. It wasn't until a month later that Abigail realized she was pregnant. Barbara was more supportive than

Abigail expected. Her mom knew something was up when Abigail asked her to come over for lunch.

"What's wrong? Something's wrong," said Barbara. "I can hear it in your voice."

"I'm fine, Mom," Abigail said. "Will you just come over today for lunch, please."

"I'll come. But not until you tell me what's wrong." Barbara's voice was mixed with love, worry, and anger.

"I'm pregnant," Abigail said and started crying.

"I'm coming right now." Barbara hung up the phone and had Robert drive her over. Barbara hated driving anywhere too far. "Come back in three hours," she said to Robert and slammed the door behind her.

Abigail collapsed in her mom's arms as soon as she saw her. They made their way to the couch, and Abigail tried to tell Barbara the story, but her sobbing got in the way.

"Does the father know?" Barbara asked matter-of-factly.

"No. And I'm not going to tell him. He's out of the picture." Abigail looked down at the creams and reds of her flowered rug and said quietly, "I'm going to keep it, Mom."

"Of course, dear. We'll help you. Don't worry. We'll help you."

Nine months later, a healthy, happy Hannah was brought into this world. It was Barbara's idea to lie about Hannah's true father. Barbara practiced the story she'd made up once to her sister Eileen and her sister ate it up without question, so she called Abigail and told her what she should tell people.

"I said his name was James and he had gone to Africa to help at a makeshift hospital. I never met him, but you told me he was a good guy, always trying to help others. I told Aunt Eileen that he caught malaria there and died and you are heartbroken and don't want to talk about it. But you're blessed to have his baby."

"Seriously, Mom?"

"Yeah, what's wrong with that? I thought you'd be pleased."

"I mean, I am happy not to have to talk to anyone about it. But I don't know if I should lie. Or say he's dead."

"Look, Abigail . . ." She could hear her mom's voice getting terse. "You wanted to have the baby. And you don't want the father to know. People are going to ask about the father. And I didn't want them assuming you were some . . . some . . ." She lowered her voice and said, "Tramp."

"Mom!"

"Well, that's what people think when they see a girl with a baby and no father. I'm sorry. I'm just trying to protect you. And besides, it was a nice lie. I made him a nice guy; what's the harm? A little pity thrown your way, and it's done."

"Okay, Mom. James died of malaria helping out in Africa. Was he a doctor?"

"Oh, I don't know. Your aunt didn't ask. I just said he was helping out, whatever that means. I feel like a doctor is stretching it, don't you think?"

Abigail sat at the other end of the phone, holding her tiny pink baby girl, and wondered how her mother was capable of being so helpful and hurtful at the same time. She knew by Barbara's tone she thought she wasn't capable of landing a doctor. Even a pretend doctor. Luckily, Hannah cooed, and Abigail left her frustrating thoughts of inadequacy and smiled down at the tiny wonder. Her small hands, barely-there eyelashes, pink, soft skin. She had made the right decision to keep her.

"You are mine." Abigail smiled. "All mine."

***

Abigail took care of Hannah just as she would her favorite possessions. She kept her clean like her silk-cashmere sweater. She bought gourmet baby food that came in cute containers. She adorned her with flowers and bows on her tiny sprouts of hair. But motherhood did not come easy to Abigail. It wasn't instinctual. Her battles with breastfeeding left her feeling unmotherly and incapable. Barbara was little help. "You kids were all fed formula, and you came out fine. What's the big deal?" was often her response to Abigail's sadness at the failure. Abigail would pump morning, noon, and night to keep Hannah stockpiled with the milk. She pleaded with her mom not to tell Serena about her troubles. Somehow her sister's knowledge of this lack of bonding seemed like the ultimate disgrace. She would feel judged. Abigail scoured websites to figure out how to help Hannah latch correctly and how to make it work, but Hannah wanted no part of it.

When a local breastfeeding organization came to her house, Abigail had unbuttoned her blouse and put both breasts in the woman's hands, pleading for help. The woman, without batting an eye, got to work and did a quick move to get Hannah attached. The women assured Abigail it would get easier. And that she could come back whenever she was needed. But Abigail felt shamed, bare-breasted in front of a woman she didn't know who could use her body better than she could. Every time Abigail fed Hannah breast milk out of a bottle, she cried softly. The thought that Abigail could try her hardest but still fail made her feel absolutely terrified as she held the small baby in her arms. Abigail looked at Hannah's perfect skin and she couldn't help but feel the imperfectness of herself.

Abigail's failure at breastfeeding haunted her long past those early days. She'd shudder every time she read how healthy it was for a child. When Hannah got an abnormally large number of colds, she felt like it was her fault. "Breast milk helps the baby's immune system," all the reports would say. It was her first failure as a mother, and she held dear to it. Like a scab she could pick anytime something went wrong with Hannah. The immense pressure that Hannah was all hers and hers alone sometimes overwhelmed her. There was no father to blame her OCD on. No bad habits Hannah could pick up from someone else. If Hannah turned out well, it would be Abigail's triumph. And if Hannah had problems, there would be only Abigail to blame.

When Serena had Maggie, Abigail wanted to be happy. Even though Abigail had struggled with motherhood, she still thought it was something she could claim for herself and not have to share with Serena. Serena was into her career, trying to discover the next big breakthrough in cancer. There was no room for kids in that dream. Abigail wasn't prepared when Serena got pregnant. She had blotted out the thought of it long before. But right away her competitiveness overcame her. Maggie and Serena had an easy bond; it was obvious to everyone. Somehow, Serena made it all look easy. Abigail thought it was because Tom was there to help. Lately,

Abigail didn't like to do things with the two girls, because she felt like the difference was so obvious. Hannah and Abigail's bond was a lot of work. Abigail adored everything Hannah wanted to do and tried her hardest to appease her. If she liked ballet, Abigail would sign her up for the best classes. If she wanted to paint, she'd go out and get her an easel. Abigail felt like she spent her whole time trying to keep Hannah happy. It was a one-sided love. Whereas Maggie showered Serena with love. She'd run up and hug her and kiss her constantly. She had never seen a little girl give a parent so much constant love.

While Abigail's stomach was feeling sour over this thought, Serena called.

"I thought we should do another mom outing in honor of her birthday."

"Oh, yeah, where?"

"That steak place."

"The weird small one with the Russian guy?"

"Yeah, that one. She loved it. What was that one she liked called? The garlic steak or something."

"It's kind of expensive."

"I know. I'll treat," said Serena, trying to be nice.

"No, it's fine. I have money." Abigail's hackles went up at the thought that Serena felt like she needed to buy her a charity steak.

"Just us obviously. No girls," said Serena.

"Yeah, I figured. I'm not sure kids and nice linens go together," joked Abigail. "Plus, there's something I want to show you. Something I found at Dad's."

"What? Is everything okay?" asked Serena, noticing her

sister's obvious tone change.

"Yeah. Just want to show you in person," Abigail said coolly so her sister wouldn't push it. Abigail wanted to tell Serena about the birth certificate. But she wanted to do it in person. She wanted the secret all to herself for now. Because knowing her sister, Serena would stop at nothing to figure out why the date wasn't right. Serena never let anything slide.

Abigail put on her best breezy voice and said, "When do you want to go? I'll need to see if Lainey can watch Hannah."

"Thursday?"

"Sounds good. See you then." Abigail hung up the phone and took out Dorothy's folded-up birth certificate from where she hid it in her cupboard. She touched Dorothy's name. Even though the mother outings were Abigail's idea, sometimes they seemed like work. She loved Serena, but sometimes she felt like Serena and she had two different mothers. And Abigail always felt like Serena somehow blamed her for that.

***

The steak place was just as they remembered. They had been there four times as younger girls. Always for Barbara's birthday. For some reason, Robert was never a big fan, but he would give in when Barbara would say, "It's my birthday. Let me choose."

The linens were purple, maroon, and soft. The tables were oversized squares. Barbara always liked this. "There's room to spread out," she'd say. "I hate being cramped into tables." Serena always secretly thought her mom liked the tables almost as much as the steak. The waiter handed the two sisters a wine menu.

"You want to?"

"If you do." Abigail glanced down at the prices.

"Let's do it. In honor of Mom."

"She never drank wine."

"I know, but she should have. She would have been a lot more fun." Serena was happy to see that she had made Abigail laugh. Her sister looked tired to her. Her cheeks a bit chubbier. Her eyes a bit heavier. The light behind them a bit dimmer.

The wine went down easy, and both girls relaxed and fell into the comfort that was sisterhood.

"What was it you wanted to show me?" Serena didn't waste any time. She always liked knowing everything.

"Okay. But it's a bit odd." Abigail reached into her purse and unfolded the birth certificate. The two sisters peered down at the paper.

"Dorothy's," Serena said quietly.

"Yes, I found it in Mom's drawer. But do you notice anything...?" But before Abigail could say anything, Serena's Nancy Drew eyes had already spotted it.

"The date is wrong. That's two years after I was born. Why would the date be wrong?" Serena searched Abigail's face for clues.

"I have no idea."

"People don't just get this wrong, Abigail. This is weird. There's a process. A registrar has to verify it." But Serena could see that Abigail wasn't listening. She watched as her eyes followed a man sitting down. Serena realized it was Abigail's ex, Andy.

"You okay?" Serena asked.

"Yeah. Of course. That was a long time ago," Abigail lied, not wanting to let her sister know that she had seen him recently. But Abigail couldn't help glancing over constantly to check out the blonde girl he walked in with. She was pretty. She wore fancy shoes and painted toes. They ordered champagne. *She must be paying*, Abigail thought to herself.

Abigail barely touched her steak. She spent a lot of time cutting it into small pieces and feeling the knife get stuck in its flesh. Both girls ordered ketchup in honor of their mom, who would always piss off the best steak places with the request. But the ketchup just looked like pooled blood to her. Her blood. Her sadness. And she couldn't stomach dipping the meat chunks into it.

Andy and the blonde woman ate quickly. They chatted happily, and she seemed surprised when the waiter brought out a cake with a sparkler in it. Both Serena and Abigail had always enjoyed the sparkler cake for Barbara's birthday. Barbara never ate the cake. "Too rich," she'd say, and the two girls would happily devour it and even share a forkful or two with their dad. But the blonde girl looked confused.

"How dumb can she be? It's a birthday cake," whispered Abigail to Serena.

But then both girls watched as Andy stood up and got down on one knee and proposed. The white sparks of light flying seemed to move slower. The din of the restaurant turned into a loud hum.

"We need to go," said Abigail.

"I'll get the check. You go now so they don't see you," said Serena. Abigail was grateful for her sister's understanding of how awful this was for her. She didn't want Andy to know she was there.

The two sisters drove home in silence.

Serena dropped Abigail off at home and said, "Do you want to talk?"

"No," said Abigail, and she closed the door with a quick, "Love you."

Abigail let her babysitter leave. She was glad to know Hannah was asleep upstairs. But Abigail couldn't sit still. She went into the kitchen and started cooking. She pulled out the beets she had roasted earlier and started to remove their skin. Thin layers of red like maroon finger tissue. The red juices flowed off the cutting board; her hands stained with the reds and purples of their flesh. She chopped them in half, hard, and the juice splattered all over her arms. She sobbed as the drips of beet juice stained her clothes.

Outside, Serena waited in her car. She took out the birth certificate and looked it over again. She didn't know why the date change bothered her so much. It was probably a mistake. But something deep inside her told her that there was more to the story. She decided she needed to go in and ask Abigail if she could pursue it.

But when she entered Abigail's home—all she could see were Abigail's hands covered in blood.

"Abigail!" Serena screamed as she ran toward her. Abigail had not heard her come in. She didn't even think that her sister would come into her home. "What have you done? What have you done?" Serena screamed.

"They're just beets. They're just beets," Abigail said as she cried into her sister's shoulder. Staining it with red where her hands wrapped around her.

"I saw the red and the knife and I thought you had done something to hurt yourself." Serena's heart was racing so fast it was hard to get her words out.

"I can't do this anymore, Serena."

"Do what?"

"Everything." Abigail sat down on the floor, and Serena sat down next to her. Their backs to the cabinets and heads resting together.

"I know what you mean," said Serena. But Abigail didn't think she really did. *It's never me*, Abigail thought to herself. *I'm never the one someone asks to marry. It's never going to be me.*

"I've never kissed someone," Abigail said softly.

"What? Yes, you have. Um, hello, you had Hannah."

"No, that's not what I meant. I've always been kissed. I never kissed someone. I never took the initiative. I was never in control."

The two sisters sat with the silence between them. Abigail wanted to divulge further, to tell her sister how she watched movies sometimes and when female characters were emboldened to kiss someone, it made her cry inside. How deep down if she had to do it all over again, she'd be the type of female who took control, who would stop letting men decide her love and her worth. If she could just go back and build herself back up again, she'd be different. Not that she didn't love Hannah, but the truth was, she just didn't love herself these days. How she wished she could go back. And yet at the same time, how she wished she could fast-forward and find out if everything was going to turn out okay. If she was going to be okay.

But instead, she just said, "I love you, sis," and leaned her head on Serena's shoulder.

"I'd let you kiss me but that would be weird," Serena joked, trying to make Abigail smile.

"Not funny."

"No. Not funny. Scientists aren't known for their humor. But for you, I'd try anything. Hey, can I ask you something?"

Abigail nodded her head.

Serena took out the folded birth certificate. "Can I keep this? Just for a bit? I have a hunch and I want to look into some things."

"Serena the scientist, always on a quest for truth," Abigail teased. "Sure, keep it. I doubt Dad will notice it's gone. And I'm sure it's just a misprint or something."

"Yeah, probably," said Serena although she didn't think it was a mistake. She thought it was the beginning to answers that she had waited her whole life to learn.

The next morning, Abigail woke up early so she could attend services. There was something soothing about sitting in the wooden pews, surrounded by the sound of others. There was beauty in the old couple who held hands, dressed in nice clothes, the rhythm of the service part of the fabric of their daily lives. Hannah was happy to get dropped off at a playdate while Abigail found herself among the goers. Her family was not religious. Both her mom and dad had been brought up attending synagogue but rarely attended services with the kids. Abigail remembered her mom had a falling out with one of the members, and after that day, they never attended except for Passover and Yom Kippur. "We give our money," Barbara would say as if to explain that was enough support.

Abigail was searching for something. There was a restlessness in her that she had never felt before. During the calm of the service, Abigail had a vision of a stream. Standing hand in hand with her mother and staring down at the water. She could almost feel her mother's hand in hers, as they stared at the small stream practicing Tashlikh during the Jewish High Holidays. She couldn't visualize if Serena was there. If she was, she wasn't in her memory.

***

"Throw a piece in, Abigail." Abigail listened and threw a tiny piece of challah in the water.

"You can say goodbye to whatever you don't like from this past year. We can start anew again. Doesn't that sound wonderful," Barbara said.

"I didn't like that Serena stole my nightgown and now she wears it." Abigail chucked a huge piece in and watched little fish gobble it up.

"I don't like that I'm always angry and I can't let go of what happened," Barbara said and threw a piece in.

Abigail looked up at her mom and saw that she was crying, so she ran and hugged her. One arm around her knees, Abigail threw in more bread. This time she just thought in her head over and over, *Help my mamma. Please. Please help her be happy.*

***

Abigail was jarred from her memory when it was time for the congregation to stand. Her palms were sweating. Her hands clenched.

chapter 8: applesauce

When Tom called to say he was going to be late again, Serena was cleaning the ceiling of the kitchen. "Do you have any idea what's on the ceiling? It's, like, dried stuff," said Serena.

"Applesauce," said Tom. "It was an accident. Last week I squeezed a pouch. I thought I got it all."

Serena hung up the phone. She was always cleaning up after Tom's accidents. There were dots on the ceilings. And then she realized there were hardened applesauce specks on the cabinets, too. She scrubbed them hard. And it seemed like everywhere she cleaned, she noticed more hidden applesauce debris.

She couldn't help but think of the other mess of a relationship she had with her mother. Serena went and grabbed the cookbook where she had hidden Dorothy's birth certificate. She touched the perimeter with her fingers. She moved her hand across Dorothy's name. Her father's name. Her mother's name. The round seal of the hospital where they all were born. She stared at the date of birth, date filed, file number. Information that might lead her to answers.

She wished she could ask her mother. But then she laughed at herself; she would never have asked her mother. Could she ask her dad? Maybe. Her aunt? She should start with her dad. After all, he was Dorothy's father, too. She circled the hospital seal one more time with her finger, and her friend Nina popped into her head. Nina's wife worked at the same hospital Dorothy was born at. Maybe she could help her get some answers, too. Or at least point

Serena in some direction where she could get answers. Why was she already planning ahead and assuming her father would give her no answers? "A good scientist looks at more than one data point," Serena assured herself. She got out her phone and sent a quick message to see if Nina wanted to meet up for lunch or coffee at work. Right away, she got a response, but sadly it was an out-of-office message that Nina was away on vacation until the following week. Serena folded the birth certificate back up and slipped it back in her cookbook. Tom had never opened a cookbook. And to be fair, Serena hardly did either. Barbara had bought her the thirty-minute recipe cookbook. She had handed her the yard sale find and said, "Because you work so much and don't have much time to cook." A double-edged sword of a compliment and gift. And now a safe spot to hide her dead sister's birth certificate.

Serena put the cookbook away on the shelf and stared at the purple spine. Just another example of how their relationship wasn't easy. And yet she missed her terribly. After so many years of hate, there was love when she became Maggie's grandma. Barbara was a different person as a grandmother. But then again, as soon as she held Maggie in her arms, Serena was different, too. Maybe Barbara was trying to make up for the past? Or maybe just the sweetness of a new life broke Barbara's years of coldness, but whatever the reason, Serena and Barbara's whole relationship changed when Maggie was born.

Barbara was excited, indulgent, and sweet, with never-ending interest in Maggie. Whereas before, Serena knew all the answers and didn't want her mother's help, with Maggie, Serena was vulnerable and appreciative. Before Barbara got sick, she'd stop by unannounced with diapers and toys. Sometimes she'd stop by four times a week and Serena never minded—she needed the company.

It was a whole new world being home with a child, and she was happy to have someone there. It was the first time she and her mother fit in the world right together. Sometimes, Serena wished she had never experienced that, because it was that year she missed the most. She had a lifetime of memories with her mother that she wouldn't miss. Like the time Barbara slapped her before she opened the door for her first date and then rolled her eyes as if to say, "Don't think you're all that," and walked away. Or the countless times she made Serena feel guilty for going to a college out-of-state and wasting their money. Or the many times Barbara would shine her love on Abigail and say, "We just have a different bond."

But damn her, she was an amazing grandmother, and Serena missed her presence there. It was a space that her father had not filled since Barbara's passing. Serena thought Robert would take more of an interest in doing things with Maggie, but he hadn't called once. Every time Serena tried to invite him to the park, he had other plans. But Serena felt the questions of Dorothy's birth certificate weighing on her. She wanted answers. Even though she didn't know how she'd get them out of Robert. The day was rainy, and Maggie had grown tired of Play-Doh, books, and coloring.

Today's as good a day as any, thought Serena. She smiled at Maggie and asked, "Want to go visit Grandpa?" And deep down, she wouldn't have been upset if Maggie had said no and saved her from the nervousness she was feeling.

"Grandpa!" Maggie shrieked excitedly and started fiddling with her horse doll to bring with her.

"Here's your coat. Let's go." She scooped Maggie up and slid her coat on her little arms while Maggie flailed around to hold onto her horse. Serena felt anxious as she drove to her father's. *Maybe he won't even be home*, she thought. But as she pulled into the familiar driveway, his car was there. The door was open, and Maggie ran in. Serena followed her and whispered in Maggie's ear, "Say 'Grandpa, where are you?'"

Maggie happily repeated as much as she could, "Grandpa, where you? Grandpa, where you?" as her little feet ran through the house. Maggie gave up looking as soon as she saw her favorite puzzle that Barbara had bought her at a garage sale. Serena looked around the house. It looked very orderly. Every book was aligned, the vase had flowers in it; at first, Serena thought her father must be cleaning and doing well. But then the sunlight caught the table just the right way, and she could see a thick layer of dirt and dust. She wondered if her dad hadn't dusted since her mom had passed. Serena went upstairs and saw her father lying in bed, fast asleep.

"Dad," she said. The same brass alarm clock that she'd played with when she was little was ticking on his nightstand. It was next to the same old Raggedy Ann lamp that was from Abigail's room when she was younger. The fact that they didn't buy a new lamp and just used a child's lamp was the undeniable work of her mother. The dark green flowered bedspread looked more masculine now that there was no woman to lie beneath it.

Robert did not stir, so Serena went back downstairs and left a note:

We stopped by to say hi, but you were asleep.
Maybe we can go to lunch sometime?

Love, Serena and Maggie

Serena stopped by the playground on the way home just so she could feel the air. She needed the air today. Was she relieved that she didn't get to talk to her dad about the birth certificate? Yes. But why was she so nervous? Did this mean she didn't believe the date was a mistake? Or, somewhere deep in her gut, did she think somehow it helped explain more about her childhood?

It was a hot day at the playground. Serena watched Maggie play. *Dorothy never got to play on a playground*, Serena thought. Suddenly there was a whole lifetime of things Dorothy never got to do. Is that what Barbara saw when she looked at Serena? All the things Dorothy would never get to do? She looked at Maggie, sweaty from play. Her hair wet against her neck. Behind her kneecaps were sticky, moist pools from too many runs down the warm, green slide. She slid down right into Serena's arms and gave her a big hug. Maggie's little chopstick arms stuck to Serena's. Serena kissed them and got a mixture of sunscreen and salt on her tongue. Maggie smiled. *Will I always know you, child?* Serena wondered. For surely there are days to come when my mouth cannot kiss your body freely.

***

"What is it, Serena?" her mother asked, frustrated and busily putting away laundry.

Serena sat on the bed, staring down at the flowered comforter.

"I've been . . ." But that's all Serena could say. Her face turned red, and the words just couldn't come out. She couldn't even look up at her mother.

"What, Serena?"

"I've been sweaty lately."

"Yes." Her mom's voice now impatient, ready to move on to the next chore.

"And . . ." Serena hid her head under her arm, so she didn't have to make eye contact with her mom.

"I think . . ." Serena tried to start again. Why was this so hard? What was she so afraid to talk to her mother? Isn't this what little girls are supposed to do? But she had never really felt like a little girl who could say anything to her mother.

Finally, in an almost-whisper, Serena got out the words, "I smell."

Without looking up, Serena could feel her mom's eyes on her. Her tone was cold and matter-of-fact. "I will pick you up deodorant next time I go to the store." And with that, her mom left the room.

Serena felt relieved. Slightly stupid. But mostly relieved her mom hadn't yelled at her. She was always yelling at her.

***

Serena felt something wet oozing across her hand. She looked down, and she had squeezed the sunscreen without realizing it.

When Tom came home that night, Serena tried to be nicer to him. He sat and watched Maggie and Serena talk in their secret way, Maggie with her half-words, gestures, and grunts that Serena somehow instantly understood.

He went to hand Maggie the doll he thought she wanted.

"No, she's asking you for the blue doll," Serena said.

"How do you know?" Tom asked, but Serena had already handed Maggie the doll she had wanted, and Maggie already cradled it in her little arms.

Serena was trying to not be mad at Tom's newfound passion for biking, but it was hard. Of course, she never said this to him. She was mad when she rushed home from work to pick up Maggie, never once stopping at the gym she joined. But most of her anger came out while she was vacuuming. The vacuum had broken last month, and Tom offered to pick one up on the way home from work. He bought a heavy, old-fashioned canister vacuum. The kind where there is a separate rolling contraption that follows you around as you vacuum.

"They said it was heavy-duty," said Tom.

"Was it on sale?" Serena asked.

"No. It just looked good, like powerful. The guy there said they use it for, like, businesses and stuff," Tom said.

Every time Serena struggled with the vacuum, she got mad. Every time it bumped into a wall or got stuck in some chair behind her, she got furious. Maggie thought the vacuum was a great toy. She rode the canister like a prized bullfighter. The vacuum symbolized everything that was wrong with their relationship right now. Tom always said Serena didn't let him make decisions. Yet look what happened when she did. She wanted to yell at him every time she took the stupid five-hundred-pound vacuum upstairs. She held on with two hands and hoisted it up one step at a time, feeling the weight of everything.

Tom knew Serena wasn't happy with him, but she was distant lately, and he felt like he never did anything selfish before. Never went out with the guys to a bar like some of his buddies did every Thursday night. So, he was exercising—who cares? And yes, he was exercising with a young twenty-something, but why should that matter. Nothing happened. He was always courteous not to pay attention to her spandex or whatever she was wearing. He just enjoyed having a friend. Someone who wasn't Serena.

Serena had never needed friends like he did. She had a few close friends like Natalie, she had her research, and now that she had Maggie, it was like there was no need for anyone else, including Tom. He thought about that a lot when he was riding. Sometimes he imagined himself riding farther and farther away from Serena and Maggie and wondered how they would react. Would they be sad? Would they care? Maggie loved Serena more. She had fun with Tom, but when Maggie was sad or scared, she'd reach out for Serena, and it bothered him. His love was not enough for her. His love was not enough for Serena. And so, he looked up at Kara and pedaled faster.

Serena was working later and more intensely at her lab. She was starting to see results. She knew she hadn't been able to save her mother, but she was driven to help others. She was analyzing sequencing data on her computer when she first spotted it. Several recurrent breast tumors had the same mutation in the same gene, a mutation that wasn't in the original cancer. Serena's pulse quickened. This is what she had been searching for. A mutation that arose specifically during tumor recurrence. Could this mutation be what caused these cancers to recur? If so, a drug designed to target this mutation might help stop breast cancers from coming back. Could this be the breakthrough her career and, more importantly, other cancer patients needed?

And when Serena wasn't putting her focus on her research, she was putting newfound passion into mothering Maggie. It was her only solace from the confusion she was still feeling about her mother and the frustration she was feeling toward Tom. When Maggie wasn't in daycare, Serena crafted the day with Maggie like a very intense protocol. One-part reading books. One-part fun activity. One-part music or tumbling class. One-part art. And then one-part Serena trying hard to focus tender hugs and kisses on Maggie and make her realize how much she loved her. Serena took the same approach to Maggie's meals. She felt proud when Maggie's lunch had been a perfect combination of vegetables, fruit, whole grains, and protein. It was like the meal was proof that Serena was a good mom. In the back of Serena's mind, she knew that all these fun days meant that Maggie and she were becoming more and more of a close unit, and Tom was just something that came home at night for an hour. She knew this hurt him. But Maggie's love was what Serena needed more than anything right now.

It's why every Thursday, Serena went into the lab late so she could take Maggie to music class. The music teacher was full of light and exuberance. The teacher complimented Maggie when she sang or when she drummed her sticks appropriately. Serena knew it seemed lame to need her praise for her child, but with her mother's absence, she felt like no one noticed Maggie anymore except Serena. There was no one to cheer her on or laugh at her when she was silly. There was no one to call when Maggie was sick. Tom's parents were retired and in Florida. They had six other grandchildren and had done the grandparent thing already. Once in a while, Serena sent a picture to them and she'd get an obligatory phone call commenting on how much Maggie had grown.

Today, Serena sat and counted how many grandparents were in class. Five. Five grandparents laughing with their kids. Some of them with their daughters, some completely on their own with the grandchild. Smiling, encouraging; it broke Serena's heart. Serena loved watching the different types of moms interact with their children. All of them different. None of them wrong. But in her head, she had nicknames for them all. There was the dog mom, the mom who would snap her fingers or pat her leg and say in her stern voice to "come" or "sit down" as if the child were Lassie. There was the Starbucks mom who talked with the other Starbucks moms holding their double mocha vanilla soy lattes while their kids stole toys from the younger ones or pushed them. Serena was always jealous of their coffee.

There were the exasperated moms, usually the moms of young boys who ran around screaming, throwing themselves down and biting the other kids, while their moms would profusely apologize as they watched their kids repeat the behavior over and over. Serena always wanted to tell them it's okay, and that she was tired, too. There were the prim and proper moms, their kids well-dressed in smocked clothing, oftentimes with script initials on all pieces of their matching outfits. They treated music class like it was high tea and always made sure to loudly say thank you for their child even if they were three months old and couldn't speak for themselves. Proudly showing that manners start before speech. There were the organic moms, who fed their children kale chips and other overpriced foods while adorning them in hemp clothing and environmental onesies. Serena wished she had more time and always admired their commitment to the Earth. The bookworm moms always knew the latest FDA recalls and didn't wipe their child's butt without reading a three-hundred-page book about which method was the best. Serena listened in on what they said, in case she could learn something. And then there was Serena. She wasn't sure what kind of mom she was. Half of these moms made her feel insecure about her parenting choices. She knew she was probably too overindulgent, too huggy or kissy, too obvious about showing that her child was way too important to her. She didn't quite fit in with any of the moms.

Serena smiled at Maggie and whispered how proud she was at Maggie shaking her maracas. She twirled Maggie as hard as she could and danced to make her laugh. The grandmother she normally sat next to was named Sarah. She had short brown hair and cool glasses. She was sixty and fabulous. She wore yoga pants and expensive shoes from mountain climbing stores, and she drove a Prius. She took her granddaughter, Evi, to wonderful places like the farmers' market, political puppet shows, and art museums.

Sarah plopped next to Serena and said, "My knees are killing me."

Serena smiled. "Yeah, I'm always tired by the end of this class!" Maggie clapped her hands along to the music, and Serena watched with pride.

"She's excited today," Sarah nodded to Maggie, who was doing her jumping dance. Evi sat next to her grandmother, with one hand resting on her knee—always cautiously sitting for most of the class until she warmed up or saw an exciting instrument that made her feel comfortable not shying away.

Serena watched the teacher and tried to mimic the rhythm patterns on her daughter's back so she could feel the distinction between a big beat and a little beat. She watched a young boy run around the class without a care in the world and then looked down at Maggie, who was concentrating without smiling. Sometimes in those moments, she felt the enormity of raising a girl. How hard it is to be a girl growing up in this world. The feelings, the struggles of love, boyfriends or no boyfriends, the pregnancy worries, the way Maggie would have to fight harder to get what she wanted, to be paid equally to what a man made, not to be judged by the size of her breasts or the number on the scale, to get through it all and simply be happy. It seemed like an impossible feat. Serena's impending feeling of hopelessness and defeat was broken by Evi's grandmother.

"You guys have anything fun planned for this weekend?" she asked.

"Not that I know of," said Serena.

"Oh, I just thought since it is Mother's Day this Sunday."

Serena looked at her feet. "I didn't know it was Mother's Day."

Serena had noticed some displays and signage at the clothing store, but she didn't know when Mother's Day was because she no longer had to buy a gift for anyone. She used to hate Mother's Day. Barbara never liked anything and finding her a gift was so challenging. Abigail always got her pajamas for everything—Christmas, birthdays, and Mother's Day—and somehow Barbara always loved it. Barbara would always say, "You can always use pajamas." Serena would try hard to come up with a gift that meant something special, but somehow it always seemed lame. Like that one time with the peppers. Serena had taken her mom to a Spanish restaurant and was so excited that Barbara had loved these special peppers, just like Serena had when she visited Spain. Serena tried desperately to find them for Mother's Day, but could only find one website that sold them, for fifty dollars. Desperate to make Barbara happy and to have a meaningful gift, Serena bought them. The box was smaller than Serena had expected. It was plastic, unassuming, and held about twenty small, long green peppers. When she gave them to her mom, Barbara got more stressed than excited. "Do you know how to make them? You're going to have to make them for me, Serena, because I have no idea how."

On the way home from class, Serena felt small. Like her car was the only one on the road that wasn't grounded. That somehow not having a mother made her feel like she wasn't connected to the earth from below or above. That there was no one to watch over her anymore. Her little car made its way down the road like an ant waiting to be squashed. She thought about stopping at her dad's and demanding answers to the birth certificate question. But when she drove past Robert's home, his car was not in the driveway.

That night, Serena woke to Maggie's small cries. She looked at the monitor and could see Maggie sitting up in her bed, staring at her hands. Serena went to her door and opened it slowly.

"What's wrong, honey?"

"My monkey stamp! Gone. Monkey!"

"Monkey stamp?"

"Monkey gone. Gone." Real tears streamed down Maggie's

face, her sweet curls around her face catching them as they slid.

"The monkey stamp from music? Sweetie, sweetie. You took a bath. Remember? It got washed away." Maggie buried her face in Serena's shoulder, her little body sobbing heavily. Serena wrapped her arms around her tiny shoulders, comforting her body as she slowly lay her down next to her. She could feel Maggie's frame relax as the thoughts of her monkey stamp faded into dreamland. When Maggie's body had grown still, Serena counted her warm breaths against her cheek. When she reached fifty, she slowly moved her arms and disentangled her body from her little limbs and got back into bed.

"Everything okay?" asked Tom from the covers.

"Yeah, she was just sad." Serena closed her eyes and breathed deep. These quiet tragedies of motherhood, the sadness in Maggie's heart, they all seemed so much bigger than the world in these late-night hours.

That Thursday, Serena started following one of her colleagues, a medical oncologist, around to see patients. He offered this to the promising young scientists because he felt that it was good for them to see the end benefit of who they were helping. He was a small, mild-mannered man who seemed to take in everything with deep sighs. His dark hair sat atop his small head like a very neat mop. Today, as they made their rounds, Serena quietly in the background, he reminded her not to say anything but just to listen. When they got to the second patient room, he stopped.

"Not this one, Serena. Out of respect for the patient, stay out here until I'm done. I got her test back today, and I need to tell her that her cancer has come back. It's always hard to hear."

"I understand," said Serena. As she waited by the patient's door, trying to blend into the pale wooden walls and keep out of the scurrying nurses in pink, purple, and funny animal scrubs, she couldn't help but think about her mom. She never even thought about what it had been like for her to hear the news that she had cancer. Did her heart skip? Did she feel sick? Was she scared? Did she cry? None of these thoughts had Serena ever asked or thought about. When Barbara had called Serena with the news, Serena had answered back with her typical questions. Where? What stage? What was the next step? She was so matter-of-fact with it, as she had become with Barbara, that she never treated her like she should have, like someone with a heart.

Usually, when Serena went on rounds, she'd hear the type of cancer they had. She'd think of the last paper she read that detailed the research about promising new treatments. Today, for the first time, she saw the patients as mothers, fathers, someone's grandparents, and she had a hard time not feeling sick to her stomach with grief. After an hour, it was time for her to leave the hospital to get back to her lab and take her cells out of the freezer to thaw for an experiment. The warm cell-culture smells of her lab relaxed her. She was glad to be away from the living patients and instead be with her quiet cells. Petri dishes that hid their true inhabitants. Beakers with multi-colored chemicals, all with purpose—to grow, to divide, to kill. Serena found herself rhythmically pipetting into her tubes and wondering if somewhere inside of them were answers for any of the patients she saw today.

Serena's email pinged and she had an email from Nina: I'm back. Let's meet up for coffee and chat. I'll tell you about our trip!

Let me know what day and time work for you.

Serena felt relieved; she felt more comfortable talking to Nina than she did pressing Robert for details. The birth certificate question hung on to Serena like a bad day with no break in sight. She couldn't shake the feeling, and it was like she was carrying extra weight on her shoulders she couldn't shrug off.

On the way home from work, Serena picked up Maggie from daycare and stopped by the grocery store. Shopping with a two-year-old was like having a bull in your cart. And some days, there was not enough wine in the world to get a mother through it. Serena tried to coax Maggie with a cupcake if she made it through the trip without whining.

"Mamma, fish. Fish! Fish!" Maggie had spotted the Goldfish in the aisle.

"Sure, Maggie, you can have some fish." Serena grabbed a bag and opened it and handed it to Maggie. Maggie shoved three fish in her mouth and smiled. Serena moved the cart faster down the aisle, figuring this bought her more time, but who knew how long before Maggie would grow tired of the fish and start doing her normal "All done grocery store. All done grocery store" rant that always got the disapproving looks of other shoppers. Serena grabbed stuff off the shelves without looking: fruit cups, pretzels, peanut butter, yogurt, milk, spinach nuggets, frozen waffles. She chucked all the food in the cart and kept the momentum until finally, she made it to the front of the store only to see one lane open with five people waiting.

"All done." Maggie frowned.

"Almost, sweetie. Almost." Serena could tell Maggie was

tired. A full day of daycare always left her cranky at the end. If only Tom wasn't working late, Serena could have gone shopping after Maggie was in bed. Before she knew it, Maggie had grabbed three magazines and started ripping them.

"No, Maggie. Don't rip those. They aren't ours. You can look at them." Serena smiled a bashful look at the shopper next in line.

"Candy!" Maggie shouted. Serena blushed. She felt judged by the woman in front of her. Maggie didn't even eat candy. Serena had taught her letters when they stood in line at the grocery store.

Serena tried to save face by saying, "Yes, let's do our alphabet with the candy. I see an R; do you see the big R?" Serena grabbed the peanut butter cups and showed them to Maggie.

But Maggie snatched them out of her hand, bit the orange plastic wrapper, and said, "Mmmmm." She shook her head back and forth and then threw it on the ground.

"Here, Maggie, hold my store card. Can you be a good girl and help Mommy?"

Maggie seemed pleased to be holding the card and pretended to swipe it in the air. Serena started throwing her purchases on the conveyer belt as fast as she could. The kid behind the counter had shaggy hair that fell in his eyes. He had remarkably nice skin for such oily locks. Serena gave him the store card, and he swiped it three times before he finally got it to work, testing the limits of Maggie's patience. Maggie rubbed her eyes and started frowning.

"I know you're tired. Mamma's almost done." Serena grabbed a box of raisin bran and showed it to Maggie. "You want flakes, Mags?"

Maggie looked up with a half-interested glance. Serena was

already opening the box and struggling with the plastic bag. A few raisins and flakes went flying on the floor.

"Uhhh. Mom. Mommy," Maggie said as she pointed to the floor at the fallen flakes. Serena handed the box to Maggie, and Maggie flailed the box around wildly, and more cereal fell on the floor.

Serena could feel her face get warm. "Maggie, stop," she said sternly and took the box from her. Maggie promptly started screaming louder. This day felt so long to Serena. How could a day feel so long? How could one grocery trip last so long? How could she not lose her temper when a day lasts this unbearably long?

"Maggie, calm down." Serena glanced at the checkout kid, who seemed to be looking at every piece of produce like it was a foreign species.

"It's kale," she said.

"Hmm. Kale," the kid repeated as he looked down the list of numbers to type in. He picked up the phone. "What's the produce number for kale?"

"Seriously," Serena said loudly as she watched him slowly type the number in and then look at the next item on the belt with confusion.

"They're mangoes," said Serena, trying to speed up the process. The kid started to pick up the phone, and Serena noticed it was the last item and said, "Forget it. We don't need them. Just finish up."

The boy gave a "whatever" look and tossed the mangoes in a bin to be returned.

"Would you like to give a dollar to cure cancer?" the kid asked without looking up.

"Not today."

"Nice," he said under his breath.

"Listen, buddy. I study cancer every day. That's what I do for a living. And guess what, you should tell your manager that you can't cure cancer. You should say, 'Would you like to give a dollar to find cures for cancer?' Not cure. There should be an 's.' Plural. Because it's not going to be a single cure. There are three main different cancers in breast cancer alone, and really, there's more than that if you count the obscure ones. You add that to all the different kinds of brain cancer, lung cancer, bone cancer. Whatever, add a dollar donation to my bill."

The kid nervously moved the hair out of his eyes. "Okay, lady. Thanks," he said.

Maggie was quiet in the cart with her head tilted to the side, fascinated by the fact that her mother was scolding someone that wasn't her. Serena grabbed the bags and put them in her cart and left the store as dignified as she could. Maggie threw handfuls of raisin bran on the ground as they left. Like a flower girl chucking roses on a failed wedding.

Serena opened the windows as she drove. She caught Maggie's face in the back. Happily smiling, looking out at a dog that was walking on the sidewalk. Mesmerized by his small furry gait and happy tail. Maggie arched her neck to see where he was going next. *I hope she always looks out the window happily*, Serena thought. At what age do they turn into adults like me who don't ever look out the window? Serena searched the sky for something of wonder. When they got home, Serena unpacked the groceries and noticed the cleaner she had used to get the applesauce off the ceiling had ruined the paint.

chapter 9: horses

It was the least Tom and Serena had talked to each other in their whole lives. Serena hadn't even told him about or showed him Dorothy's birth certificate. She had never felt so far away from him. Even when they were younger and had midterms and were stressed, they'd still find time to talk. Serena tried to run her life as if Tom didn't exist. She didn't know what he was doing with this Kara person, but she saw her name in his email and on his phone too much not to be suspicious. When they did have infrequent conversations, it was common that Tom would drop Kara's name openly. Serena thought he did this to piss her off or to wound her.

"Kara told me there's a new yogurt shop opening in town."

"Oh, yeah. Just what we need. Another ice cream place."

"No. It's yogurt."

"Who cares? I'd rather it be a Thai place or Indian. Or maybe Mexican."

"It's the suburbs, Serena. Not much ethnic variety around here."

"The restaurants here are so depressing it kills me." Serena grimaced and felt her chest tighten. She felt trapped every time they needed to go somewhere to eat. Their choices were pathetic. There were some dark, not-well-cleaned generic restaurants where other generic suburban families went, with their too-casual clothes and ever-fattening waistbands.

"Everything depresses you." Tom rolled his eyes and smiled

down at Maggie, who was coloring away furiously with her big, purple crayon.

Maggie looked up and smiled. "It's a neigh-neigh."

"It's a great horse!" said Tom.

"I'm sure Kara is never depressed. I'm sure she's super perky," Serena said, staring at Tom directly.

"You guys should meet. You would like her. You don't have many female friends. Maybe I'll invite her over to dinner sometime?" Tom said, with his eyes suddenly looking boyishly excited.

"Oh, I'm sure you'd love that. I'm not cooking for your girlfriend."

"She's not my girlfriend. She's my friend. And with the way you've been acting lately, I need one."

"What's that supposed to mean?" Serena's face went hot.

"Look. I don't want to argue in front of Maggie."

"We're not arguing; we're having a discussion."

"Well, I don't want to." Tom proceeded to ignore Serena in the way only he was capable of. As if nothing had just happened and life was perfectly fine while he was watching his perfectly cute daughter draw two very imperfect horses.

"Horses don't mate for life. That's probably why they always look so wild and free," said Serena with a sarcastic smile. She looked at Tom and wondered how humans ever thought it was possible to mate forever. Few mammals do it, she recalled. And tried to think back to that biology paper she once read on gibbons having low sexual dimorphism so the males and females are about equal size. Research had shown they were monogamous, a rare trait for primates, and then someone had debunked the idea when mates were shown to be philandering on the side. *Even gibbons cheat*, thought Serena.

Maggie looked at her mom and said, "Hurt," which meant "heart." But Maggie couldn't always get the r right. She loved it when Serena drew hearts. So, for good measure, Serena drew a little purple heart about the two horses. Even though it felt like a big scientific lie.

That night, Maggie woke up and cried out while she was sleeping. It woke Serena up, but of course, Tom slept through it.

I wonder at what age you stop crying out in the middle of the night, thought Serena. *Is it because you realize there's no one there to rescue you? Do you give up?* Serena felt like screaming herself. She wondered who would come to her aid. Would Tom console her? Would he even wake up? Barbara had cried out in her final days a lot. It always scared Serena, but when she would go to her, Barbara would be fast asleep.

Deep in the darkness, she put her arms around Maggie and tried to comfort her. With the help of the moon, she tried to take in Maggie's smallness. Her little curls. Her soft skin. The way her eyelids closed just so. And in that cloak of night, Serena could see it all before her. The days of Maggie's smallness falling away. The joy of her first steps. The happiness from coloring and blowing dandelions. The small moments of childhood that would get further and further away until one day she would be leaving for college. Serena could feel it all in the darkness between them—a whole lifetime of distance that would continue to grow with every day Maggie grew.

Serena waited a while and watched Maggie's lungs go up and

down. Once she was sure she fell back into a deep sleep, Serena slowly walked out of the room—making sure not to hit any of the creaks in the floorboards. As she climbed back in bed, the darkness in her room did not comfort her. All Serena could see in the blackness was her mother's face after she died. It scared her when she thought about it. She had always thought of death as some abstract thing. She had killed hundreds of mice in her research. Read countless details on cancer and death. But as she lay there staring at the ceiling, the thought of herself dying and not knowing what happens next terrified her. She believed in God enough to appreciate the Earth and all the wondrous things in it. She sometimes saw him in all the intricacies of science. But it had been a long time since she had spoken to him. She realized at that moment how far she had grown apart from the comfort of believing in him. Now her comfort was in the things she could touch, in the facts of science, in the things she could prove.

When she was little, she used to talk to him all the time, as if God were her fairy godmother. She'd tell him—because for her, he was a man, and for some reason, she pictured God to look like Moses—when she was upset or scared. She felt comforted by knowing that he was up there, so large and powerful, looking down on her, so small in the world. But in the darkness of her bedroom, between the soft cries of Maggie in the night, she felt no comfort. The blackness encompassed her like a coffin and Serena felt scared and alone. Like the whole world was going on around her and she was just a small unnoticeable speck on a pillow. Serena closed her eyes and felt herself succumbing to the blackness, and she let her body fall toward sleep.

The next day, Maggie really wanted to pet a horse. So, like good parents, Serena and Tom decided to take Maggie to a farm where she could pet the animals. On the way, Tom held Serena's hand in the car. It was always instinct that his hand fell over to hers and held it while they drove. Serena wondered if he even realized he still did it. It seemed so tender, so sweet, when their relationship these days didn't seem like either one. Serena left her hand there, and she wondered if this was how her mother felt when she held her hand in those final days. Stiff and unmoved and doubtful of the love behind the gesture.

At the farm, Serena and Tom looked like normal parents. Smiling at Maggie, who squealed in delight at all the animals.

"Horsey!" Maggie ran down the pebble road and climbed up the fence with her little outstretched hand trying to get a pet of the horse's mane. "Mane," she declared proudly.

"Very good, Maggie. It is his mane," Serena offered. "There's sheep down there if you want to see them."

"Sheep!" And off Maggie scrambled, her thin legs trying hard to move fast with her head bobbling as if her whole body couldn't quite keep up with itself.

"So, do you think it's over?" Serena asked matter-of-factly, as if she had just asked about the weather.

"What?" Tom asked as he watched Maggie run to a chubby brown sheep who had no interest in giving up his nap to the intrusion of being petted.

"Us. Do you think we're over? Things are bad. I don't like living like this." Serena looked down at her sneakers and kicked a pebble down the path.

"Like what?" Tom's face looked like a combination of overwhelmed and confused. His eyes couldn't decide if they wanted to glare at her or open wide in shock.

"Unloved. I don't like living where I feel unloved and that everything I do annoys you."

"You? Do you have any idea how much you tell me I'm doing something wrong, or not how you like it? You paralyze me. I can't do anything for fear you're going to get mad that I'm not doing it your way."

Maggie bent down and found a piece of hay and tried to shove it in the old sheep's mouth to no avail. The sturdy cotton creature was not going to wake up for her or for an old piece of hay.

"See, that's exactly what I'm talking about. You paint me in the worst light. I paralyze you? Why would I want to stay with someone who describes me like that?"

"I don't want to talk about this here."

"Of course. You never want to talk about anything, anywhere." Serena left Tom and made her way to an old cow. Its big brown snout greeted her. Serena petted it rhythmically, trying to get control of her anger.

Maggie scampered up next to her and pointed to the bottom of the cow. "Udders!" her little voice said confidently.

"Very good, Maggie. Mommy thinks you are so smart. You know how much I love you?"

"Yes," Maggie answered definitively.

"Good," Serena said and kissed the top of her sweet head. Serena watched Maggie's happy curls, thinking of all that those curls would have to endure in their lifetime. Mean kids, broken friendships, love, loss, job failure. Maggie was Serena's little ripple of DNA in the world, making its way in what seemed like a never-ending scary challenge. How did people create more kids without worrying about all the struggles these tiny people would face? In this moment of absolute happy skies, the odds seemed so much against them. The skies would not always be blue like today. The sun was not perfect. No beams of light are guaranteed for long.

Yet every parent goes into parenthood thinking they'll be different than how their own parents were. That their kid will escape the odds, be kinder, and love their siblings. Their child will never fight with them or give them an eye-roll. Their kid's childhood will be different than their childhood. Brighter. More loving. And yet every parent finds themselves in a moment of anger. Maybe it's over the third stupid spill of the day. Maybe it's during the exhaustion of a sleepless night. But even the best parent, even Serena, had done it. Lost herself in the moment to anger. And every time, it shocked and scared her when she was faced with the boil of inner rage. Every time she wondered, *Am I that different from my mother?*

That night, the normal bath ritual felt anything but normal. The smallness of their bathroom had never been so evident. Tom washed Maggie down with her frog washcloth while Serena soaped up her hair. Their knees and elbows would awkwardly hit each other like two strangers who were crammed together.

"Turn off the water. We're killing fish." Serena heard herself say the words and all at once she realized how much she sounded like her mother.

"I'll put her to bed," said Tom.

"No, I want to," said Serena.

"I was just trying to help."

"It makes me feel happy when I do it."

"Fine."

Tom walked out of the bathroom and grabbed Maggie's towel. He threw it to Serena and said, "You finish up. I'm going to go for a bike ride."

"Fine," said Serena without looking up.

She wrapped up Maggie's soft body in the towel, hugging her gently and using the ends of the towel to catch any drips off her nose and chin. Her sweet little body, innocent to the demands that would come to it one day. As Serena dressed Maggie in her snuggly pink pajamas, she couldn't help but remember her own struggles with her budding body. She was uncomfortable talking to her mother and would try to ask her about things. Serena had noticed everyone else had started to wear bras, but her mother had never broached the subject. In gym class, Serena would make up lies when the other girls teased her about still being a baby. She would tell them she had rashes that made her unable to wear brassieres.

Finally, one day, she went into Abigail's room when she wasn't home and looked in her drawers and found some old training bras stuffed in the back. She pulled them out and hid them under her bed. Every day, she'd sneakily put them on, making sure to go to the bathroom at school first thing to put one on and go to the bathroom at the end of the day to take it off. Somehow afraid she might get in trouble with Barbara for wearing something she had never asked for. She hid a small bowl with soap and water under her bed where she would secretly wash them and dry them. This went on for a year before she had the nerve to ask her mom for bras of her own. Serena looked down at Maggie's precious skin and kissed her belly. *I will talk to you*, she thought. *You won't have to be scared of me or your body. I will try harder tomorrow to see you. To delight in you. To not let the stress of the day make me forget how sweet you are.*

The next morning when Serena came downstairs, she could tell by Tom's shoulders he was not happy. His lips looked unwelcoming.

"She's not eating," he said and rolled his eyes at Maggie.

"You didn't rip her pancakes in half. She doesn't like them whole anymore."

"When did that start?" said Tom.

"Last week. That's a kid. They have silly rules."

"It's because of you. She takes after you."

"What the hell is that supposed to mean?" Serena was mad and tore Maggie's pancakes quickly. Maggie picked one up happily and began chomping.

"Syrup?" Maggie asked. Tom opened the fridge.

"No syrup," said Serena and glared at Tom.

"Mommy says no syrup," Tom said.

"Why do you say it like that? You know we don't give her syrup."

"No. I know you don't give her syrup. I would. Who the hell cares about a little sugar?"

"Sorry that I care to have our daughter eat healthy."

Tom took out the syrup and put a huge dollop on Maggie's plate.

"You're an ass," Serena said.

"Syrup!" shouted Maggie, forgoing the pancake and dipping

her little fingers directly into it and then sliding her gooey fingers into her mouth.

"Come on, Maggie, hurry up and eat, and Mommy will take you to daycare."

"No, Daddy take."

"Of course, you want that. Daddy gives you syrup. Of course, without Mommy, you wouldn't even be eating your pancakes. But Daddy is so great, isn't he?"

Tom and Serena glared at each other.

"Just go to work," said Tom. "That's what you really care about anyway."

"Thanks a lot." Serena left and slammed the door. Her heart hurt that she didn't say goodbye or kiss Maggie.

On her way to work, Serena stopped by her favorite coffee shop. The barista smiled and was ready with her favorite drink, a café au lait. Sometimes Serena even put on lipstick before getting coffee because she thought he—the coffee man named Jackson—was cute. Today, she didn't care about cute. She wanted to hide and make her way through the glum world until she got to the lab and could disappear in a world of science and routine.

As she waited for her coffee, Jackson commented, "You look nice today. Big day?"

"What? No." Serena looked down at her clothes and wondered if they were communicating something she didn't understand.

"Aw, another pretty girl who can't take a compliment." Jackson smiled and Serena wasn't in the mood to see it.

"I'm just logical. I'm not pretty. I'm athletic and smart." And before she could stop herself, she said, "And I have a symmetrical face. Research shows people prefer symmetrical faces and label them as more attractive. It's proven."

"I've heard it's a fact that people find horses more beautiful than most people." Jackson smiled, not dissuaded by her attitude.

"Horses, huh. I'd believe that. They don't talk." And with that, she took her coffee and headed out to face the world.

When she got to the lab, she pinged her friend Nina. Could she meet today? Serena was agitated and ready for answers. Serena often got tumor cells from her, so they had gotten close over the years. Nina's wife worked in the pediatric NICU, and Serena was hoping she could help her understand more about the birth certificate date or at least verify records for her.

But first, Serena wanted to check on one of her experiments. She was testing whether a drug could be effective against tumors with the mutation she found. She also needed to set up breast cancer cell lines that didn't have this mutation as her negative control. She got lost in the sequencing of cells—searching for the gene in those cell lines that had the mutation or didn't. Growing these cells would take some time before she treated them with the drug. But within each petri dish, Serena was sure she was growing hope and answers. When her cell phone buzzed, it was Nina, ready to meet. Serena cleaned up and washed her hands diligently. She took out the birth certificate and made a copy to bring to her friend. Serena felt connected to the original copy; she didn't want to lose it. It was like a piece of Dorothy was near her. Now, it was time for some other answers.

"Hey there, Nina." Serena smiled at her friend. Brown hair, tight bun, and warm nurse's smile.

"Hey there, Doctor," Nina teased. Serena was not one to flaunt her Ph.D., which is why Nina could so casually do it.

"Hi. No muffin today?" Serena had grown accustomed to a coffee and muffin date with Nina.

"No. Jen's on a no-sugar diet, and I, for some stupid reason, told her I would do it, too."

"Good for you." Serena smiled, even though she wanted a muffin but now felt like she shouldn't eat one either. And the cafeteria had decent chocolate chip muffins.

"I have a weird question for you. It's actually for Jen."

"Everything okay with Maggie?" Nina was used to fielding questions for her friends with kids. She was proud of the wealth of knowledge her partner had about pediatric health.

"Yeah, not a Maggie question. It's about this." Serena opened up the copy of the birth certificate.

Nina peered down at it, not sure what she was supposed to be noticing.

"The date is wrong," Serena said. Her heart skipped fast, even though Serena was trying to will her body to be calm.

"Huh, really? I suppose it happens."

"Does it? I mean, could you talk with Jen? Any chance she could look up the record of birth at the hospital? I mean, I'm sure they did at least a blood test, right? They do that on all babies."

"Hmmm. I know the hospital moved a lot of the old records to digital. This one is pretty old, though. I'll see what she can do."

"Thanks. It means a lot."

"This was your . . ." Nina got quiet.

"She was my sister. She died before I was born. That's why

I know the date can't be right." But even as Serena said that, she knew she wasn't as sure as she sounded. She went back to the lab to distract herself. She looked up if people really do find horses more beautiful than most people.

chapter 10: woodworking

"Is marriage like war?" Serena asked.

"No, that's not what I meant," said Robert. They were standing in front of a wooden carving that depicted an Indian chief with a bow and arrow. Serena was happy Robert had chosen her to go on this excursion.

It was to a local woodworking exhibit that turned out to be not-so-local, as they discovered after driving over an hour to find the place deep in the woods, off some curvy road, in a tiny town with mailboxes that all had flags on them.

For being such a quiet man, Robert enjoyed looking at other people's work, especially artistic endeavors. Serena was sure that it all spoke to Robert in some way that her ears couldn't hear.

"Can you see how intricate that bow is? Imagine this was once a tree. Look at that one over there, the bear with the fish." Robert walked over and slid his hand over the smooth side of the fish and delicately moved the price tag to see how much it would cost. "Your mom would kill me," he said sheepishly.

"Do you like it?" Serena asked, still trying to understand the basis of their marriage. She wondered if that's why Robert had picked her to go on this particular journey. Because of what she said last night at dinner when her parents were snippy.

"Jenny's parents are divorced, and they actually like each other more now. She sees them every other week."

Barbara looked up, mid-spoonful on her plate.

"What? We aren't getting a divorce." She laughed dismissively, as if their family were a shining example of love and grace.

Serena hadn't thought it was anything her parents hadn't thought about before. Divorce seemed so casual these days, like whether or not you wanted an extra shot of espresso in your morning latte. It was just another choice.

"Marriage isn't a choice," said Robert. "It's a commitment." His nostrils flared, and Serena knew she should be quiet. Robert wasn't one to raise his voice; he didn't need to. A change in tone was enough to give his words merit and weight.

Serena bent down and pet a wooden dog as if it were alive. Robert bent down next to her and followed the groove of its tail.

"This is what marriage is. You get shaped in different ways."

"But you let her shape you," Serena said and realized her voice gave away too much of her hurt toward her mom.

"Your mom is a tough woman. But I respect that. It's . . ." And he quieted down as an older lady stood by the wooden dog and said out loud, though not necessarily aimed at anyone in particular, "Reminds me of my Charlie. He was a golden retriever. Used to lay just like that."

"Serena. Marriage is not a choice," Robert said, barely audible.

Robert stood up and walked away. A signal that their conversation was done.

***

"Marriage is not a choice." Those words still stuck with her now as she contemplated her relationship with Tom these days. Sure, old-school marriage was forever. But nowadays, marriage felt more fluid. It felt like a choice. A choice many people walked away from. But with the holidays coming up, she wanted to make it different for Maggie. How had she let her relationship get here? How did it get so cold? Why did it feel so hard? She always imagined her version of the holidays being different from what she grew up with. She imagined a warm fire, hugging, playing a board game on the carpet. She could see it all. But what she couldn't have predicted was the wide gulf that would exist between her and her husband. The frustration she would hold inside her that would clench her belly so tight she couldn't sit on the floor without being uncomfortable. Serena couldn't have possibly known the cracks that would spread within her marriage, that she would spread inside herself, that made every day so much harder. Harder to try to get back to ground zero where there was a chance at love again.

But Thanksgiving was coming, and Serena wanted it to feel like a home. She bought seasonal pillows and a burgundy tablecloth. She made little turkey hands with Maggie and then wrote all that they had to be thankful for on the paper feathers. She collected recipes for the best mashed potatoes, turkey, stuffing, and cranberry sauce. She bought cranberry-scented candles so the house would smell just right. She spent every night adding one word to their pumpkin with gold markers so that by the time Thanksgiving came, their pumpkin would be filled with words that showed her family was taking a moment to appreciate life. That she was teaching her daughter to be grateful. The one thing she did not prep for and did not do was talk to Tom about their relationship.

***

"Get the chairs." Barbara was always terse with her words, but on days when company was coming, her words were even sharper. Serena had just woken up and she could already smell the deliciousness of meats marinating and warm things in the oven. Barbara was standing over the sink peeling potatoes. Her hands shook a little—a mixture of lack of sleep, too much coffee, and agitation. Serena knew better than to mention breakfast. It was better to just get to work and do whatever Barbara wanted, and at some point, when Serena's blood sugar made her feel ill, she would eat something and then shower. The house always felt like the heat had been off for a long time. Serena's hands would get cold going downstairs to the basement to bring up the dusty folding chairs. The basement always smelled damp and dirty as she went down, down, down. And then as she came up, up, up, the wafts of turkey brine would greet her nose. Twelve chairs. Twelve ups and downs. Twelve ways she was trying to make her mom a little happier.

***

But marriage is a choice. A constant choice to try, Serena thought. *If anything, it's a choice you need to make every day.* Serena sat down with her coffee and stared up at the light above her kitchen table. She spent a whole week trying to find the perfect light. This light—what did it illuminate about her family? What good is a beautifully shaped wooden chandelier if it only shines down on brokenness? Suddenly the day felt heavy. Why bother with any of it? *Maybe we should fall apart,* Serena thought. Gloriously let go and let everything come undone. Undo our ponytails. Unbutton the tight constriction of our lives. Give away the uncomfortable. And just be.

Serena looked out the window, streaked with raindrops. No, that wasn't her—to give up. She watched one raindrop slide down the pane like it was having fun. She watched another slip by effortlessly. *I need to find opportunities in the raindrops,* she thought. *The possibilities at the bottom of my cup. The beauty in the light as it throws shadows.* She stared at the light and squinted her eyes, like if she looked at it just right, life's secrets and answers would unfold in front of her.

Behind her, she heard the scuffle of Tom's slippers across the floor. She stared straight ahead and felt his hand on her shoulder. A white flag signaling the possibility of a truce. *Marriage is a choice,* she thought. She reached her hand to touch his. But paused. And then she touched him for a moment. Their hands, a pact, that today they would try. They'd let the holiday bring them closer, if only for this moment. Because the day held promises of pie and family.

Serena chopped the onions for the stuffing. There was something about the rhythmic chopping of vegetables that took her back. And suddenly her hands became her mom's. One on top of hers as she pushed down the onions. "Like this, Serena," she could hear her mom say. Or on a not-great holiday, chopping silently next to her mother. With tears from the onions streaming down her face.

But on this Thanksgiving, the day was warm. The rain kept them inside. There were mashed potatoes and family. Her father joined them. Her sister joined them. Her aunt joined them. It was the first Thanksgiving without Barbara, and it felt heavy. It was as if they all just wanted to be normal for the day, but all they could feel was the weight of who was not there. Even as Serena smiled and filled her plate with stuffing, she felt the emptiness of her mother's chair. Holidays do not let you hide from grief. The loss sits with you at the table.

Her phone buzzed: it was her friend Natalie. She was at the hospital with her grandma who had been sick. Serena didn't want to just write, "I'm thinking of you." She knew how empty those words felt when Barbara died.

Filled with so much at the moment, she wrote what was in her heart and texted: I've been there. Hold her hand so you can remember what it feels like. Thank her for the little things that made a big difference for you. Forget the rest of the world and just be with her. Just be her granddaughter for as long as you can. It will never be long enough.

Serena looked back at the table with tears in her eyes that no one noticed. She looked at Maggie. Would she ever be ready to die and leave her child in this world without her? What would Maggie remember about her? Would she remember the laughter and coloring together? Or would she remember the times Serena got frustrated and wanted the toys cleaned up? As she sat there, Serena felt like she was already in the past. Just an adjunct to Maggie's story. An anecdote of how she forgot dates and maybe the remembrance of a favorite birthday party. What would Maggie remember about her? What would be her twelve chairs of pain to go along with her childhood? Maggie climbed out of her chair and ran to Serena. Serena instinctively pushed her chair back so Maggie could climb on her lap. Serena felt thankful for the moment to have Maggie in her arms. Maggie wrapped her body tightly around Serena. It was as if they were carved out of one piece of wood, no space between their arms, no air between their hearts, just love on top of love.

chapter 11: maggie

This is what Serena remembered when she got the call: she hadn't said goodbye. She hadn't kissed Maggie. She hadn't hugged her but only touched her shoulder gently as she left. She was in a rush to get to the lab and was annoyed that Tom gave Maggie pancakes again because she took forever to eat them. Tom said he could drop Maggie off at school so Serena left quickly before Maggie could get upset.

This is what Serena remembered when she got home from the hospital: Maggie's pink piggy plate was still there. One half-eaten pancake with a little nibble—a Maggie-sized nibble—was still there. The perpetual mess of their life was openly displayed for Serena to see in every crumb of breakfast that was still there waiting to be cleaned up. An empty water cup. Butter on the counter. Maggie's plate. Tom's edge of toast sitting on a napkin. All the symbols of their hurried and messy life. Still there on the counter. What wasn't there? Maggie.

It was 5:47 p.m. when Tom called her. She was finishing up splitting cells at the lab and was running late. Lately she was always running late from an experiment that went longer than she had expected. But she was so close to learning the truth about whether or not the mutation in the breast cancer cells she found was actually a big deal.

"I was in an accident," he said. "I was going down Tyburn Road."

Serena stopped him. "Tyburn Road? Why the hell were you down there?"

"Kara needed a ride home."

"Of course." Serena almost hung up.

"Maggie was in the car." Serena stopped and put her pipette down. Her hand shook, and she looked around the lab to make sure no one could see her.

"You need to get down here. I'm at Saint Christopher's." Tom started to explain the accident, but Serena hung up. She felt sick. Her heart felt like she had drunk five hundred cups of coffee. She ran out the door with her lab coat on.

The hall of the hospital was long. At the end was Tom talking to a male doctor. The doctor had large arms. That was the only thing Serena could see. She passed Kara, who was sitting on an uncomfortable blue plastic hospital lounge chair.

Kara opened her mouth to speak, and Serena put her hand up and said, "Don't." Serena's face twitched with anger, and Kara sat down quietly.

Tom put his hand on Serena's arm, and Serena moved it away violently.

"Where is she?"

"Serena," Tom said, looking at the doctor.

Serena screamed, "Where is she?"

The doctor looked at Tom and walked Serena into the room where Maggie's little body lay on a stark white bed. Her body was half the size of the big hospital bed. She looked so small. There was a machine hooked up to her, helping her breathe. A tube choking out of her little mouth. Serena was struck by how Maggie still looked so unbearably cute even with all that was entering and exiting her body.

"The impact of the accident caused a lot of internal bleeding and injury to her spine. Your husband and his passenger are lucky to be alive." Serena didn't hear his voice. She couldn't hear his voice. Instead, all she could think of was a fact she had read in a research paper: "The spinal cord ruptures if stretched more than a quarter of an inch." She thought of the pictures she'd seen of outstretched spines that had occurred during accidents.

She put her arms around Maggie. Her warm body couldn't bend to her curves like it normally did when she lay with her at night—like two measuring cups nestled inside of each other.

She began to sing softly in her ear, "You are my sunshine, my little sunshine. You make me happy when skies are gray."

Maggie always liked that song when she was sick. The doctor left the room quietly. Serena took her finger and traced it up and down Maggie's tiny arm just the way she liked it. She grazed the side of her cheek and nuzzled into her neck. There was no place on Maggie's body that Serena didn't know. Every nook. Each toe, kneecap, and squishy thigh.

It had been a large truck. Tom was making a left on Tyburn, a notoriously busy road. Serena never liked to drive on it and would even forgo the good Italian gelato place just to avoid it. Kara lived three streets away from Tyburn. Her car wouldn't start after work, and she called Tom. Tom hadn't left work yet, so he agreed to take her home. They picked up Maggie from daycare, or as Maggie called it, "school," and drove toward Kara's house. Tom said they were just talking when he made a left. He said he wasn't distracted.

Serena would go over this countless times in her head, as if thinking through it could change the outcome.

**

Two months later, Maggie still could not walk. Her days of Play-Doh and going up and down the driveway on her scooter were now replaced with hours of physical therapy. Doctors. Medication. Endlessly working toward the goal of getting Maggie able to go home.

But home was no longer home. Serena sat at their dark wooden kitchen table and stared at the lines in the wood. Her eyes followed the circles, the crannies, the imperfections of age. She searched out the small blue marker stains that were left from an attempt at craft time with Maggie. She remembered picking out this table. She had looked through catalogue after catalogue. The different colors, shapes, all seemed to depict a different style of family life. The kitchen table, to her, represented all that she wanted of her family. The meals she'd cook, where they'd sit down to hear about Maggie's day. She had always wanted a house that meant something. She dreamed of flowerpots bursting with flowers and bright colors that screamed stability, vitality, and happiness. She wanted a fireplace with an idyllic and cozy rug in front of it for cold winter nights filled with s'more making. And now, as Tom ate his cereal at the end of the table, it felt like a joke. The beautiful table and her not-so-catalogue life were looking back at her as Tom ate his granola with flax seeds. Each chew louder and louder—making the table uglier and uglier with its sound.

"I think you should move out." Serena kept her eyes on the tiny blue marker lines. She lightly traced them with her finger.

"What?" Tom stopped crunching. His spoon hit the side of the bowl with an unnecessary force. "How is that going to help Maggie?" he asked.

"It's not. It's going to help me," Serena answered coldly. "We can discuss it again when it's time for her to come home. But for now, I think you should stay at Mike's."

Tom got up and left. Serena stared at his cereal bowl for a while. She wasn't sure if she was hurt that he didn't argue back. She wasn't sure of anything, but she hoped the distance would somehow make her hurt more. She imagined the distance between her and Tom opening her heart even wider, spreading like a lily at the end of its bloom. In that pain, she found solace. That she was hurting, that she was somehow carrying the equal weight of what Maggie was feeling inside as she looked down at her immovable legs.

The house seemed to know that Maggie was different now and sought to remind Serena of the pain. Her little handprints whispered on the walls. Tiny socks were found underneath furniture. An old Cheerio between cushions. A small hair bow tucked in the bathroom drawer next to the extra soap. Serena slept with Maggie's favorite stuffed monkey doll at night, but it was losing its smell of outdoor dirt, cheese crackers, and strawberry detangler spray.

Serena went to Maggie's room and put all her stuffed animals away in her purple bin. It looked neat and tidy now—all the soft animals and dolls hidden away. Serena picked up a random hippo that Tom had won Maggie at a carnival. How much had he spent trying to win this? She flipped it over and saw its stitches were showing. How many stuffed animals does one little girl need? How long does it take a stuffed hippo to decompose in the trash? She threw it in the purple bin and exhaled. The world seemed like one big bin holding everyone's consumption. Her house suddenly felt overwhelming. Are stacks of stuffed animals any different than stacks of beets?

On Thursdays, Serena would sneak into the old community center where she used to take Maggie for music. She hid in the bathroom so no one would see her. She listened to the happy kids' songs through the walls. Songs about dancing clowns, mischievous rabbits, and choo choo trains combined with the sounds of hands on drums, rhythm sticks slapping, and the crash of noisy cymbals that were completely offbeat. Serena's long, lean legs perched on the old white toilets. Instinctively she'd tap her hands on her legs to keep beat like she'd do on Maggie's little legs to teach her about rhythm. She didn't cry. She just sat there until class was over and waited exactly thirteen minutes to give everyone enough time to put on jackets, locate any missing sippy cups, and hold hands while steering the slowest of dawdling first-time walkers. Serena did this every week for two months. A painful scab she could pick every Thursday.

Serena had not been returning Abigail's calls. She ignored Robert's sudden attempts for company. She was letting herself fall apart a little. Wasn't that healthy? Wasn't her life of holding everything so tightly together not healthy? The one place Serena could focus was the lab. She felt her purpose at her lab bench. She had outsmarted men to get here. Outlasted inappropriate conversations where she was the only woman in the room. Her lab was a testament to how much she had prevailed. And she would stop at nothing to do her best science and help other female scientists and grad students do their best. She was filling out a grant for one of her students when she got Nina's phone call.

"I've got some news for you. But it's all a bit odd. The good news is the hospital had put a lot of patient files in a database, and Jen was able to locate your sister. The date isn't wrong, Serena. She found the bloodwork. And the bloodwork and everything checked out normal."

"Well, that doesn't make sense. My sister had trisomy. There's no way the bloodwork would have been normal." Serena shook her head as if to get the information out of it. She had been concerned about the date; she never expected the bloodwork to not match either.

"Could someone have entered the date wrong in both places?" Serena asked.

"Jen doesn't think so. I mean, anything is possible. Mistakes happen. But the bloodwork matched the date, too."

"I appreciate Jen looking into this. I'm not sure what it all means. But . . ." Serena stopped there, because her brain was scrambling, trying to wrap her head around why the date would be wrong and the bloodwork would show a normal baby.

"Okay, got to get back to work. Coffee next week?"

"Yep. Let's plan sometime next week. Thanks again. And thank Jen."

Serena knew she needed to talk to Abigail. And she was about to call her when she got a text from her aunt Eileen. She wanted everyone to meet up that night. Eileen had always understood her. Acceptance somehow spilled out of her aunt's reddish-gray hair. Approval came from her extra big eyelids. Through the years, Serena always felt comfortable around her, and she wanted to feel that for a few moments again. Abigail was bringing pizza. They would all meet at her father's house. Yes, it was her father's house now. She wondered what her aunt and father would say about her birth certificate finding. Surely, they knew the truth behind it.

Serena knocked lightly on the door she had entered for so long without having to knock.

"Anyone here?" she asked as she opened.

She could hear her aunt talking to Abigail in the kitchen. Serena walked in quietly, and her aunt stood up and gave her a big hug. A hug that took her entire body into hers, hard. Not one of those half-shouldered insincere ones where bodies hardly touch.

"You hanging in there?" Eileen asked, her eyes working hard to find Serena's.

"Could be worse." Serena laughed uncomfortably and enjoyed the tension she put in the air.

Abigail put her hand on Serena's shoulder, and Serena shot her a look that indicated she had news to share. But Abigail didn't pick up on it.

Dinner was quiet. Abigail inspected the pizza crust and tried to focus on the flour as if it were the most fascinating specks of white she had seen. Robert bobbed his head up and down in an agreeable fashion to Eileen's discussion about the current state of politics and the need for more funding for small businesses. Serena felt somewhere between sick to her stomach and nervous. She wanted to bring up the birth certificate, but when was the right time? And should she tell Abigail first? Instead, she gave them an update about Maggie and her progress with therapy. But stopped before she mentioned Dorothy's birth certificate. It was like her words were stuck in cement inside of her. Serena put down her curved crust, which seemed to be smiling at her on the plate. She turned the smiling crust upside down so it would frown.

Serena escaped to the bathroom to collect her thoughts. *It's dirty*, she thought. A dust trail around the molding. Her mother's collection of hand soaps now had snowcaps of dust on them. She traced her finger around the delicate pink heart her mom had gotten from Serena's wedding shower. Serena had gotten it as a gift, and her mom put it in her purse before Serena had time to claim it as her own. "This will go great in the bathroom, don't you think?" Barbara asked. Serena smiled shyly, hoping no one else at the shower noticed the interaction.

She washed her hands repeatedly. Trying to rid herself of her uncomfortableness. Why did this feel like such a big deal? Was it because she knew it meant something bigger? Something that included her mother? A woman she would never understand. She tried to soap away the dusty bathroom and all that its dirt reminded her of. As if each speck of dust screamed, "She is gone. She is dead." The hot water splashed her again, uncomfortably reminding her skin that she couldn't scrub away seeing Maggie's legs move as if they had forgotten how to play. Like drunken deer legs wobbling weakly. As if chasing bubbles was something they had never done or would never do again.

Serena looked down and saw a little spider making its way up the handle of the toilet bowl brush in the corner. The brush sat in a silly-looking wooden duck that her mom had gotten at a craft fair long ago, its beak and neck now home to a web. She couldn't fix Maggie. She couldn't fix her mom. But she could find out the truth. She needed to find out the truth. And she knew deep inside that Dorothy's birth certificate wasn't a mistake; it was a lie.

When Serena returned to the table, she opened up the birth certificate and said, "I want to talk about Dorothy."

Eileen's eyes looked up and darted around to her fellow pizza eaters.

"Where did you find that?" Aunt Eileen said, trying to make her voice sound as pleasant and normal as possible, which only made it sound slightly high-pitched, uptight, and uncomfortable. Suddenly, Serena felt them all staring at her. Abigail with confusion. Her dad with shame. And her aunt with fear.

"Why is the date wrong?" This time Serena stared back with boldness and directness. She was not afraid of their eyes. She was not afraid of the truth.

"Your mom loved you. More than you know," her aunt said as she looked over at Robert for some sort of approval. Robert's eyes fell low.

"Why is the date wrong?" Serena repeated.

"Maybe it's time you heard the truth."

"Eileen." Robert was suddenly awake now, his body wrenching with agitation.

"Your mom spent her whole life protecting you."

"Protecting me?" Serena said wildly. "Protecting me from what? From her hating me, finding fault in me? Ha. If there was a car speeding down the street, Mom would have thrown me in front of it and said it was to teach me a lesson."

"Look, it's complicated," Eileen said.

"So, explain it to me." Serena put her hand on her aunt's arm.

She had been nothing but tender to her aunt. But right now, Serena knew her aunt held the truth. And suddenly words bubbled out of her aunt, unstoppable like a volcano.

"Your mom lived her whole life protecting you from the truth. Because she thought it'd be better for you. I'm not saying I always agreed with her. Maybe it wasn't right. I don't know, maybe, she . . ." Her aunt stopped and got quiet.

"I don't know what you're trying to tell me." Serena felt frustrated, tired of all the feelings her aunt was stirring. Feeling everything—that's all she had been doing every day since losing her mother, since the accident with Maggie. Feeling sad when she saw Maggie's small toothbrush. Feeling angry when she drove past that street where the accident was. Feeling annoyed when Tom's magazines came in the mail and their subscription cards fell out like snow on the carpet.

"Dorothy didn't die of that disease like your mom said." Her aunt's words came out quickly.

"I knew it. Her blood tests were normal."

"You checked her blood tests?" Suddenly, Abigail's voice broke into the conversation.

"I was going to tell you. I just found out." Serena's eyes filled with an apology to her sister.

Robert's eyes opened and his mouth gaped, but he said nothing. Instead, he turned his back and slumped his shoulders down.

"What? Just tell me. Please tell me the truth." Serena wanted more than anything to quench her thirst for the truth. The truth that hung silently around her whole childhood. It was on her mother's face. It was hidden in the hate between them. The quiet reminder was always there that something was not right. She wanted to kick the couch, to do irrational things to make all of them talk.

"Dorothy didn't have something wrong with her kidneys; your mom heard about that disease on a talk show or something." Her aunt's words were slow now. "You were just two when Dorothy died."

Serena noticed her father's shoulders shaking. It took her a minute to realize they weren't shaking because he was cold; he was crying. It hadn't dawned on her to look at Abigail. But at that moment, she could see in Abigail's eyes that she was scared and didn't have any idea what was going on.

"But Dorothy died before I was born, didn't she?" Serena asked, her brain not ready to take in the birth certificate date and her aunt's words.

Her aunt repeated her words, "You were two when Dorothy died."

Serena looked at Abigail. The two sisters' eyes met and looked for clarity in each other. Abigail's face was frozen.

"Abigail." Her aunt paused, as if suddenly realizing she was a part of this, too.

Abigail said nothing. And Serena saw in her a quiet recognition of something. She couldn't tell what, but she saw her face change.

"Barbara repeated over and over that Dorothy had died

before you were born, Serena. You were young; you didn't even speak. So, you grew up knowing only that. But Abigail, it took you longer. Barbara would correct you over and over, and soon you believed it, too. You stopped trusting your memory about which baby was which."

"Why would she lie to us about when our sister was born?" Serena asked, suddenly feeling so angry at her mother. And anger was a feeling that came easily to Serena when she thought about how hard her mother made so many parts of her life.

"For you, Serena. She did it for you." Eileen's face looked different. Suddenly her whole face looked hard, her cheeks like marble floors.

"Robert?" Her aunt looked at him as if this was his curtain call, that suddenly he would spring to life and tell the rest of the story. But his eyes stayed down at his feet. He reached into his pocket and grabbed a stained hanky and wiped his nose.

"She loved you. She did, Serena." Serena waited for her aunt to say more. She waited in the silence. She imagined swirls of sun dust all around her. She felt sick to her stomach. She felt exhilarated. She felt everything and nothing. She didn't look up at Abigail; she didn't have room to take in her sister's emotions, too.

"You were so excited when Dorothy came home. Your very own baby doll. You loved nothing more than carrying baby dolls around back then. You would stare at her all day. You loved her so. One night, you snuck into her nursery. She was in a bassinet. You scooted your little red stool over and brought Dorothy into your room. You must have been so gentle with her; she didn't make a peep. You had a little wooden bed that you used for your dolls all ready for her. You didn't mean to do anything. You loved her."

"I didn't mean to do what?" Serena asked. Suddenly her heart felt large and pulsing. This was not the truth she was looking for. She hadn't prepared any hypothesis in her mind where she was a part of this lie.

"You went back to sleep with Dorothy in your room. You put a cover on her and gave her a stuffed animal. The wooden bed wasn't meant to hold a real baby. The slat broke slightly, just enough that Dorothy rolled a bit. She was swaddled super tight. But she was facing downward under the cover. You hear more about it these days. She died of SIDS."

"What?" Serena was feeling angry, and for the first time ever, she wanted to hit her aunt.

Abigail was now bent down, squatting on her back legs. Serena gave her one glance, but it felt like all of the words were coming directly at Serena and attacking her. Never before had she been aware of every cell in her skin.

But her aunt kept talking. Slower now, as if this freight train of a conversation could not be stopped and there was nothing to do but let each of the words out along the track.

"Barbara woke up and couldn't find the baby. She was in hysterics. She checked your room to check on you and found her."

"You were just a kid." The change in voice alerted Serena. Her dad's eyes looked full and heavy. Something in the tone of his voice made her feel like he had repeated this line many times before, sticking up for her. Was this the line he fed to Barbara when she accused Serena of being a killer as they went to sleep at night?

A thousand years of anger came out of Serena. "You knew

this. And you've been lying to me my whole life. And to her?" Serena suddenly felt the need to get Abigail involved in this. To share the misery of the situation.

"I need to go." Serena felt Eileen's arm pulling her back, but for once she didn't care if she hurt her. She pulled her body away from her, from everyone. She had learned the truth, and she had never in her life wanted to run so far from it.

"It's because she loved you. She protected you your whole life. Don't you see how much she loved you?"

But Serena did not see love. She saw hate. She saw lies. She saw all the times as a child she put her hand out to her mother, only to have her recoil.

"She hated me," Serena screamed, and all at once felt like a two-year-old girl having a tantrum. She wanted to stomp her foot through everything in the room on the ground. *Love? This is love?* she thought.

She ran to the car and could hardly control her keys. Her hands were shaking. Her whole body was shaking. Her mind couldn't think. She just needed to drive away somewhere. But it was too quiet. The road, the night, everything. She turned on her radio and spun the dial. A CD started to play: one of Maggie's music CDs. "I love the mountains. I love the trees," rang out in a syrupy sweet voice as Serena drove to nowhere.

***

"I want this for my birthday, Mommy." It was a beautiful pink doll cradle with little white hearts. Just like a little real one. It looked soft and cozy and magically sweet.

"No. No doll stuff. That's for babies. You're a big girl. You know that. How many times do I have to tell you?" Her mom's face looked hard. Her *No*s had an air of disgust to them. Serena knew she was in trouble. Serena put her hand up to hold her mother's. But Barbara was already in front of her.

***

Before long, Serena couldn't help but find herself on familiar roads. She pulled into a rocky parking lot and listened to the low rumble under her tires. It was her favorite playground when she was little. She got out and sat on the bench. It was a wood bench that had been repainted many colors over many years—from orange to green to now an earthy brown. She sat and looked down at her legs. She could remember how her mom's legs were always crossed, the top one always kicking and moving slightly like it couldn't rest. She stared ahead where her favorite bridge used to be. It was black and you could jump on it. Sometimes big kids would get on there and jump so hard Serena would go flying forward. Now in its place was a solid structure that no one could jump on. It looked safe, but less fun. When Serena closed her eyes, she could still see the bridge. The sound of laughter woke her from her memory.

"Catch it. You can do it. Look how beautiful!" She watched as a dad scampered after a toddler who was trying mightily to catch a white butterfly kissing the tops of the grass. The emphatic excitement that only parents could muster up, as if the world were reborn anew when they saw it through their kid's eyes. The sight of a butterfly suddenly became a moment to teach, to embrace, to find joy. *How it all fades away*, Serena thought. That excitement and push to see the world with beauty. Where does it go? *It is all killed. One day at a time*, Serena thought. The sun was going down, and suddenly the air had a chill to it. The cold filled Serena, but she could not move. To move was to accept what she just heard. To move was to live in a world where she had killed her sister. To move was to have to think about the life of lies.

She searched the sky. She found no answers. She watched a man walk his small brown dog. The dog's short legs moved quickly, yet went nowhere. The dog's thick brown fur was matted in odd ways, like he had stuck his head out the window and enjoyed the wind all the way to the park. His black eyes had that special blend of crazy small dog—the kind of crazy that bites mailmen and chases bikes riding past. The owner talked to the dog and smiled at him. Serena couldn't hear what he was saying. She knew that she should see companionship, but as she watched the dog and the man following behind, all she could think was that he held his leash like he was a prisoner. Like it was a ball and chain that was stuck on him. The man marched slowly behind the dog, a bag of poop swinging side to side, letting out puffs of defecation. A slave to the dog's whims of stopping, sniffing, and marking. *Are we all prisoners to others?* she wondered.

She went back to her car and turned on the radio, searching for a song, for anything. She turned the dial over and over and over. From song to talk to static to song to song to song. Nothing was right. She just kept turning the dial and not even listening to what came on the speakers. In the few seconds of silence before each new song, she felt like she was drowning. That the air wasn't getting to her lungs. She could feel her lungs; she breathed deep to make them expand and tried to imagine the process. She tried to focus on the air traveling through her nose down her windpipe. She couldn't feel it reach her lungs. Her bronchial tubes weren't working. Her alveoli weren't getting air. She could picture her seventh-grade science book. The diagram that showed the blue illustration of how lungs worked. She closed her eyes and tried to pretend she was that flat diagram, nothing but a nondescript blue scientific picture. *Just breathe,* she thought. She wished nothing more than to be a diagram in a book. Flat. Unfeeling. Closed after a moment's glance of learning. Her hand rested on her leg. She was not flat. She felt her skin. There was no hiding from this. In her head, she thought about how just yesterday she was overwhelmed by the pile of life. The dirty dishes in the sink. The laundry stack in the basket waiting to be put away. Just yesterday life had felt so overwhelming. So much needing in so many places. Just yesterday the needs of her child and chores had taken her strength. And now today. Well, today. All had changed.

She got out her phone and texted Tom: Are u there? She held the phone and stared at it.

It buzzed quickly. Yes. Everything okay?

Serena wrote two letters: No, and tears streamed down her face. She walked back to her car and hid in its darkness. Her phone buzzed angrily.

What's going on? Is it Maggie? Can I call you?

Serena texted: Not Maggie. It's me. Are you alone?

Yes, wrote Tom. Mike is out of town.

Can I come over?

Yes. Are you okay?

Need to talk. Be there in 10.

Serena started driving. She wasn't sure she even wanted to talk to Tom, to tell him. But she knew if there was one person who would understand, it was him. Well, she knew Abigail would understand, too. But she wasn't ready to face her sister yet. She looked at her watch. She promised Maggie she'd be back to the clinic by seven-thirty after her physical therapy. She hated that they encouraged Maggie to do it by herself. Empowerment without Mommy.

Serena parked and could hear the sound of an instrument in the distance. Was it a violin? A cello? It sounded beautifully sad. How she longed to play an instrument. To learn something new. When do we stop learning? We fill our early lives with learning, concerts to prove our worth, dance recitals, awkward school plays on a stage. For what? To become adults where we don't do anything? Where we take fewer chances and spend our days working? It all seemed as lonely as the stringed instrument she heard playing. *But at least they are playing*, she thought. Suddenly it sounded more like a rallying cry. A not-giving-up sound. A note fighting against the dullness of the adult world.

Serena listened for a moment more as she stood in front of the door. The music quieted, and she knocked. The knock that would mean the words were true. The knock that would begin her story that ended with death.

"Hi." It was all Tom said. But it was enough to unravel her. She had been holding her breath. She hugged him and cried. Cried like a child. Hard sobs, snot dripping—it was not like her at all to be such a mess, but she didn't care. Her snot ran into her hair, got on his shoulder. After a few moments, her embarrassment set in, and she regained her harden shell. "I'm sorry. This isn't fair. I don't know what I'm doing." She pulled back, straightened her shirt, and pushed back her hair with both hands, neatening her ponytail.

"You said it wasn't Maggie? Maybe you need a night off from her? I can stay tonight? We only have one week left until she gets to come home, right? We're almost there."

"No, I want to stay with Maggie. I don't mind. I even sleep decent there now. I promised her."

Serena thought she should just leave. Keep her secret. Keep her shame. But the thought of living in the world with it alone seemed too big.

"Come sit down. I can make you tea? A drink?" offered Tom. He seemed so formal for someone who had spent the last seven years with her.

Serena sat on the couch. She didn't lean back. She sat on the edge of the brown cushion and stared forward. She didn't know where to start. And then she did. The words just kept tumbling out of her. They didn't even feel real. But the changing look on Tom's face showed her they were real. All of it. The birth certificate. The wrong date. The death of her sister. The conversation with her aunt and father. The lies of her mother. The strange relationship that twisted back from love to hate that plagued Serena all her life. That feeling like her mother always thought she had done something wrong. It was all so clear, yet it was all so awful. It was like the whole landscape of the world had suddenly shuffled and reappeared before her. Not more beautiful, but more confusing and darker. She didn't even realize she had stopped talking. That no one was talking until Tom came over and hugged her. He said nothing. She said nothing. They sat there together, his arms around her. Serena's arms were down at her side; she let him hug her and finally rested her hand on his arm. The arm of the only person whom she could trust to talk to. Even though her heart still questioned if she really could trust anyone.

"I don't know what to say. What did your dad say?" Tom finally spoke.

"Nothing really. My aunt did most of the talking."

"I can't believe they kept this a secret."

"I can. I'm a fucking killer. No wonder she hated me."

"You were a kid."

"I was never a kid. My mom made sure of that. And now I finally know why."

"What if it was Maggie?" Tom asked.

"What?"

"If it was Maggie, would you tell her?"

"I don't know." Serena thought for a moment how odd it was to think of her mother as loving her as much as she loved Maggie. She would do anything to protect Maggie.

"What now?" Tom asked.

"I don't know," said Serena, and they both stared at the floor as if each step forward seemed impossible.

"Will you kiss me?" Serena asked.

"Of course." And Tom kissed her sweetly on the lips because he missed her, too. He kissed her lips, her cheeks, her forehead, and her neck. It reminded Serena of when they were younger and the world seemed better when they were together. When new restaurants were new adventures, and the possibility of owning houses, having careers, and going on vacations all seemed so exciting. She kissed him back and pulled him onto the rug next to the couch. She didn't know why, but she needed him at that moment. To know that he still loved her, wanted her, needed her. To touch something real when all the world suddenly seemed very strange. His shoulders felt stronger than she remembered. She kissed his neck, and his body tightened in a good way. His breath deepened.

She stared up at the fan and tried to imagine it was something beautiful. Like if she could look at it a different way, it could turn into one of those artsy photographs from the fifties where inanimate objects suddenly looked cool. An opened door could look both mysterious and deep. But she could not find the beauty in the fan. The lightbulbs didn't match. The glass surroundings looked like misshaped flowers. The white was rusting.

Before long, it was done. They never took their shoes off. His brown pants were barely down below his waist. She felt sheepish, and the world turned back to cold.

Serena pulled up her pants and looked at her watch. "I should go. Maggie is waiting for me. Don't tell anyone, okay?"

"Of course." Tom stood up and touched her arm. "Serena?"

"Yes?"

"I'm sorry." His eyes looked soft. The creases around them frowning.

Serena looked at him and wondered what Tom was sorry for. What he did, what Serena did, or for the road ahead. As she walked out the door, Tom grabbed her shoulder.

"I'm going to go with you," he said.

"I'm fine. I don't need you to go with me." Serena's posture was sunken. Her back was suddenly tired. Her words sounded stronger than she felt.

"I'm going with you," he said again as he casually grabbed his jacket and walked out the door. "I'll drive."

Serena didn't feel like fighting, and she realized, in that moment, she didn't feel like driving anyway. She lived in a world where she constantly took on more, never saying no. Juggling a job, motherhood, a failing marriage. She took it all on and walked forward with her heavy load because in her mind, that's what strong women do. They balance all of life in one hand and a glass of wine in the other. But in her strength, she had forgotten about herself. And for once, she let Tom make life a tad bit easier.

"Mommy! Daddy!" Maggie's little arms grabbed them both and pulled them close into her hospital bed. She sat up as high as she could on her braced legs. "Family hug," Maggie said as she closed her eyes tight.

Are we still a family? Serena wondered to herself. In her daughter's sweet embrace, she wanted to be. She wanted to be the family that Maggie deserved. A family of love, hugs, warm family dinners, laughter, and picnics. But Serena didn't know if she could even be the same person, or even the same mother, now that she knew the truth.

chapter 12: sand

Serena watched Tom snuggle next to Maggie. Maggie was eagerly ready for a nighttime story of animals, heroics, and a princess named Maggie. Tom's stories always went on too long, but tonight it did the trick, and Maggie went to sleep.

Maggie's nurse poked her head in and waved them outside of the room.

"Not surprised she's asleep. She did great today. Really worked her hard." Nurse Rhonda had fluffy brown hair that broke apart at the top of her head from her too-tight ponytail. Her face was soft but pleasant.

She looks like a nurse, Serena thought to herself, and then internally rolled her eyes at how stereotypical that statement was. *And what if someone said you looked like a scientist?* Serena's subconscious asked herself.

"Everything's on track and the doctor feels comfortable letting Maggie go home at the end of the week."

"That's great!" Tom answered before Serena's mouth had time to process the good news.

"We'll need you both here on Thursday so we can go over exercises for therapy. And we'll talk about what days the therapist can come to your house. Have you talked to Maggie about school?"

"No, not yet." Serena looked down. Maggie wanted nothing more than to play and see her friends at "school," which was really just daycare. "I'm going to take a few days off to get her adjusted.

Thanks again for putting me in contact with Linda. I met her and she seems great." Linda was a retired nurse who was now a nanny. Serena felt relieved knowing Maggie would be in good hands when she went back to work. She didn't have the heart yet to tell Maggie her legs had to work better before she could go back to school.

"She's doing well." The nurse squeezed Serena's hand in assurance. Serena nodded.

As the nurse walked away, Tom said, "I want to move back. I want to be home when Maggie comes home."

Serena opened her mouth to say no, but she closed it and said nothing.

"It would be best for Maggie," Tom said, and Serena knew it was true. "I'm willing to do the work, Serena. To get our family back. To get you back. Therapy, anything. I'll change jobs. I told Kara we can't be friends. And that's all we were, Serena. Just friends. It was stupid. You were just distant. And now when I see her it just reminds me of how I hurt Maggie. I can't." When Serena looked at his eyes, she saw they were wet with tears. "Look. We need to talk about this. But not here. Not now."

They went back into the room and stood at Maggie's bed. Her little lungs going in and out. Her eyelids so lightly closed. Her curly hair behind her head making it look shorter and her even younger without the length to give away the passage of time.

"You don't have to stay," Serena said softly as she eyed the makeshift family cot in the corner where they'd be sleeping. It was more of a bench than a bed, but it was all the children's hospital offered.

"I want to stay," he said. And they shifted their bodies to their sides so they could both fit. Tom propped up the pillow so his neck wasn't as cramped. He put one arm around Serena to hold her close. It reminded her of the tiny beds in college and all the nights they had slept so peacefully in the dorms.

How did I get here? she wondered to herself as she felt her husband's arms cling to her so tightly. It should mean something, his arms. After all, it was his arms that she chose out of everyone else's on the planet. Did she choose them? Did they choose her? She was never into relationships. She was more interested in things like apoptosis and gene regulation than the opposite sex. And now, here she was in the wasteland of her thirties, alone on a couch, yet not alone. Her mind dissecting the value of marriage instead of falling asleep, instead of thinking about the death of her sister, anything to avoid thinking about that.

Evolutionarily it makes sense, to couple, to make sure your DNA or child makes it through. Serena did what she always did when she thought about it. She tried to recount the species that stayed together. Didn't vultures? The plight of the emperor penguins came to her head. Their miraculous mating ritual was something she showed Maggie a video of on YouTube. But surely the rampant divorce and cheating in human lives proved that monogamy was not right for the species. If anything, marriage was more like cancer. Where small, everyday disagreements poison the cells around them until the whole relationship is one big tumor of hate.

Marriage seemed like an unattainable goal that only resulted in the quiet desperation and monotony of everyday life. And yet all throughout high school and college, it seemed like this was all her friends aimed for. The invisible drive to find a mate. For what? The angst, the heartbreak, the need, and then it was over. A boyfriend found. The journey of desire stopped. What for? The ease of two incomes to buy a house? The quest to have a child? To not be alone? Tom's hand found hers, and his fingers dangled before hers. Even in his sleep, his hands found hers and made their way to hold on. He loved her. She didn't know why, but she knew this was true, and somehow, in the comfort of his arms, the only arms she had really known, she fell asleep.

On the way home the next day, she called her friend Jill who had just had a baby. "I'd like to bring you over some dinner. Can I stop by today?"

She had met Jill through music and knew this second child would not be easy. Mainly because her first child, Nathan, had been a bundle of energy and emotions, playfully biting her shoulder most days in music class and leaving little bruises of love all down her arm. Through exasperated and sometimes embarrassed eyes, she loved her little monster as only a mother could.

"Yes, that would be great. But the house is a disaster," said Jill.

"It should be a disaster. You just had a baby!" Serena tried to comfort her friend.

"No, really. It's, like, disgusting."

"Good," said Serena. "It'll feel like home."

Serena swung by Whole Foods and picked up some prepared food. Chicken. Salad. Garlic green beans. Everything prepared better than she had the energy to cook. She could cook, but the thought of cooking for someone else seemed tiring, when just taking care of her family seemed hard enough. She focused on her food choices. She was glad to focus on anything other than what her aunt had told her yesterday. She caught a glimpse of herself in the shiny display of the prepared foods. She never liked to look in mirrors. She was a casual observer of her hair, her face. Any closer inspection always brought out her flaws. But from far away, Serena could almost see a glimpse of something. Not quite beauty, but an intensity and security of who she was that made men take notice of her. Was that still there? She looked at her unremarkable hair. Not too shiny, not curly, not silky straight. She couldn't make eye contact with herself. Instead, she grabbed a tiramisu and headed to the grocery line. Two aisles over, the sight of her caught Serena's eyes. It was Kara. She could tell her even from the back. Serena's heart started racing. She felt sick and weak. Her adrenaline shot up.

"Do you have your own bags? Ma'am, do you have your own bags?" The grocery girl looked at her expectantly.

"No, I forgot them," Serena said, not taking her eyes off Kara. Her heartbeat finally slowed down as she watched her walk out of the store. She was not in the mood for a confrontation. It wasn't until she got to her car and took out her keys that her hands gave her away. Shaking badly, she could hardly press the button on her key fob.

Jill was happy to see her. Serena made herself useful by putting away the food she had bought. Nathan hung on Jill, climbing over her body like it was a jungle gym. Every inch of her skin was his to touch, kick, and love however he wanted. His little sister Jayne was pink and preciously wrapped in a little pink-and-white polka-dotted blanket. The shiny white satin on the edge alone gave away its delicate newness.

"You can hold her," said Jill, her voice a combination of excitement and relief to pass off the beautiful but overwhelming bundle to someone else.

Serena smiled and gently skimmed her finger along the baby's cheeks. She moved her hat slightly to see her whisper of brown hair. "She's beautiful, Jill. Really. I don't want to wake her. She looks so peaceful. Is she sleeping well?"

"No," said Jill. And her eyes fell, giving away the struggle of what had been the last few weeks. "And this boy"—she gave Nathan a little tickle—"has been waking up, too."

"Oh, I almost forgot, I have something for you, Nathan. The big brother." Serena dug in her pocketbook and took out a little tan-and-blue car made out of recycled parts that she saw as she was checking out of the store, remembering the advice she had read that siblings have trouble with new arrivals. *I wonder what Maggie would be like with a brother or sister*, she thought and then quickly shook the thought out of her head as she thought about what she had done to her sister.

Nathan, amused by his new car, started vrooming it all over the rug, giving Jill and Serena a moment to talk. "How are you really?" Serena asked.

"Tired. People say two isn't that much harder than one. But it hasn't been easy. Jayne wants to eat every three hours, and Nathan's been all over me. I try to read him books when I'm nursing, but he just moves around so much he practically squishes the baby. I don't know . . ." Her voice trailed off.

Suddenly Jill raised her voice, "Nathan, no!"

Serena watched as Nathan pretended to zoom his little car

over the baby's stomach, making its way to her little red face. Jayne stirred and started crying. Nathan started crying from his mother's outburst, his emotions oversensitive from the invasion of his sister.

"I'll get her." Serena picked up the baby and patted her rhythmically. How it all came back so quickly.

"And of course, the kitchen sink broke yesterday," Jill continued, letting out a dam of emotions and words that had been stuck in her. "Jason started to fix it, but he didn't have the right part and so now I don't have a kitchen sink today."

"At least he can fix it," said Serena, wondering to herself if Tom would be able to fix their sink. These were the things no one prepared you for. There was no class for couplehood. No college courses. You came together full of expectations without practicality—not knowing who can fix the plumbing, the electricity, the refrigerator.

"Ahh, she likes you," said Jill as she quieted Nathan in her arms. Nathan hit her shoulder and Jill reacted, "Ow, Nathan, no hitting."

And suddenly Serena was filled with such amazement at her friend Jill. A woman who always seemed a bit scattered, never on time, and always failing to keep Nathan in line. In this moment, Serena could only see her strength. In the solitude of her home, she loved and cared for two people. Never sleeping when she needed it. Never getting a break. Everywhere, women did what they needed to. Out of love. *We are the stronger sex*, Serena thought. And as she looked down at this baby with the promise of everything in life ahead of her, Serena got a sick feeling in her stomach that maybe this was the age her sister was when she killed her. The baby started to cry, and Serena quickly handed her over to Jill.

"She's probably hungry again." Jill rolled her eyes at the early exhaustion of being an on-demand cow.

"It's okay; it's time for me to get going anyway," said Serena.

"Thanks for the food. For stopping by. Gets a little lonely, you know," said Jill, her eyes giving away the emotions of motherhood.

"Hang in there. You're doing great. If you need more food, or want me to pick up Nathan for a playdate—" Serena stopped herself. *Could Maggie still play?* she wondered. It would be different now that she couldn't run or really walk, but she still needed to play. As Nathan jumped on his mom as she pulled in to nurse Jayne, Serena thought, *Maybe Nathan isn't the best one for Maggie to play with in the beginning.*

As Serena walked to her car, she checked her phone. Two missed messages from her sister. Did she want to talk? Right now, Serena wanted to go home to her bed and curl up in a ball. She drove home, walked to her bed, and, without taking off her coat, lay down, pulled up her fluffy comforter over her head, and fell asleep, feeling like a small snail hiding from the world.

"Serena?" She heard the voice somewhere in the distance. She was warm, and her hair was wet with sweat. How long had she been asleep? She poked her head out from the blanket and saw Abigail sitting rigidly in a chair.

"I'm sorry. The door was open. I tried calling." Abigail looked down. She looked like hell. Hair not washed, a bulky college sweatshirt with dirty sleeves that were too short.

Serena just stared at her. What could she say? The two sisters sat in silence, neither one wanting to break the wall of air between them.

"I don't remember," Abigail whispered after some time.

"What?" Serena asked as she took a deep breath, knowing that this conversation would require knight-like armor to get through.

"I don't remember Dorothy. I should. I keep wracking my brain. And sometimes I think I see her, a small brown-haired baby. But I don't know. I mean, I remember her being dead for years more than her being alive."

"Mom probably confused you so much, you can't remember," said Serena sullenly.

"In my head, I wonder: am I remembering you or her? I just don't know." Abigail twisted her fingers.

"What does it matter?" said Serena, suddenly annoyed that her sister was making it all about her. "You're not the one that killed her."

Yes, there it was. In the room. Those words. The two sisters said nothing. Because they were no longer just sisters; one of them had now been responsible for Dorothy's death.

Abigail got up, flustered. "I don't know why I came. I just thought you might need to talk. That we could talk." Serena stood up and took off her coat finally. She was warm, too warm. She felt like she needed to shower again. Abigail went to touch Serena's arm, but Serena flinched. "Look," Abigail said, suddenly finding her posture. "It could have been me. We were kids. I could have easily been the one to put the baby somewhere. It was an accident."

"But it wasn't you," said Serena.

"I know. I'm still processing this. I was lied to, too," she said softly.

"But it wasn't you," Serena repeated again

"I don't know what to say. I'm not trying to fight. I'm just trying to..." Abigail looked up at Serena, searching somewhere on her face for any indication of what to do, but Serena was not ready to let her in.

"There's nothing to do." Serena's face went cold, her cheeks taut as the feeling of dread filled her stomach. Abigail waited in silence, not quite ready to take a step away. Sisterly love kept her close.

"I'm here if you need me. To talk."

"Okay," Serena said.

"Okay," Abigail said, and Serena walked her to the door.

"I'll call you over the weekend when Maggie's home." Serena put on her most normal voice.

"Hannah is excited for her to be home. She made her a present." Abigail smiled and hoped Serena could accept her smile.

"Great," said Serena.

Abigail looked up once more, her face and mouth twitching to find the words, the right words, any words to make all of this somehow change, but there were none. And so she did the one thing she could do: she hugged Serena tight and left.

***

The next day Serena tried to focus on what mattered most— her daughter was home. Tom was home. Her family had a chance. Even if she wasn't sure what her past meant, she was beginning to be surer of her future.

In the normalcy of their living room, Tom hugged Maggie tightly. Maggie held on to the biggest butterfly balloon Serena had ever seen. Bright pink, almost fluorescent orange and blue. It was three times the size of Maggie. A ridiculous gesture of Tom's, as always.

"Guess what, Mags? We're going to have a big party for you tomorrow," Tom exclaimed, catching Serena's eye.

"What?" Serena gasped, trying to hide her feelings from Maggie.

"It's time you face them, and what better reason for everyone to celebrate than Maggie coming home?" Tom whispered, his voice sounding hard and sure. It wasn't like Tom to do anything without Serena. He was never bold, never made plans. Suddenly, Serena felt like his whole personality had shifted. She was mad. How dare he take control at this moment and make her face her family? How dare he use Maggie as a way to force this situation? Her face felt warm; anger boiled and raged inside her.

Maggie clapped her hands together. "Party! Party!" With eager eyes, she asked, "Grandpa come?"

Ugh, Dad, Serena thought. She had already had one awkward phone call filled with silence and sorry.

"Yes," voiced Tom, his cheerful voice trying to overcome Serena's scowl. "We are so proud of you, Mags. And we love you so."

"My room still purple?" Maggie asked, breaking Serena from her mood.

"Of course, silly. Why wouldn't it be?" Serena kissed her forehead and smelled the strawberry detangler in her curls. But

Maggie was looking up, making her balloon go up and down, her little hand having fun grasping and releasing the blue string. Suddenly, the string bobbled away from her and was just out of reach. Maggie's arms reached to get it. Her legs locked in braces wouldn't give way. The sight tugged at Serena's heart, but she did not let the emotion show.

"Here you go, silly goose," Serena said as she handed the string back to Maggie. Maggie resumed her play, unbothered by the moment of frustration.

"Kids are resilient," the nurse's earlier voice echoed in Serena's head. *This will probably make her stronger in the long run, tougher,* Serena thought. *Is that what Barbara thought, too?* wondered Serena. She shivered and pushed her mother out of her head.

Tom came over and rubbed Serena's shoulders as if it were an apology for what he was about to put her through. "It'll be good to see everyone." But Serena didn't say anything; she was still mad he was forcing this step, this big step, without her consent.

The next day, the house was cleaned, Tom's clothes put back in drawers. How easy it was to play this game. As if marriage was just a collection of his and hers clothes in the appropriate places. Serena instinctively bent down and recovered Tom's sock next to the hamper. Misplaced socks. Yes, Tom was most certainly home.

As she went downstairs, the smell of chocolate cupcakes filled the air. The beep of the oven reinforced that they were indeed done. Serena pulled them out and placed them out of reach, in case Maggie's hands came near. Could she even reach them now?

The knock on the door made her quickly scan the time. *Must be Dad,* she thought. Her father was always early to these things. She opened the door, and it was not her dad. It was her aunt.

Serena could feel her heart pounding, but she kept her words cool. "Hello, come in."

They had set up Maggie on the floor, her back against the couch with toys all within reach. She couldn't yet get up on her own from a sitting position. She handed Maggie the little sand timer she loved. She would turn it over and over and watch the sand go from one side to another. Serena sat with Maggie and watched the sand slide effortlessly down, wishing she could somehow make time return back just like it did. Back before she knew what she knew now.

"Can we talk?" Eileen's voice interrupted her sand trance.

"I'm not sure I want to," said Serena. "Today is about Maggie. Not about me."

"I don't want this hanging over us," Eileen said quietly.

"Hanging over us!" Serena's voice squeaked high, and Maggie looked over.

"Mamma?" Maggie looked over at her mom to see why she looked upset.

"Sorry, Mags, Mommy didn't mean to startle you." Serena gave Maggie a reassuring smile. The smile didn't quite meet the corner of her eyes, but it was enough to convince Maggie to go back to her toys.

"Come with me," Serena said softly and harshly to Eileen. They walked to the sunroom, and Serena closed the door. "Sit," Serena said coldly as she sat next to Eileen on the sofa. She picked at the dark red cushion. She remembered sitting on it at Target with Maggie. They had it on display with a wooden fence around it and little white lights scalloped around it.

Serena remembered how Maggie's eyes had lit up. Maggie had sat on the cushion and leaned against Serena. Serena had checked the tag, and it was on sale. She had bought it in some ways because she wanted to buy that moment for her family. She even bought little white lights to hang around her sunroom. The lights hung, but they were never turned on much. Serena stared at each bulb, trying to look at anything but her aunt.

"Serena," Eileen went to talk first, touching her arm lightly. Serena moved it quickly away and placed it in her lap. She said nothing but stared down at her black shoes as if she were a child. "Serena," Eileen started again, taking a deep breath. "You wanted to know the truth. You're the one who pushed about the birth certificate and blood test. And, well, you had thrown Tom out. You've been working yourself to death. And to be honest, you haven't been the same since your mom's death or Maggie's accident. You seemed to be spiraling. I thought it was time. Your whole life I felt like you were always looking for answers. And I just felt like you deserved to know the truth. That it would help you understand Barbara. Maybe help you understand yourself."

"Who doesn't want to know they're a killer?" Serena rolled her eyes sarcastically.

"You were not—you are not a killer. You were a little girl who loved her sister," Eileen said, grabbing Serena's hand. Serena pulled her hand away and tried to keep her tears in her eyes.

"I don't know what to do with this information. Yes, it explains a lot. It explains why mom was always so distant. I always felt like she hated me."

"I know. And I always tried to tell you she loved you. She changed after Dorothy. She tried her best, but . . ."

"But what?" Serena felt angry at her mother, at her aunt, at her father. The list was too long to count.

"I took care of you." Eileen's face seemed to register some awful event. Her eyes suddenly looked tired. "After the funeral, your mom just wasn't doing well. I had suspected she had some postpartum depression after Dorothy was born, and then her death just escalated it. She called me one day. I remember the call like it was yesterday. Her voice was low and just sounded off. I mean, I knew it was my sister but, in her voice, something sounded really wrong. For a moment I was worried she had done something."

"Done something?" Serena asked and shivered as if she knew what her aunt was alluding to.

"'I have to go,' is what she said. 'I have to go.' Just once. And then she didn't say anything more and just stayed on the line while I tried to get her to talk more but she wouldn't. I told her I was coming and that I would take care of you girls and she could go, go wherever it was she felt like she needed. I could hear her breathing. I hung up, called your father, and rushed to your house. I don't know what I expected to find. But you girls were upstairs playing; she had locked you in a room. I don't think you knew that anything was wrong. I think she locked the door so she wouldn't do anything stupid. But when I saw her, her face, her eyes, it was like she wasn't there. She was sitting on the couch with a knife."

"What?" Serena felt sick to her stomach. "Was that knife for me?"

"No. No. No," said Eileen. "I keep telling you. She loved you.

A mother would never hurt her daughter."

Serena looked down and thought, *Except mentally for years*.

"She was going to use it on herself," Eileen said quietly.

"Have you told this to Abigail?" Serena suddenly wanted her sister there. There to hear everything. There to hear that their mother wasn't the perfect thing that Abigail always thought she was. After all, she wanted to leave Abigail, too.

"Yes, Abigail has called me a few times since last week," said Eileen.

"Of course she has," said Serena, with snark in her tone. Abigail always liked to talk. Communicating feelings was on her list of accomplishments. "What did Abigail say about all this?" Serena gestured her hand as if the air in front of her contained all of the words she had just heard.

"She listened. She cried. She felt bad for your mom." Eileen picked at a red thread on the couch.

"Of course she did." Again, Serena couldn't help the tone in her voice. Just then she heard the doorbell.

"Serena, I want to talk more. After the party. I want you to understand."

Serena looked back and nodded her head slightly to indicate she may be open to hearing more. "Today is about Maggie," she said, and she pulled her shoulders back and walked to the front door.

The rest of the guests came quickly. Her father, Hannah and Abigail, the neighbors across the street with their little daughter. The house was filled with giggles again. Most conversation centered around Maggie or playing with Maggie. Everyone was good about hanging out on the carpet, so it almost seemed like Maggie wasn't broken at all. Maggie ate her pink-frosted cupcake with her normal happy abandonment, so her face, chin, and cheeks were covered with frosting war paint. Every so often, Tom would come and give Serena's shoulder a reassuring hug or she'd find his arm around her back. Serena was so tired of feeling alone that she welcomed Tom's gestures. When the neighbors and her dad had left, Tom walked over and gave Serena a big hug and said, "You're doing great."

Maggie looked up from the carpet and gave Serena's leg a big squeeze. "Family hug," she said. Serena bent down and put her arms around Maggie. The leg hug seemed sad and an obvious indication that Maggie was different. Maggie didn't seem to mind and accepted a bigger hug. Tom bent down, too, and hugged them.

"Can we do bubbles or something outside?" Their family moment was interrupted by the ever-eager sound of Hannah.

"Um, yeah," Serena said, searching Tom's face for a "do you think Maggie can do bubbles" answer.

"Yeah, outside is fine," Tom answered. He scooped up Maggie and helped her to her walker. "It'll be fine," he said softly to Serena. "Why don't you go . . . ?" He paused and looked up at Abigail and Eileen, who were in deep conversation in the dining room. Serena followed his gaze.

"Bubbles! Bubbles!" Hannah was chanting loudly to get Maggie even more excited. Tom took the madness outside.

"Pop!" she heard Maggie scream with glee, and Serena's whole body relaxed a little. She walked up to her aunt and sister.

"Okay," she said. As if those were all the words she needed to say to open the drawbridge to the conversation that lay before them.

"Let's go sit," said Eileen. The three women walked back to the sunroom. The warmth of the afternoon sun made the room bright and offset the coldness of their conversation.

Serena's aunt didn't look nervous. If anything, her shoulders looked square, her small stature erect and strong. "I know this isn't easy. But I think it's time for the truth."

The two sisters stared down at their hands, both their heads angled down in unison. As if in their body language they had accepted the strangeness of what they were about to hear.

"Abigail, you know some of this. That day when your mom called me—afterwards, I made sure you kids were okay. And you were. You were playing. Robert called their doctor and found out where to take your mom. You know, nowadays, you hear about postpartum. There's more dialogue about depression. But back then, it was like, oh, she has the baby blues. It wasn't taken seriously. It was a throwaway comment as if it wasn't a big deal. Your mom had just gone through a lot. She wasn't herself."

"How long did she stay away?" Serena looked up. Her eyes peering at Eileen, ready for answers. Eileen closed her eyes as if she were hiding something or just searching for answers. Serena wasn't sure, so she asked again, "How long did she stay away from us?" This time her voice was stronger, ready.

"A few months."

"A few months!" Both girls' voices screeched in unison.

"It was on and off. We tried to make it fun for you guys. You stayed with me. Robert took you to the beach."

Serena stared at the wall. Her thoughts went back to Maggie's first beach trip. A total parenting fail. They had packed so much stuff—blankets, snacks, umbrella, lotion, toys. Their new-parent anxiety overcame the tranquility of the beach. They had walked up to show their daughter the wonder of the ocean just to have her scream in horror. They didn't even get the pink octopus towel down for a second before Maggie cried so hard that she coughed and puked. Her feet didn't even touch the sand. She would just point away, signaling "go, go, go," to get far away from the big, scary wave monster. The walk back in the extreme heat and the slog of the burden of parenting contraptions in their arms seemed to represent all that was wrong. "Maybe we can get ice cream," Tom had offered. As if he could fix the day. But Serena knew when Maggie was done. And inside, so was she. She could feel the familiar pull of cognitive dissonance inside her—when the ideals of the world weren't reality. The picture in her head of them holding hands and jumping the waves like some postcard was just that—only a picture. The truth was in the oppressive heat of the day. The sand on their feet that wasn't worth its mess in joy. Each grain a millimeter-sized evidence of the defeat of the day. And now, she had just one more reason to hate the promise of the beach.

"I remember that beach trip," Abigail said quietly and broke Serena from her thoughts. "We had never been away with just Dad before. I remember thinking it was special." She wrinkled up her nose and shook her head, trying to get her brain to remember more. The sun, the blue of the ocean, the undivided attention of her dad—it all stayed with her. She could practically feel the sand between her toes. The hours they spent building sandcastles. And yet, it was all a ruse.

"And what, she came back and you both trusted her with us?" Serena still felt mad. She wasn't sure who she was most mad at. Mad at the lies, mad at her mother, mad at her aunt and father for all the hidden stories.

"No. It wasn't that simple. Your mom went on medication. That helped. She started seeing a therapist. We had a nanny to help."

"Deb!" Abigail said happily. "I remember her!" Memories of baking brownies, coloring, and hanging out on the swing set with Deb played in Abigail's head. How was it she had remembrances of some things but not of Dorothy? *If only I had remembered*, Abigail thought. But what would she have done as a child? She would have never upset her mother. Even now, Abigail knew she would have believed anything Barbara wanted her to believe.

"I don't remember Deb." Serena's brow felt tight. She had been furrowing it during the whole conversation, wracking her brain, her memory, for something, anything that would help see this more clearly.

"I remember the first time I heard your mom correct you about Dorothy. I called Robert immediately. And I could tell he wasn't telling me something," Eileen said. The girls listened quietly and tried to picture who their dad was back then. "They thought it was for the best. For all of you. And for a while, Barbara seemed renewed by it." Eileen's face darkened.

"For a while, until I started growing up," Serena said for her.

"Robert and I talked about it. She would get hostile if we talked to her about it. I remember one time she wouldn't talk to me for a week. Screaming, yelling at me about how dare I make it sound like she treated you differently. She changed the whole world for you, Serena. To her, that was her biggest act of love." Suddenly her aunt looked sick. "Is any of this helping? In my heart, I thought this would answer questions in your heart. But maybe I've just ruined everything."

"It was already ruined," said Serena. The truth was all she had at the moment. And she clung to it like the mother she never quite had.

"If we hadn't found the birth certificate, would you never have told us?" Abigail asked. Serena looked up to figure out if Abigail's voice sounded mad, frustrated, but she couldn't see any clues in her face.

"I don't know. It wasn't just up to me. It hasn't been easy. The countless conversations trying to reassure Serena about Barbara. To watch you struggle. To watch Barbara struggle."

Abigail interrupted, "Is that why we moved?"

"No—yes. I mean, it just turned out that your dad was offered a position to manage the new production line in Maryland. It seemed like a fresh start. But the company didn't do well, and you guys moved back a few years later. I was glad. I had visited you often, but it was nice to have you close to home again." And as if to answer Serena's unspoken question: "You girls seemed good. Happy. I felt like we all had made the right decision." Eileen looked at the two girls to gauge their faces, their hearts. She grabbed Serena's hand tightly as if her life depended on it. "You've been struggling. Barbara's death. Maggie. Tom. I felt like I owed it to you. If it was me, I'd want to know the truth. We've always been kindred spirits. I just wanted you to know before . . ."

Serena accepted her aunt's hand. Her internal thoughts

reassured her, *You are a scientist, Serena. You seek the truth in everything you do.*

"I'm glad I understand. I'm not happy. I don't know quite what to do with it all. But in some ways, I feel like I'm relieved. I've gone my whole life feeling like I did something wrong. And now, I know."

"You were just a kid," Eileen said.

"Yes, but my mom never let it go."

"She tried her best." Eileen put her arms around Serena. Serena accepted the hug but couldn't make her arms return the gesture. Eileen opened up her arms to include Abigail in the hug. The sudden burst of childhood glee and singing broke the exhaustion of the room.

"Girls are back," said Serena, standing. "That's enough. Enough for today."

Eileen smiled graciously up at her. "We should keep talking. All of us. Have you girls talked to Robert yet about this?"

"No, he hasn't said much," said Abigail.

"No," said Serena, remembering their silent, strange phone call and how he seemed to not look her in the eye the entire time he was here today at Maggie's party. Constantly shining his attention on Maggie so he wouldn't have to face Serena. Leaving early with an excuse.

"This all happened to him, too. He loves you all. Keep trying. He's mad at me," Eileen said before Hannah bounced into the room with a thump and ran next to Abigail.

"Mom, I'm thirsty."

"Okay, okay, let's go get you a drink." Abigail smiled, her

body returning to mommy mode.

That night, Serena went to bed as soon as she put Maggie down. She knew she should talk to Tom, but she just didn't want to. Her chest felt cold, and she welcomed the pain. She curled up her body as tight as she could and tried to process what she learned.

Was she happy to know the truth? Yes. Not happy with the actual truth. But relieved to finally understand this thing that had plagued her all her life. This feeling that she could never figure out. The unspoken feelings that existed between her and her mother. At least it all made sense. It swirled around her in the dark of the night. She tried to remember her sister, but she shuddered at the thought of thinking about her, for she knew what a baby felt like. The warmth of Maggie's body when she was little was still a memory she could feel. Her snuggly body asleep on her chest. And she had taken that away from her mother. She could feel her stomach churn. She went to the medicine cabinet and found some cough medicine. She did not have a cough, but she desperately wanted sleep. The warmth of the liquid coated her throat. She went back to bed and squeezed the fluff in her pillow. She heard Tom's footsteps coming up the stairs, and she closed her eyes tight, pretending to be fast asleep.

Tom walked into the dark room and searched for the lamp beside the bed, causing the shade to rattle. He took off his shirt and grabbed a book to read. Serena flipped so the light wouldn't bother her.

"You awake?" he asked quietly.

"No," she said grumpily. If she was asleep, he certainly wasn't doing a great job of letting her sleep in peace. Tom always read before bed. A much-needed habit that often stirred Serena when she went to bed first.

"If you want to talk, we can talk about things."

"Thanks. I'm not in a talking mood."

"We could have sex," Tom added, half-kidding and half-hoping.

"Uh, no. I have a lot on my mind. Not really in the mood."

"I understand." His tone sounded kind. Serena didn't have room in her mind to think about him tonight.

She felt his hand crawl under the covers and find hers. A squeeze of "I love you," and then he let go.

"Maybe we could get away? The beach?"

"No. Definitely not the beach," said Serena strongly. And then changed her tone, "It wouldn't be easy for Maggie."

"I know. I thought we could stay on the boardwalk, enjoy the view, ice cream. Nowhere near the sand." Serena shifted her body, trying to welcome sleep. "Serena," Tom said quietly, almost like a question. "Nothing has changed. You're the girl I fell in love with. I just wanted you to know that, because I know you and the way you think. And think. I love your mind. And whatever happened when you were little—it doesn't change who you are today."

"Thanks," Serena said sheepishly. And because she had so much to say but didn't know what to say, she said it again, "Thanks," and closed her eyes.

She felt Tom's finger on her back, and he slowly made out the letters into her skin: I and L-O-V-E and Y-O-U. A tear rolled down Serena's cheek, but she kept quiet and fell asleep. She dreamed of swimming in the sand timer, trying desperately to go backward but never getting anywhere.

chapter 13: needles

Serena woke up to the smell of French toast. She hadn't woken up to the smell of someone else cooking for so long. Only the scents she had put there. She rolled over to see the covers messed up on Tom's side of the bed and remembered he was home. And then she sat up in bed with a start.

"Maggie!" But her body relaxed when she heard the sounds of Maggie's giggles and Tom's voice below.

She made her way down to the kitchen and said, "Hello, you two."

"Mamma!" Maggie squirmed and squealed, but she could not move from her chair. The sudden remembrance of her not-quite-working legs brought a pout to her face. Tom distracted her with the one word that was magic, "Syrup?"

"Yes!" said Maggie, her legs forgotten as her eyes looked at the stack of French toast. Tom oozed syrup all over.

"That's probably enough," said Serena.

"How about some snow?" asked Tom as he took out the powdered sugar.

Serena rolled her eyes but said nothing as she watched Maggie pound the powdered sugar holder with her hand, sending sugar snowflakes all over her syrupy French toast.

"Can you give me twenty minutes? I just need to check my email," Serena asked Tom.

"Yep. No problem."

When Serena started her computer, she tapped her fingers, impatient at the time it took to boot up. Why must everything go so slow? After a quick scan of the normal emails from lab techs asking about mouse questions, she noticed one from Sarah. Her former advisor.

Hi Serena,

I hope this email finds you well. I just saw an article in *Nature* about gene downregulation, and it made me think of you. How are things going with your lab?

You were born to rock. Don't you forget it.

Sarah Cagnette
Department of Pharmacology
Vallor University School of Medicine

Serena read the email again and smiled. Born to rock. Amazing how her advisor always believed in her, saw something in her. It almost made her believe it about herself. Somewhere inside she felt it, that gnawing curiosity that drove her, that passion for answers that led her to choose science. The words in that email somehow unlocked her spirit and reminded her that it was not time to stop. No matter what, Serena was a scientist, and scientists always pushed for the truth. Even if this time it was within herself.

When Serena returned to the kitchen, she found a mess of syrup, powdered sugar explosions, and egg and milk drips. On a small plate was her French toast à la Maggie—a little wet, a lot of sugar, and a few blueberries for good measure. Serena ate bites in between washing dishes and cleaning the counter. Her cell phone rang. It was Abigail.

"Hey there," her sister said.

"Hi."

"Can we meet up today?"

"Um, maybe. I have to talk to Tom. See when Maggie's therapist is coming today."

"I just really want to talk. I can't sleep. I just want to talk."

"Okay, okay. I hear you. I feel like we've talked a lot."

"No. Aunt Eileen has talked. We haven't talked."

"Okay."

"Talk to Tom. Text me a time and a location we can meet up." Abigail hung up the phone.

When did she get so bossy? Serena thought to herself. She went up the stairs to find Maggie and Tom playing in her room.

"Hi, guys." She walked over to Maggie and sat down beside her, conscious that Maggie could no longer run squealing into her arms. "Whatcha doing?" Serena asked. Maggie beamed.

"You're probably not going to like this," said Tom.

"Why is it you guys are always doing things you don't think I'm going to like?" asked Serena.

Tom shrugged his shoulders and gave a delicious grin to Maggie, who returned it with a giddy smile.

"Do it. Do it, Daddy." Maggie clapped her hands.

"Okay, so we have this brown monkey. And he likes to climb, but what he really wants to do is fly. He wants to be a butterfly. So . . . we throw him up in the air."

The fan blades in Maggie's room caught the monkey and

shot him against the wall like a rocket. Maggie giggled so hard she snorted. "Again!"

"How do you think up this stuff?" said Serena. Her eyes gave away her smile behind her statement.

"You want to do it?" asked Tom, handing her the monkey.

"Uh, sure. Okay, monkey. Fly like a butterfly." Serena whipped the monkey up, and it shot back at her. Putting her hands up instinctively to stop the reflecting monkey from hitting her in the face, Serena shouted, "Ow, bad monkey."

Maggie's laughter filled the room.

Maybe it'll all be okay, Serena thought to herself. The laughter was a Band-Aid for all the healing that still needed to happen.

"Hey, would you be sad if Mommy went to see Aunt Abigail for a tiny bit and you kept playing with Daddy?"

"Daddy. Daddy," Maggie chanted.

"Okay, got my answer." Serena smiled. "You okay with that?" She looked at Tom.

"Yeah, no problem." Tom started walking the little monkey up Maggie's braced legs. Serena turned to go.

"Hey, wait."

"What?"

"We need more syrup."

"Ha. Yeah, I saw that. We do. I'll pick some up on the way home. Text me if we need anything else." As she walked down the stairs, she thought how normal that conversation had seemed. Could things return to normal? Was she happy with normal? She looked down at her phone and texted Abigail: Your house? Ten minutes?

Within a second, her phone buzzed: Yes! I have coffee. She grabbed her coat out of the closet and let her hands linger on Maggie's soft red coat. Its littleness on the hanger made her smile. She remembered how her mom had been adamant about getting Maggie that coat.

***

"I took Maggie to the mall today and she wants a coat," her mom said.

"A what?" Serena was fixing her mom tea as she came into the room.

"A coat. She saw it and her eyes lit up."

"Really? She got excited over a coat? Let me guess... Was it sparkly?

"Nope. It was red. A little red peacoat."

"Huh, that's funny. She has a bear with a red coat. I wonder if that's why? What store?" As Serena asked the question, her mom's face filled with mischief.

"I bought it."

"Mom! You are crazy." Serena stopped herself and said, "Thank you." Amazing how Maggie had changed the space between them to feel more comfortable. "It's a beautiful coat, and she'll love wearing it."

"I was afraid there wouldn't be another time, you know." Barbara's face looked down, and Serena knew what her mom was afraid of. The uncertain path that cancer was leading her on.

***

Her mom never got to see her wear the coat. She became grandma on the couch, not grandma who could play outside. And now the little red coat was living on.

Serena paused before she knocked under the big puffy wreath on Abigail's yellow door. She could faintly smell the dried lavender that weaved its way through the circle branches. She knocked hard, twice.

"Good morning," said Abigail.

"Is it?" asked Serena, her sarcasm bounding out of her mouth before she could stop it.

"Do you mean is it good, or is it morning?" said Abigail, smiling, trying to ease the awkward air between them.

"Not sure. How are you? Why aren't you at work?"

"Working from home today. I have a proposal due for a new project."

"Cool."

"Could be. Come in."

Abigail's house always looked neat; she was one of those moms who always made Hannah pick up her toys. She had little bins specifically marked for puzzles and coloring containers that neatly held markers and kept crayons from escaping.

"Want cream in your coffee?" Abigail asked politely.

"Yeah, sure. I can do it." The two sisters found themselves in the kitchen, working side by side, grabbing cups, putting in cream, a touch of sugar. A casual, comfortable rhythm that felt so normal Abigail almost doubted talking to her sister about what she wanted to talk to her about.

Once back to the cream couch with light blue flowers, Serena snuggled against a large throw pillow and drank her coffee comfortably. The yellow mug was oversized and felt nice in her hand. The type of thick lip to the mug that made it cozy.

"So." Abigail smiled and took a sip of her coffee.

"So," Serena replied, looking up at the newest picture of Hannah framed on the mantel.

"I had a thought. And I wanted to talk." Abigail felt nervous, like she was asking someone out on a date. She shook her head as if to get the uncomfortable feeling out of her.

"Yeah, what?" Serena took another sip of coffee. Damn, it was good. She wondered if Abigail spent a lot on her coffee beans.

"What do you want to tell the girls?" Abigail spit out the words like they were hot.

"What do you mean?" Serena put down her coffee.

"Hannah, Maggie. What do you want their truth to be?" The words hung out in the air as the two sisters stared at each other.

"Their truth" stuck in Serena's head. Was the truth something they could create? Was that what her mom did? Treated it like an object, some science experiment that only she controlled?

"Hmm. I don't know." Serena still didn't feel comfortable with the question.

"I just started thinking last night, that this is our story now. Our lives that we get to tell. Not Mom's story. So, what happens now? Do we tell our daughters what really happened when we talk about it? Or do we tell them what Mom said? I don't know. I thought we should talk about it." Abigail paused, then said, "I'll do whatever you want. Obviously, you've kept my secret about," and she mouthed the words that she was too afraid to say out loud, "Hannah's dad." And then she stopped and looked at Serena.

Serena was quiet. How hadn't she thought about it? Maggie, what was she going to tell Maggie? She had spent so much time just digesting what it meant for herself, she didn't think about what it meant for Maggie.

"I don't know," Serena answered honestly. "I hadn't thought of it in that way." And suddenly she felt like a shitty mom for not thinking about her daughter in this.

"I didn't know either. I've lived with the untruth for so long it just seems easier."

"But it's not true," Serena said quietly, but she didn't have any force to her words because she did think the untrue story was much easier. "I need to think about it."

"Of course." Abigail sidled next to Serena and gave her an awkward hug. "I love you, Serena."

"I know. I love you, too, Abigail." Serena let her shoulders slump and leaned into the hug, and for a second, the two sisters hugged without any distance between them.

Serena broke the comfort and stood up. "I have to go. I'm going to stop by the lab. There's a result I want to check on."

"Oh, good," Abigail said, blushing from her overzealous voice of encouragement.

Serena rolled her eyes.

"Is it ever hard?" Abigail asked.

"What?"

"Staring at the disease that killed Mom."

"Sometimes. But lately, I just think of it as helping her. I couldn't save her. But I can save others. And, well, Mom . . ." And in that silence lived all the complexity that was their mother and now this huge new reality of their childhood.

"It's complicated," Abigail filled in. "We'll get through this, Serena. You don't always have to be the strong one. I'm here for you." Abigail's eyes stared down at a frayed edge of the gray carpet.

"Yeah, maybe it's time I gave up that role." Serena tried her best to give a smile, but her lips were not convinced.

When Serena got to the lab, the familiar smells of chemicals greeted her. She opened a few deep freezers to thaw some cells for upcoming experiments. She checked on her mice to see how their tumor growth looked. It all felt familiar. Mouse. Injection. Mouse. Her hands worked quickly, the needle going into their pink skin and out.

She took a look at her plates to check on the cell lines that she had treated. These cell lines were ones she knew had the mutation she had identified in recurrent breast tumors. All the drug-treated cells were dead. Could it be? She took out another plate. Dead. And another. Dead. She took out her untreated cells, and they were all fine. The drug had worked. It had killed the cancer cells with the mutation that she had identified in recurrent breast cancer. This was a huge breakthrough—her breakthrough. And not only would this mean a paper for her, it might mean a better chance for women with breast cancer.

As Serena walked through her lab, she felt ecstatic. She felt proud. There was acceptance in her limbs—less to prove to others. She was a woman, and she had just made a major scientific discovery. Her brain was powerful. Her body was powerful. It had created Maggie. It had been on journeys her younger self had no idea were possible. All at once, her head filled with the amazing scientific facts of how mammary glands produce milk and then shut down. At that moment, she was overcome with contentment. Maybe it's because she knew she had just made a significant breast cancer finding. Maybe it's because she knew the truth. She had always been Serena, the child who came after. The child who came after her mother's heart was destroyed. The child who never knew her mom when she was happy. The child who somehow knew every milestone was a marker in her mom's heart. Some torn moment of the future caught up in the past of a sister who would never reach that same mark. A bitter battle that happened at every birthday that she would see in her mom's eyes, never quite understanding but feeling it in every candle lit, every breath Serena blew. Pain mixed with anger mixed with love. A heady combination that sometimes made Serena's heart ache for love she knew her mother couldn't give. Hugs that never felt warm. Tears that made Serena quietly hide as a child, not knowing why her mom was crying, but knowing somehow, she was the reason. But that was not who Serena was anymore. That was not her story. That was not her skin. And in this brief moment, she felt her body accept this new truth. Her skin was finally true. No lies lurked beneath. Serena was a truth-teller for herself and for the future of breast cancer. Serena was no longer the child who came after. She was a woman who was living in the now.

She decided to go down to check in with Professor Chen about a clinical trial collaboration, and because she had to share her finding with someone. She walked down the long hallway, bustling with patients, doctors, and family. How different this hallway looked to her now. She had pleaded with her mother to do a clinical trial, to at least look into it, but Barbara wasn't interested.

"I don't want to be a guinea pig. I don't want to be stuck with needles and not know if it's going to work," she'd say adamantly. Serena used to think this hallway represented all that she worked for. Science at its best, working to help those who had lost hope. As she made her way past the many doorways, she saw a familiar head go into a door. It looked just like her aunt's. Serena walked up to the door slowly and saw the name of the doctor.

Wilson, why does that sound familiar? What does she study? She grabbed her phone and typed in a search for her name and papers. The first one caught her eye: "The effects of the immune system on reducing amyloid plaques in Alzheimer's disease." Serena grabbed the handle to go in but stopped herself. She instead walked in the opposite direction to the elevator. She got in and pressed the button for the fifth floor for no reason other than to get as far away as possible from what she just saw. Her mind started working rapidly.

It all made sense to her. The impetus for her aunt telling her the truth didn't just have to do with Serena, it also had to do with her aunt. She was losing her memory. But how much? How long? She knew she needed to talk to her. Maybe she could help her? Why didn't she tell her about the Alzheimer's? It was too many questions at once.

She grabbed her phone and sent a text to her aunt and Abigail: Dinner this week? I can tell you about Maggie's progress and we can chat. She read over the text a few times. It felt nonchalant, not obvious. She pressed send. Her phone buzzed quickly.

Her aunt replied: Sounds good. Thursday works for me.

Two seconds later, Abigail chimed in: Thursday is fine. Has to be late. Hannah has ballet. 8:30 at Vinos?

Serena typed: Yep. Works for me.

Serena sighed and tried to let her head rest knowing Thursday would bring answers.

Thursday, of course, brought a change of plans. Serena's phone buzzed with a text from Abigail: Hannah's sick. Can we do dinner here? I'll order in.

Serena rolled her eyes. Did she want to have this discussion where Hannah could hear? Suddenly she didn't want to have this discussion at all. But then her phone buzzed again; this time it was her aunt: Works for me. Love you girls.

And then Serena looked at that word. Love. Such a good word. Surely, she needed to talk to her aunt, to understand what was going on. If there was one thing Serena felt in all this confusion, it was that her aunt loved her.

When Serena got to her sister's house, Hannah peeked out from upstairs. "Hey, come here," she said quietly. "Come up here."

"Just going to go say hi to Hannah real quick," Serena called to Abigail around the corner. She walked up the stairs to see Hannah. "What's up? I thought you were sick?"

"Can I ask you something?" Hannah said.

"Of course." Hannah sat next to her on the bed. Her legs awkwardly splayed in front of her. Her posture slouchy. Her head bent down, and she did not look up at Serena.

"What's up?" Serena said, realizing Hannah was having a

hard time finding her words.

"Does my hair look stupid?" She said the words quickly, then tucked her head back down so she couldn't see Serena's face.

"Of course not. I think it looks really cute!" Serena said with truthful excitement. "I thought you wanted your hair cut short?"

"I did. Well, my mom wanted it, and I thought I didn't care, and there was that whole Locks of Love idea, and I was proud to do it. But someone at school said something."

"What?" Serena suddenly felt angry. Why are kids always so mean to each other?

"She said I look like a boy. And some other stuff."

"You don't look like a boy. I think you look cool. Unfortunately, second graders are still learning to be nice. Did you know your brain isn't even fully developed until you're twenty-five?"

"That's old."

"Yeah, well you and the kids in your school have lots of learning to do until then and even after. Besides, sometimes people say stuff when they are jealous."

"Jealous?"

"Yeah, maybe that girl wishes she could get her hair cut. Or maybe she thinks you were brave for donating your hair to Locks of Love. Or maybe she was just having a bad day. The crazy thing about people is they usually say one thing but have three hundred other things going on in their head. I do that sometimes."

"You do?" Hannah asked. Her eyes suddenly welcoming Serena's. Her posture relaxing as she took a deep breath. "Me, too. I guess. So, I don't look like a boy?"

"No. You look awesome. Did you tell your mom what the girl

said? Is that why you didn't want to go to ballet?"

"No. Yes. You know, Mom, she'd get upset, plus you . . . you always tell me the truth, so I wanted to ask you."

And it was with those words of an insecure kid who would have to face her own truths one day that Serena knew what she wanted to do. The truth, the real truth would be the answer. The accident, Barbara's cover-up, it was all the truth now, and if she painted it just right, the girls could learn from it and see the love that was entwined within each layer. It made Serena and Abigail who they were today. And the truth of understanding what lies beneath their mother was the most important truth Serena could give them.

"Your secret is safe with me. You are great. Your hair and in here." Serena pointed to Hannah's heart. "Now get under the covers and milk this sickness while you can. You want your iPad?"

"Yeah, thanks."

"Love you, kiddo."

"Love you, too. Thanks."

Serena smiled and shut the door behind her and went down to find Abigail and her aunt.

She found both of them on the couch. Two plates were in their lap filled with food. She smiled to herself as she looked at her aunt's plate: perfectly arranged gnocchi, salad, and bread—all with clear circumferences around them so no food would touch another. Abigail's plate was the opposite. Generous amounts of gnocchi spilled into overdressed salad with a piece of bread balancing on top of the gnocchi mountain. *What one could learn by studying people's food arrangements*, Serena thought to herself. She consciously fixed herself a plate, now too aware of herself to be deemed a good experiment.

Her plate was somewhere in between—not quite as severe spacing around the food, but not a heap of food entanglement. She ripped a piece of bread and nibbled as she tried to read her aunt's face.

"Good food," said Abigail, chowing down her gnocchi before touching her salad.

"Yes, lovely. I do like their sauce," said Eileen. Her smiling eyes gave away some tension that she was getting ready for more talk than just tomatoes.

"So," said Serena, ready to start whatever discussion was going to start. Her heart beating fast as she thought about what she already had seen of her aunt in the waiting room.

"I wanted to get you girls together again. I know this hasn't been easy. Some nights I wonder if I've done the right thing. I felt so adamant at the time. And your mother." Eileen looked down and her voice grew quiet.

"Mom?" said Serena. This wasn't what she thought they were going to talk about.

"I went to visit your mom a few days before she passed. And she was upset, hysterical really. And I tried to calm her down. And she grabbed my hands and asked me if she had made a mistake. She doubted all of it—hiding the truth from you. At first, I thought she was just out of her mind. But we talked. We talked for a long time. The nurses kept coming in and checking on her, and I just wanted to get her to relax. I hated seeing her so upset. I asked her if she wanted me to tell you the truth. She lay back, nodded yes, and closed her eyes. She fell asleep. I left while she was asleep, hoping to talk with her again. But well, she passed away two days later."

Eileen looked up at Serena and quickly looked down.

"I don't get it. She went her whole life living some lie. Why question it now? Why?" Serena tried to search Eileen's face for more answers.

"I don't know. Who's to say what facing death does to someone? But I felt like she opened the door to the truth. And, well, you had the birth certificate. I feel like she wanted me to tell you. I feel like me just taking the weight of the truth off her shoulders is what brought her peace."

"Oh. That's not why I thought you told me." Serena hid her gaze from her aunt's face. Suddenly she filled with anxiety. Should she make her aunt confess her secret?

Quietly, Serena said, "I saw you. Last week at the hospital." She peeked her eyes up like a child afraid to make eye contact.

"I was going to—" Eileen stopped and looked at Abigail, who looked confused at all that was going around her.

"What's going on?" Abigail asked, annoyed she was being left out of whatever was happening.

"I have the beginning stages of Alzheimer's," Eileen said, with more dignity and poise than she felt.

"I'm sorry," Serena said softly.

"It's okay; it really is. And yes, maybe that was why when your mom pleaded with me, I knew it was the right time to tell you. I didn't want to forget the details. The details that might be important to you. I didn't want to forget the . . ." Eileen stopped, looking for the right words.

"The truth," Serena said.

"Yes," Eileen said kindly and reached over and grabbed Serena and Abigail's hands. "This doesn't change anything. I've just noticed some early signs. I'm involved in a great clinical trial, which I'll be talking to you more about, Serena. I go in every two weeks for bloodwork. It's not a big deal. A needle here and there."

"Yes, please, any way I can help," Serena added.

"Does Dad know?" asked Abigail, her face splotchy and red, her skin revealing the true emotion underneath.

"I've talked to him a little about it, yes," said Eileen.

"Dad's a vault. Who knew? All this time holding information in," Serena said, glibber than she meant to be. *What good is it being a vault?* she wondered. *Who does it help?*

All these secrets, lies, and withholdings. All these things people keep hidden from each other. All the lies seemed so tangible to Serena in that moment. Like she could see the universe and its dark, hidden underbelly.

Serena went home and listened to the monitor. It was a blend of static and Maggie's quiet inhales and exhales. She saw Tom's light on in his office, and she pulled out a bag from the closet. Inside was a little mermaid dress. A surprise for Maggie. But as Serena looked at its tapering body, she knew there was no way it would fit over Maggie's leg brace so she started ripping the bottom. She ran into the kitchen and found her needle and thread. She plopped back on the carpet and got to work. About a half-hour later, Tom walked in. Serena had the needle in her mouth as she examined the cloth.

"What are you doing?"

"Making Maggie's princess costume work. It's too tight. It won't fit over her leg." She kept her eye on the seam and didn't look up.

"I didn't know you could sew." Tom laughed.

"I can't. I haven't moved, and I'm still not even close to finished."

"What are those?" Tom looked and saw cutout pieces of fabric on the floor. "Are those our sheets?"

Serena looked sheepish. "Yeah, I had this idea that I could cover up her crutch and put, like, fishes on there so it's a part of her dress-up. I thought she'd like that. I can buy us other sheets. I just thought they'd make cute fish." Serena's voice was a mix of annoyance, concentration, and frustration. She kept trying to thread the needle. She licked the end of the white thread and tried again to put it through the hole.

"I hate needles," she said. "It makes me want to puke trying to get it through."

"Want me to do it?"

"No. I can do it."

Tom walked over and took the thread from her hands.

"Let me help," said Tom.

Serena laughed. Not a happy laugh. The type of laugh where Tom knew Serena was annoyed but not too annoyed to give in and accept help. He picked up a wannabe fish cutout and looked it over.

"Give me that. Stop judging. I'm doing my best." Serena grabbed the fish.

She went back to poking the needle through the fabric as fast as she could. She poked her finger and made herself bleed. She sucked her finger and stared at the dress.

"I want to finish it so she can have it tomorrow."

"Cool, but I'm helping."

"Great. Sit down. Start cutting fish."

"It'll make her happy," Tom said, assuring his wife he understood why she felt the need to do it. Tom touched Serena's arm.

"I just want to fix her," she said. "I mean, I just need to fix the dress. I meant the dress." Serena sighed and hated what her words revealed.

"Serena, you've been through a lot. I can't imagine what your brain is doing, knowing your brain." He smiled. "But you should know, I can't sew. But I can glue. Can't we glue them? I have the gorilla stuff. It'll hold."

"Good idea."

Tom came back in the room, and Serena put her hand up without looking to take the glue. But it was cold.

"Not glue. Ice cream. And two spoons. You need a break."

Serena opened the lid, and Tom sat beside her.

Serena dug into the ice cream while Tom waited.

"It's so good. Don't you want some?" Serena asked.

"I usually let you go first since you like to eat out all the good bits."

"I do not eat out all the good bits," Serena argued back playfully, but then looked at her spoon, which had three big chunks of cookie dough on it. Her eyes widened as she realized, "I do eat all the good bits."

"It's okay. I let you." Tom winked and dug his spoon in. "I love you like that."

After a few bites, Tom leaned over and kissed her. It was a mixture of ice cream and warmth. He kissed her harder, and her back instinctively went to the ground. Tom carefully took their spoons and ice cream and placed them on the coffee table so Maggie's costume wouldn't get dirty. Serena smiled at him. And there between the scraps of costume material, Serena and Tom's bodies pressed in and out of each other like a sewing needle goes in and out of fabric, binding them together tightly.

***

After, Tom and Serena spent the rest of the night laughing at their bad crafting. Serena filled in Tom all about her exciting discovery and what this meant for her career—she would write a paper about the data and aim for a prestigious scientific journal like *Nature*. By midnight, the new dress and crutch decorations were done. As they got into bed, Tom kissed her forehead and said, "We were a good team today."

"We were."

"And I'm proud of you. You know, you've always been the scientist I believed in most," Tom said.

Serena stared at the ceiling feeling accomplished. She couldn't fix her mom. She couldn't fix her aunt. She couldn't fix her past. But she could make the future better for women with breast cancer. And she could make tomorrow better for Maggie with that dress. And that made all the difference.

chapter 14: robert

"The doctor said it's common for people to change past events to deal with things. He felt like it's her way of coping." Robert's eyes didn't meet Eileen's. "I don't want to push her. I don't want to make her snap. What's the problem with her thinking that? What's the problem with anyone thinking that?"

"Because it's not true," Eileen said quietly.

"Look. I don't know what to do. I'm doing my best here." He stood up and paced around the room and left. He found the girls and said, "Who wants to play?"

"Me, me, me." Abigail ran to his arms as Serena hugged his leg tightly. Serena giggled as he walked with her attached to his leg.

"Hmm, what's this on my leg? Is it a big shoe?"

"Noooo," Serena said, laughing.

"Is it a monster?" Robert asked.

"Noooooo," said Serena.

"Yes, it is." And Robert tickled both the girls. "Tickle monster!" Abigail cried and surrendered to the onslaught of chin and tummy tickles.

Every day it was more of the same. Robert tried his best to bring laughter into the girls' lives. Even when he was bone-tired from working, he pushed himself to play. Over time, he could see Barbara getting more tender with her children. Hugging and giggling again. And when Abigail mentioned Dorothy, Barbara calmly said,

"No silly, Dorothy died a long time ago. She was sick."

One night as he was lying in bed with Barbara, she sat up, soaked in sweat.

"What? What is it?" Robert touched her arm, but she didn't move. Her skin felt clammy and cold.

"We're never going to tell them." Barbara stared straight away, looking at the wall like it was a beautiful angel.

"Barbara, are you okay?" Robert turned his body so that he was facing her. Her eyes stayed straight.

"They don't need to know the truth. Serena is so young. It's too horrible." The tears tumbled out of her eyes, a never-ending waterfall of big, splashy tears that soaked her already-wet nightgown. Her crying got louder and frantic. Robert's pulse quickened.

"Shhh. Shhh. Don't wake the girls. It'll be okay."

Suddenly Barbara grabbed Robert hard. All sadness gone from her face. "Promise me. Promise me this. It's the only way I can face them. The only way I can wake up tomorrow. Do you have any idea how hard it is to wake up each morning? Every morning I wake up to her, Dorothy. Wondering where she is. Listening for her cries. Every morning I relive it all." Her hand was gripping Robert's arm so tight that her nails were leaving red marks on his flesh.

And that was it. The past was changed. Serena was young, and when she did mention her sister, it was changed to, "Dorothy died before you were born. She was sick. But then we were lucky, and you came along." For Abigail, it took a little longer. But both Dorothy and Serena had brown hair. Robert always felt slightly guilty when Abigail's eyes would show her confusion, but he felt like it was for the best. Serena could grow up without this terrible incident, and Barbara seemed to have renewed energy. In his silence, he felt like he was saving his family.

One day he came home and Barbara was sitting on the floor in a praying position. She sat about five inches from the television. It wasn't until she turned that he could see the tears down her face. Her eyes lit up, and she said, "They were talking about what Dorothy had. Edwards syndrome. That's what she died of, too." Abigail was playing in the background, her eyes looking up at her mom and dad, quietly taking it all in.

Barbara said it again, this time with a stronger, more defiant tone. "Edwards syndrome is what Dorothy had." And that was it. A talk show feature now became their daughter's past.

***

And now here he was, staring at Barbara's grave; everything seemed like a big dream. A strange world that wasn't any better. But was it worse? Was he mad at Eileen? Had he betrayed Barbara in not stopping Eileen? Had he betrayed Serena all these years? Robert prided himself on being a simple man. He was straightforward and honest with his friends. He had been through so much that he didn't have the energy to be mad at Eileen. She'd always been there for his daughters. Relieved? He didn't feel relieved by the truth. Uncomfortable would probably be the best word to describe him. But he had always felt uncomfortable with the world around him.

"I don't know what I'm doing," he said to Barbara's grave. "I don't know what I should do. I don't know if what we did was right. I just wanted to make things better. To fix you, the girls. But it never was right. How could it be?" Robert stared silently at the grave. He was not a man of words, and he felt odd to have said those words to Barbara out loud. They were a couple who did things, nagged, but didn't talk. Their relationship had been about not talking in some ways. This painful wedge between them. An invisible scar that was always felt, but never discussed in detail.

And now here he was, standing in front of her, although she was not really there. And suddenly he had words. Words he wanted to talk to Barbara about. Words they hid from for so many years.

"Dorothy died. And so did you. Maybe even me. Things were never the same. And Serena. I don't know. I don't know. But the truth is there now. For better or worse, at least it's there in the open. No more secrets. No more." Robert put his hand in the air to signify everything. Because somehow the whole air around him seemed different, less constricting. "You never asked me what I wanted to do. You just talked and I listened. And I loved you." Robert couldn't find the words, his heart filled with anger, sadness, and frustration. "You were so damn headstrong. And the funny thing is, Serena is just like you. She just doesn't realize it. And now, you let this truth come out. Letting your sister do your dirty work. You didn't even ask me. You never did. But I let you. I let you."

Robert stared down at his hands. A little brown bird flew down and perched on a gravestone nearby. It tilted its head at Robert as if to say, who are you arguing with? Robert wasn't sure if he was arguing with Barbara or himself. But he was done talking. And he smirked as he said to the little bird, "Barbara probably isn't listening to me anyway."

As Robert drove away from the cemetery, he knew where

he should go. The contents in his trunk gave him a good excuse anyway. He pulled into Serena's driveway. It was not a driveway he visited often, even though there wasn't much distance between their two houses. He opened his trunk and took out two large boxes. He fumbled his way up to the door, balancing the awkward shapes, and knocked on the door with his elbow.

He heard Maggie's voice, "Mamma, door." He peered inside and could see Maggie trying to grab her canes to get up. The door opened, and there was Serena, staring at him as if the whole world was between them.

"Hi," he said.

"Hi," she said. "Come on in."

"Grandpa!" Maggie exclaimed, warming the whole house with her voice.

"Hi, Mags." Robert put down the boxes and knelt down to give Maggie a hug.

"Presents!" Maggie said as she saw the boxes.

"Maybe, I don't think so," Robert said. He looked up at Serena and said, "I've found these. I don't know why your mom kept them. Thought maybe you or Abigail would want them? If not, I can just throw them away."

Serena opened the boxes and sat down on the ground, tears streaming out of her eyes. Robert ran over to her and put his arm around her. He hadn't meant to upset her. As he put his arm tighter around her, through the awkwardness of their closeness he realized Serena was not crying, she was laughing. Hard.

"What? What is it?" he asked. Feeling confused and relieved all at the same time to see her expression of absolute amusement.

"I don't get it. Why are these funny?" Robert asked. He felt left out of the joke.

"I'm sorry. They're not. They are to me. Mom saved these damn doilies all her life. As a kid, I can still remember taking them out for special occasions. One time I used them for a tea party, and she freaked out on me. 'They are only for special occasions.' I can still hear her voice," said Serena as she fingered the white lacy paper. "She kept them all this time. Saving them for a special day."

Robert shuffled his legs back and forth, the way he did when he got nervous. Serena tried not to notice it, mainly because in her heart, that shuffle is what she'd think about most when he was gone. Those little idiosyncrasies that she knew so well would haunt her with a mixture of happiness and sadness long after he was gone. His collection of tiny pencils. How he never threw away an old flowerpot. He could always glue back, repaint, and accept the cracks as room for roots to spread through if need be.

"Do you want them, then?" Robert asked.

"Uh, yeah. I'm sure Maggie could make something with them."

She held it up to Maggie who grabbed it instantly and said, "Snowflakes!" Serena grabbed a bunch of the doilies and threw them over Maggie's head. Maggie laughed as they swirled around them. Serena didn't stop. She grabbed more and more as Maggie laughed and laughed as three-hundred-forty-seven white paper doilies covered every surface of her living room. Her brown couch was littered with them. One fell between the leaves of her green plant. They were under her chair, couch, and peeking out beneath the rug. Maggie used her arms to pull them around her like she was building her own paper snow fort. Robert, caught up in the moment, gave a half-smile at the ridiculousness of it all. Maggie went to use her crutch to get up, but it slipped and knocked over the vase on the coffee table.

"Sorry, Mamma. Sorry." Those were the only words Maggie got out before an avalanche of tears started.

Serena put her arms around her and stroked her hair. "It's okay, Mags. It was just an accident. I never liked that old vase anyhow." Maggie peeked her eyes out at her mom, searching her face for forgiveness.

"You still love me?" Maggie asked.

Serena hugged her harder and said, "Of course, of course. Don't you know mommies always love their little girls?" And then, there it was. Those words out in the room taking up all the space. Serena looked up at her dad, his eyes wet with tears. She buried her face in Maggie's hair to hide from her father's eyes. She peeked out at the white doilies all around them, escaped prisoners who, like Serena, had finally been set free.

chapter 15: zygote

"Is she asleep?" Tom asked without looking up from the couch.

"Yep. Took her awhile. But she finally gave in," Serena said and sunk into the couch cushion next to him.

"I don't know how you do it."

"I just scratch her back. She's different with me. She relaxes easier."

"Yeah, I know. I hate that."

"You hate that she relaxes?"

"No, I hate that she's different with you," said Tom, scrunching up his eyebrows.

"I'm her mom. It's supposed to be different," Serena said and picked up the remote, flipping until she found a cheesy romantic movie that they used to watch in college.

"Ha, I remember this. Remember that crappy old theater?" asked Tom.

"Yeah, with the slimy popcorn."

"I liked the popcorn. I thought it was good."

"Of course you did," said Serena.

On screen, the couple embraced. All hands, fists, and lust. Serena watched for a second and got up. Tom grabbed Serena's hand before she could leave the room and looked at her with intensity.

"What if?" he asked.

"What if what?" Serena asked, and she glanced down, evading the strong, pleading look in his eyes.

"What if we were that for each other? What if we tried harder? What if we looked at the other person and said, 'I'm going to make this work and put this person first in all that I do?' What if we chose each other? Every day." Serena opened her mouth to talk but couldn't decide what to say. "We spend all this time looking around and wondering about life, other people, if things could be better, worse. I don't know. What if we stopped looking and just focused on each other? What if what is good is right here? We just have to try harder. What if us is the answer?"

"What if us is the answer?" Serena let the words linger on her tongue.

"I just want..." Tom stopped and pulled Serena in for a deep hug. "I just want this. Love doesn't have to be perfect to still be love," Tom said.

Serena played those words over in her head, softly turning them over like pancakes, examining the edges. "Love." She held on to it.

"Love is our truth. We just need to believe in it."

Wrapped up in Tom's emotions and arms, Serena wrote on his arm the letters O-K.

Tom sighed with relief.

Serena let him hug her, longer than she liked. She counted in her head to fifty-eight seconds to distract herself from the impulse to move. And in those seconds, she let go. Really, let go. And let her body relax like Maggie's. She let Tom's love overtake her, and for a moment, her world felt different. She knew where she had to go.

"There's something I have to do. To clear my head."

"Okay," Tom said. He held on to her hand hard as if this

were goodbye for a long time.

"I'll be back in an hour," Serena teased, but she could see in Tom's eyes there was no room for teasing.

On the drive to the graveyard, she passed a car with a window down. She followed suit and put her window down just to let the air remind her to breathe. In the car next to her, a dark brown dog's shaggy head was sticking out. His tongue and ears were flapping in the wind. Serena put her head out the window and let it blow her hair and stress away.

Serena walked quietly up to her mother's grave. She could feel every grass blade bend at her feet. She paused, shifted her body to turn around, and then twisted back. Uncertainty confused her movements.

Serena stood at her mother's grave for a long time and said nothing. Her face turned wet before she realized she was crying. Tears streamed down her face as her internal voice talked with her mother. *I loved you. And all I wanted was for you to love me.*

And then real words escaped into the air. "I needed you," Serena said. She felt like her chest was going to explode. She took a deep breath and continued the conversation. Each word felt like it was going to bust out of her heart. "I still need you. I hate it. But I do. You should have loved me. I was your daughter. I was your baby, too!" The words escaped from her mouth. "Did you love me? Could you love me?" Serena stared at the ground and kicked a pebble with her foot. Too ashamed to make eye contact with the grave. "You tried," she said quietly. As if the words in the air made her final evaluation true. The wind kicked up and seemed to agree with her. There is no stopping a mother's love, Serena knew it deep down. Maggie had taught her that. And she knew, somewhere in Barbara's confused and angry heart wrapped in bands of sadness, there was also love.

"Love doesn't have to be perfect to still be love," she could hear Tom say. Was Serena going to carry her mom's years of hate forward? Or could she carry the spark of love that made her mom lie to her in the first place? That lie came from love.

"I can't change you. Or the past. But I'm going to change myself. And I'm going to change a lot of women's futures. Moms who deserve to love their kids for as long as possible."

The breeze blew and reminded Serena of all that was awaiting her. She stared at the hard rock of the cemetery stones around her and took a breath. She knew love was the right choice. What Serena didn't know was that deep inside her, tiny cells had begun to multiply and divide. But it would be weeks until her baby would have a heartbeat.

Thank you for reading

The Things We Keep

Please consider posting a rating or review. Reviews not only help other readers find books, but they also let readers know which books may end up their new favorite!

ABOUT THE AUTHOR

JULEE BALKO is the author of *The Things We Keep*, her first novel. She's also a freelance writer who has helped many companies find their brand swagger. While she started her career in advertising, she now finds herself writing for all sorts of creative endeavors. But her favorite creative project will always be her three daughters who inspire her every day.

Julee believes in interesting characters and complex relationships. She wrote her debut novel *The Things We Keep* because she wanted to write a book for women of the "sandwich generation" who are trying to take care of their parents while balancing motherhood, a job, and multiple glasses of wine. After being thrust into the world of grief when her mother and father died, Julee knew there needed to be a book that showed this often not-talked-about journey—and then she added a dash of science, mystery, motherhood, and of course, love into the mix.

Growing up Julee always had one dream, to have a book with her name on it. (And to own a pet pig.) There's no piggy yet. But she happily has a rescue hound, an inquisitive bunny, and fosters as many kittens as her husband will agree to.

For more information on Julee Balko and her writing, please visit www.juleebalko.com.

ABOUT THE PUBLISHER

GENZ PUBLISHING is on a mission to bring new authors to the world.

It can be nearly impossible for writers with promising talent to be recognized in the publishing and digital media industry. There are many unheard voices in the publishing world because of the often costly (for time, energy, and money) requirements for breaking into it.

Since there often seems to be an under-representation of new and innovative voices in the publishing world, we decided it was time for change.

GenZ Publishing emphasizes new, emerging, young and underrepresented authors. We're not a vanity press. Instead, we're a traditional, indie publisher that focuses on mentoring authors through each step of the publishing process and beyond: editing, writing sequels, cover design, marketing, PR, and even getting agented for future works.

We love to see our authors succeed both with the books they publish with us and with their other publications. That's why we call it the "GenZ Family."

OTHER GENZ TITLES YOU MAY ENJOY

A Confession by William F. Aicher

Dry World by Dylan James Brock

Those We Trust by Marie Jones

The Blackwater Phenomenon by Chad T. Nelson

Take My Whole Life Too by Justine Ruff

Escaping to the Country by E.A. Stripling

CPSIA information can be obtained
at www.ICGtesting.com
Printed in the USA
LVHW032346240522
719627LV00007B/1215